DEADLY POWERS

A Tapped In Novel

Written By
Mark Wayne McGinnis

Edited by:
Lura Lee Genz
Mia Manns

Avenstar Productions
Print ver. ISBN: 978-0-9861098-9-8

Chapter 1

I've had a few hours now to think about my current situation. Presently, I'm precariously perched, straddling a wet, wooden balustrade—a flimsy handrail, old and creaking—that constantly shifts backwards and forwards with no particular regularity. The trick is to keep my feet in constant motion. That, though, in and of itself, is not the problem. Well … not my only problem. Hell, the saloon's top floor balcony lies only a few feet below and behind me. Nope, it's the thick rope fastened around my neck. My hands are tied behind my back, which has me more than a little concerned, and the simple fact that I'm far more likely to fall forward, rather than backward—toward this small Western town's Main Street below. Either way—falling two feet backward, or pitching forward, toward the street thirty feet below—will lead to the same inevitable outcome: Dead is dead. The noosed rope around my neck is affixed high above, about ten or so yards up, to a metal bar—like a horizontally-extended flagpole—and is canted-out several feet in front of me, so I'm awkwardly leaning forward. If my feet slip off this slim railing I'll fall forward and commence doing the Irish jig until my tongue turns black and I piss myself. How I constantly place myself into such precarious situations has crossed my mind more than a few times over the last hour or so.

Did I mention that I'm going through withdrawals? I'm not a drug addict, but the symptoms are just about the same—maybe worse, in my case. I too get the sweats, the blinding headaches, and the shakes. *Whoooa … almost lost it there.* My left boot slipped from the railing and I watched several large, splintered-off pieces of railing free fall toward the muddy street below. Oh, I forgot to mention another reoccurring symptom … nausea. I retched again and felt hot bile at the back of my throat. Just one of a thousand dry heaves I've experienced over the last three or four hours, while stranded helplessly on my narrow perch. I *really* need to tap in.

To explain what my *tapping-in* process is, you first need to keep an open mind. Seriously, this can be hard to swallow, so put the rational part of your brain on hold for a bit, because what I'm going to tell you is … well … unbelievable.

I can read minds. More than that, I can influence others' thoughts. It all came about over a year ago on a desolate highway near Kingman, Arizona. I was on the run. An agent, who'd just spent a year hiding out in Russia with everyone—and I mean everyone, from the FBI, CIA, and DHS to the SVR, the CIA's Russian counterpart—looking for me, all wanting me dead. I'd been set up … accused of killing an American agent. In their defense, yes, I actually did kill her. But it was in self-defense. She was going to shoot—so it came down to who fired first—her or me? I shot first. The truth of the matter was she was a double agent, secretly working for the SVR. She was also the wife of Harland Platt, a co-CIA undercover operative and friend, working undercover with me in Moscow.

Back now to the desolate Kingman highway accident: I awoke, hanging upside down and injured, with my rental car wrapped around a telephone pole. I had no recall of what caused the accident to happen—no memory, either, of my identity. Total fucking amnesia. It didn't take long for another vehicle to come along. But it was not fortuitous for me. It was an eighteen-wheeler and it, too, ended up as a giant heap of scrap metal splayed across the middle of the highway. It had crashed into another vehicle, one left stranded on the roadway; that, in turn, plowed into my already decimated rental car. That crash triggered the high-voltage wire, hanging down from the wooden pole above me, to plop down beside me—into what was left of my car. Thirty thousand volts of raw electricity radiated mere inches from my forehead for what seemed like hours. It should have killed me. Instead, it changed me … altered my physiology. I soon found that I was peeking into the minds of the EMT workers in the process of extricating me from the car, and I was also able to inject timely suggestions into their minds. There was something else, too: While I was sitting there, strapped upside down in my car seat, with the high-voltage telephone line swinging above my head, someone … or something … was talking to me. Something out there—within the power grid—had found me and wanted my help. *Help me, please help me …*

I still don't know who, or what, that voice was. What I do know is after that I needed to tap in to a high-power line's juice within each twenty-four-hour period, or I would start experiencing what I'm experiencing now—fucking withdrawals and the loss of my ability to mind-read others.

The wind has increased in volume around me now and I'm using the tension of the noose around my neck to keep from being buffeted too far forward. As I'm swayed back and forth, nearly losing my footing, I wonder, *Christ … how much longer can I teeter here?* I need help. I steady myself and look off toward the distant foothills. How had things gone so awry?

I carefully turn my head to see someone standing behind

me at the balcony doors. One of the less attractive saloon girls, dressed in a low-cut blue dress. She glanced at me then up at the dark clouds above.

"Hey …" *shit, I've forgotten her name*. "A little help here, please? Promise you won't get in any trouble—" but she's already turned away, gone back inside.

"Steady there, Mr. Chandler. Winds come up a bit … huh?" Jude chided from the street below me.

"Hey … I want to speak to Palmolive!" I yelled into the wind, not sure he heard me.

"You had your chance, Doc, he's leaving town any minute."

I tried to turn my body to face toward the north end of the street, toward the corral, but couldn't manage it and still maintain my precarious balance.

The wind was gusting now. I looked down and saw a man's Stetson cartwheeling down the middle of the street. I slipped again and debated if I should attempt to kick off my boots—maybe things would be less slippery. *Who am I kidding?* Hell, just standing straight was nearly impossible. I retched up more dry heaves.

Again, my mind wandered. I thought of Pippa. Beautiful, amazing, Pippa. She had one rule: *Stay the hell out of my mind!*

Like myself, she was a SIFTR agent. She was also my girlfriend. She'd been there, in Kingman; then later, in Germany, when things got hairy. We survived a mission to thwart a neo-Nazi organization called the WZZ—led by husband-wife team Leon and Heidi Goertz. Although they'd gotten away, their plans for dominating the world's primary financial markets were thwarted.

I shouldn't have chanced it … peered into her mind like that. Hell, it was only a glimpse. I'd previously kept the promise to stay out, unless expressly given permission. Honest. But the problem was … is … I'm used to looking into everyone's head. It's a habit. I don't even know when I'm doing it, half the time. So when Pippa came home one evening, obviously upset about something, I peeked and she knew I'd done so almost immediately. She packed her things and was out the front door within twenty minutes, and that was the last time I heard from her.

The beam wobbled, and again, I almost lost my footing. This was getting old. I thought about the inevitable. Within the next few minutes, I was going to fall. There were no two ways about it. I would die hanging from a rope, on the site of an 1880s hotel and saloon. I supposed, eventually, my remains would make their way back to the agency. Who would claim the body? Would Pippa be the one tasked with identifying my bloated, blue-toned remains? Would that be the last memory she'd ever have of me?

Something hit my cheek. Carefully, I gazed upward. More cumulonimbus clouds converged… dark gray thunderheads. Several more drops splattered onto my face. *It's starting to rain.* My eyes settled on the railing underneath my feet. *How slick will this banister become, once it gets wetter?* I didn't think things could possibly get any worse for me, but they just had.

The sky lit up, as if a thousand flash bulbs had instantly gone off at once. Multiple lightning bolts branched out and filled the sky. Immediately, thunder—loud enough to loosen my fillings—jolted me upright and I pitched forward … too far forward. Flailing my arms wildly, I felt both boots slip out from under me.

Chapter 2

Nine days prior …

The government … specifically the IRS … wants to get their hands on my house. I have an attorney currently making a career out of keeping them at bay. I live in a modern, forty-million-dollar glass and concrete, multiple cantilevered-platform home, built into the side of a cliff on the outskirts of Kingman, Arizona. It was once owned by Drako Cervenka, a notorious, internationally known criminal, whom I eventually killed. In a convoluted series of events, which involved playing against Drako in a life-or-death chess match, his stunning property became one of the spoils of victory. With it came enough money to keep things running smoothly, on a day-to-day basis, for many years ahead, and still pay the large staff a place this size obviously required. One of those people is Cassie. She runs everything here. Not so much like a butler—more like an overseer. She looks to be of a mixed Asian-Caucasian heritage and is meticulous in her appearance and movements. To be honest, I don't know a hell of a lot about her. What I do know is she does not think about her past—she has an amazingly clear mind. I know that she is both organized and practical, and that she, thus far anyway, has been loyal. She is also a trained killer—skilled in both firearm usage and martial arts; abilities that would give most of my fellow SIFTR agents a run for their money. And that's one of the things I like most about her—she is not a SIFTR agent, so there are no mixed loyalties to contend with.

"Shall I drive you, Mr. Chandler?"

"No, thank you. I'll take the speedster," I replied, referring to the silver 1957 Porsche 356 parked in the garage—another one of the spoils of victory.

I selected several suits from the master bedroom closet and placed them into a hanging garment bag. Cassie, dressed in a white business suit, stood at the foot of the bed. Behind her, fifteen-feet-high floor-to-ceiling windows overlooked the early morning desert landscape below. I finished packing, hefted my bags off the bed, and followed Cassie through the bedroom door. "Look, if ... um ... Pippa calls or comes back—"

She looked back over her shoulder at me but kept on walking. "I told you, I'd rather not get involved in my employer's personal affairs, but fine, I'll let you know, sir." Her face was void of any expression.

I watched her hurry down the stairs ahead of me. As there are multiple levels in this sprawling home, there are multiple stairways, and since so much of the house is made of glass and concrete—a recurring theme—the stairs are no exception. The master suite occupies the highest partially-cantilevered platform on the cliff, so getting to and from this section of the house—say, to the kitchen or great room on level one—requires taking three different short staircases. I was standing on the second-level landing when I decided to *tap in* again before leaving. I never know when, or where, I'll be able to electrically connect when I'm on a mission, so it's better to play it safe now than be sorry later.

Soon after I took up residency here, I added what I've come to refer to as the Voltage Vault. It's nothing elaborate ... basically, a converted, slump stone block, large storage area on the second level. Electricians brought in a commercial, high-power, 40,000-volt electrical conduit. Next to a mounted electrical box sits a comfortable barcalounger, with a small table beside it. I entered the vault, closed and locked the door, and sank down into the old comfy chair. I set an ordinary small manual kitchen timer for ten minutes and leaned back. The way I had the chair situated, when it was fully reclined my head came within four inches of the high-power source.

Within two seconds I was tapped in. Immediately, I felt the oneness … a reunion with unknown others in a place I knew nothing about. The sounds around me, like music, carried me inward, to an elevated state of being that had no equal in my everyday life. I may as well be on another planet. Perhaps I was. Here, in this inner sanctuary in my head, I felt I was a million miles away. I stayed suspended … elevated by unknown others around me. There was a time when I looked at them … or tried to. It took away from the experience, closed down my tapping-in session. There were times, mostly early on, when some singular voice would call out to me. Plead for my help. *Help me, Rob* … but I hadn't heard it for over a month now. A part of me feared learning too much about such desperate-sounding requests. Would finding that person, that being, negatively impact my tapping in … my acquired mental abilities? Perhaps then for selfish reasons, I'd let those calls for help go unanswered. Now, it seemed, I'd never know.

Ding!

Ten minutes had passed. I opened my eyes and inhaled several deep breaths, letting them out slowly. I felt refreshed. I could now operate on a full tank and was ready for whatever SIFTR had in store for me. I continued to rest comfortably for several more moments, thinking about the powerful advantage I carried with me. With the exception of Pippa, no one knew about my mental, mind-reading, capabilities. Not even Cassie … who, I'd learned from peering into her mind, figured I meditated in here, my little closet, once a day. But that didn't mean others weren't getting somewhat suspicious: There were things I knew that I couldn't possibly know. I've slipped several times in the presence of other agents, and really need to be more careful from now on.

* * *

I arrived at the Kingman airport ten minutes later. Once a gunnery-training field during WWII, the small airport is fairly plain and nondescript. I drove up to the security shack and waited for Carl, the lone security officer, to come out and hand me a clipboard. A tall black man in his early sixties, I knew Carl once played for the Lakers and his wrecked knees were constantly on his mind. Now, seeing his perpetual friendly smile, I wondered if anyone really knew just how much this man suffered.

I signed in and handed the clipboard back to Carl.

"You want me to take care of this baby while you're gone, Mr. Chandler? Be no problem … I'll keep her safe for you …"

"Yeah … I saw that movie too, Carl, and there'll be no *Ferris Bueller's Day Off* romps around town today, my friend."

He gave me a half-hearted smile, shrugged, and waved me through.

I drove onto the tarmac and skirted the row of small private planes, mostly Cessnas. I continued forward for close to a minute, veered right, and pulled into a large, open, Quonset hut-style hangar. Parking against the corrugated metal wall, I grabbed my bags and hurried out to the tarmac. Curt Baltimore was standing by the lowered steps of a Gulfstream G650. Painted gloss-black, with no discernible markings or logos, the big jet looked strangely ominous compared to the other smaller, mostly white jets parked nearby. Its two jet engines were already revving up and Baltimore, arms crossed over his chest, looked impatient to leave.

"Nice of you to mosey on by," he said, taking my bags and handing them off to a steward standing at the rear of the plane.

I didn't reply to that. I knew Baltimore and knew that his caustic comments were just how he was. He lived and breathed SIFTR—a company man, through and through. I didn't share his enthusiasm for the agency—or any government agency. I'd recently discovered retirement was not in the cards for me; at least, not until I figured out how to do it and keep on breathing.

"And good morning to you too, sunshine," I said.

He ignored me and gestured for me to head up the steps. I did as told as he followed behind me. I was greeted by Darci, the thirty-something flight attendant, also a SIFTR agent. With a quick peek into her thoughts, I discovered this was her last scheduled round-trip flight. She was getting married and leaving the agency. Obviously, not all SIFTR agents were required to honor the same in-for-a-lifetime requirement that I seemed to be held to.

The cabin smelled of leather and newness. Thick tan carpeting, muted lighting cast from recesses above, plus a perfect complement of burl walnut accents strategically placed. No less than twelve camel-colored wide leather swivel seats were positioned down the expansive cabin. Midway back sat a handsome, gray-haired man in an impeccably tailored dark navy suit. He casually raised a hand and I headed for the opposite seat, directly in front of him. Baltimore moved past me and sat next to the window.

"Good morning, Rob."

"Mr. Calloway," I said. "Replaced the old G550?"

"No … it's still a SIFTR asset."

I leaned back into the plush seat and waited for the man in charge of the SIFTR agency to say something. He didn't look happy. In fact, he looked terrible. I peered into his mind, and suddenly found it hard to breathe. *Pippa's been taken!*

Chapter 3

I did my best to keep my face neutral. Calloway nodded toward Baltimore and I was handed a folder. Inside were a dozen color eight by tens. My heart stopped when I viewed a panel truck with white letters reading *D.C. Water and Sewer Authority* painted on its side panel. But that wasn't what caught my eye. It was a long black item being hefted either into, or out of, the back of the truck. I'd seen many of them in my lifetime. I knew what a body bag looked like. I glanced up to meet Calloway's stare.

"Just keep going."

But I remained focused on the film's image. The surroundings looked familiar. *Where have I seen that building before?* "D.C.?" I asked.

Again, Calloway nodded at me. What I was looking at, directly behind the truck, was a brown, nondescript, box-shaped building. It was obviously old … perhaps historical.

"The Lockkeeper's House," I said. I knew the building and didn't need confirmation from Calloway or Baltimore. I must have passed the two-centuries-old structure hundreds of times. Located between the White House and the National Mall—maybe even considered part of the mall—it was easy to walk past without a second glance. I brought the photo closer to my eyes. The small building was two storied, with one door and four windows. The roofline showed two chimneys, placed at opposite ends of the structure. The front door was partially opened. A date and time stamp were placed in the lower right corner of the photo: 3:31 AM.

I moved to the second image, which was nearly identical to the first. The only discernible difference was the positioning of the two uniformed men with the body bag. They were now moving across the street, each holding on to an end of the bag. The time stamp read 3:32 AM. So they were moving the body bag out of the truck. I riffled through the remaining photos; each one showed the progress of the two men, until they were finally shown entering into the Lockkeeper's House. The last photo showed the two men absent from view and the door closed.

I looked up at Calloway, then over to Baltimore. "Are you telling me Pippa is inside that bag? That she's dead?"

Neither man spoke for several long beats. Calloway eventually said, "Yes, we're fairly certain it is Pippa, but not so sure that she's dead. Why go to the trouble of transporting her this way? There's far easier, safer, means to dispose of a body."

Baltimore retrieved the folder, opened it, and scanning through the photos pulled number five out and handed it across to me. "This one shows the best view of the body bag. And, thanks to the nearby street light, you can catch the most detail." He tapped at the photo and handed it over to me.

Again, I brought it closer to my eyes. I shrugged, not seeing what he was referring to. Then I saw it: In the middle of the bag, low and long, was a smooth protrusion; a lump that looked to be cylindrical-shaped. "An oxygen tank?"

Both Calloway and Baltimore nodded.

"But why take her there? To an old abandoned historical building?"

"Do you know the history behind the structure?" Calloway asked.

I was finding it hard to keep my composure. This was Pippa's life or demise we were dealing with. "I don't know … I presume it has something to do with keeping the keys to various locks around Washington."

"No … not that kind of lock. In the early 1800s much of that area of D.C. was under water. Canals cut across, all the way to the Potomac. Various locks were set up, to raise and lower small boats. The Lockkeeper's House was constructed for the Lockkeeper to collect tolls and keep records of the comings and goings of small boats. Eventually … sometime after the Civil War, as railroads became the primary mode of transporting things, the canals were filled in and the Lockkeeper's House was given over to the United States government. It became a small police station for a while, then a public bathroom; now it's a depot for city park groundskeepers."

I felt the big jet moving along the tarmac. Outside the window, I saw we were already moving along at a fast clip. "Interesting … what does all this have to do with Pippa?"

Calloway said, "You already knew, firsthand, that there are high-speed trains running beneath D.C. The president has use of his own train, as do several other important government officials. We believe there is a second subterranean means of transportation. One that utilizes underground hydro-powered passages, leftover from the canal's era."

"Should be easy enough to check. Why don't you just look? Open the door to the little lock house and see."

"We did that," Baltimore barked back.

I waited for him to continue.

"There's nothing there. No trap door … no secret access. It's a fucking garden shack."

"Obviously, there's more to the property than is evident. Bulldoze the thing!" I said.

"It's not that easy. Our agent was discovered entering the house. Caught by security cameras, he is currently sitting in a cell, courtesy of Homeland Security. There are few things more important to them than protecting our country's national treasures, namely the National Mall, and checking out potential dangers to the public. Until cleared, he's being held as a possible terrorist threat."

I looked at Calloway, mystified. "Hell, you're a BFF with the President of the United States ... you ride together on that secret little train of his. Can't you persuade him to pull some political strings?" I asked.

Both Calloway and Baltimore exchanged looks.

"That's where things get a little murky," Calloway answered.

"Those two men carrying the body bag, at least one, we suspect, is CIA. That's probably an agency surveillance truck, as well," Baltimore said. "We can't go anywhere near that building. And we can't go to the president, either. Not yet, anyway."

"So what are we doing? Heading to D.C.?" I asked, looking out the window.

"You'll be our man on the ground at the mall. We have two other teams working this from other angles," Calloway said.

"On the ground. What does that entail?"

* * *

The thick, mid-summer eastern-seaboard humidity made the eighty-five-degree air feel more like one hundred and ten. And whoever'd worn these faded old overalls previously had a serious problem—they reeked to high heaven. Aside from the hot sticky air, and the continual wafting-up of stink every time I moved ... the fact I wasn't able to actively look for Pippa caused my foul mood to ratchet up every minute that passed.

Gustavo handed me a shovel, then picked up one for himself from the bed of the electric garden cart. Together we hoofed it over a grassy rise to the east side of the Jefferson Memorial. I was about as far away from the Lockkeeper's House as humanly possible without leaving the mall. Two Asian girls, probably college kids, were taking a selfie, with the white, domed-shaped memorial in the near-distance strategically positioned behind them. Gustavo and I walked by them and I heard one of the girls make a choking sound. A waft of my own odor rose up and entered my nostrils. I didn't need to read their minds to know what they were thinking. I glared at Gustavo's back; he'd purposely given these particular overalls to me—picked them out special. After twenty-five years on the job, he didn't like being told with whom he'd be working. Today was day three and so far I hadn't the opportunity to be in the Lockkeeper's House on my own, but I did notice it was under heavy surveillance—by cameras and plain-clothed security people, or agents.

Apparently, SIFTR had done an adequate job in providing the necessary cover credentials. I was Garry Mangus from Akron, Ohio, here on a special job-share program for the mentally challenged. Seems the U.S. government will bend over backward for the disabled; there are all kinds of opportunities for those suffering from such misfortune. Commendable, to be sure, but right now, I didn't give a shit about the unfortunate, underprivileged, or the mentally handicapped, and I contemplated hitting Gustavo in the back of the head with the business end of my shovel.

"Dig here, Mangus … hurry it up, man," Gustavo said, making an exaggerated, two-handed digging gesture just in case I didn't know what *dig here* meant.

I nodded and, keeping with my cover identity, pleasantly started to dig. The ground was soggy—saturated with water.

"Somewhere around here there's a broken sprinkler pipe ... maybe a foot and a half down," he said. He too was digging and together we piled the dirt and grass onto a growing mound off to the side. I looked into his mind for any indication he'd been involved with Pippa's abduction. Baltimore had earlier mentioned that Gustavo might have been approached—bought off. But they just weren't sure. The Lockkeeper's House was Gustavo's domain. Anyone would be hard-pressed to gain access into that place without him having direct knowledge of it. Certainly, the man seemed worried about something. Now, watching him in my peripheral vision, I saw the rhythmic tensing as his jaw muscles repeatedly clenched. He was inwardly arguing with someone, replaying the same conversation in his mind over and over again. It was dark so I couldn't fully make out just to whom he was mentally talking. Someone in a suit and tie; someone Gustavo feared.

"Just do what you're told, or your big momma's lack of residency papers will land her on a bus back to Mexico."

"She's a Spaniard ... we're from Madrid."

"Then onto a boat or a fucking plane. She's out of here and maybe your wife, too. You'll do what we want ... tonight, Gustavo. End of discussion."

I wasn't able to decipher what, exactly, the man in the suit wanted from Gustavo. Whatever it was had made him nervous. It was unethical—against his principles. I was about to leave his mind when an image of someplace dark came into view. It was a dungeon, of sorts ... perhaps in an old castle. I'd seen places like that before: cold, damp, and dreary. My mind flashed back to the Goertz's Baden-Baden castle. And then I saw her ... a glimpse of Pippa's face. Someone had partially unzipped the top section of the body bag. Gustavo was looking down at her ... he had never seen a dead body before.

Chapter 4

Pippa opened her eyes to total blackness. For a moment she wondered if she had gone blind. She felt the cold wet surface beneath her back and tried to comprehend where she was. *What's happened to me?*

Slowly, the memories of her abduction returned. She'd just left Chandler's house—had pulled off the road and was about to do a U-turn. They'd fought and she'd been overly sensitive. There came a tapping on her car window. A lost-looking man, staring at her through the glass, was holding a map in one raised hand. He wore overly short shorts and a florescent green fanny pack. *Who even wears fanny packs these days?* He couldn't have looked any more innocuous. And his very ordinariness should have tipped her off. She should have had the presence of mind to question even the slightest ordinariness. She was trained to do just that. Perhaps she'd let her relationship with Chandler dull her senses—endanger herself and others.

The needle poked into her neck's carotid artery before she had time to swipe his hand away. *Since when had she so lost her edge?*

* * *

She heard water dripping from multiple locations—sounds echoed into the blackness. Pippa forced herself to relax, allowing her heart rate to slowly settle into a normal sinus rhythm. More sounds. She heard voices in the distance—too far away to make out what they were saying. They were getting closer.

Pippa sat up, realizing her hands were bound. She wanted to rub her sore wrists, but the snug-fitting, quick-tie binding wouldn't allow her to do so. She stood and reached out with both hands in the darkness. Nothing. She took several tentative steps forward, until she felt something hard and cold … and wet … and slimy. She'd reached a wall. She used it to guide her way sideways and kept going until she came to a corner, and another right-angled wall. She followed along it until she felt a strong breeze touch her cheeks and the smell of rank water. Somewhere in front of her was an open sewer line. The voices were now loud enough for her to discern that there were two men arguing. Both had accents, unmistakably German.

Pippa saw light—the back and forth swaying of white flashlight beams. As the men approached, her immediate surroundings became illuminated. She was indeed within the subterranean confines of a sewer system. Three massive sewer pipes, easily ten to twelve feet high, converged here. She was standing on a raised platform, walled in on three sides, with a half-height wall facing out toward the three-piped junction fifteen feet below. This was some kind of water station. She could now see, up three concrete steps, where a series of massive pipes transected into valves; each was topped with a big red-painted shut-off wheel.

The two men came to a halt and stood on a concrete catwalk, five feet above where she now stood. Pippa shielded her eyes from their bright flashlight beams with her hands.

"Who the hell are you?" she asked.

Only one of the men answered her. "Friends, Ms. Rosette. You will not be harmed … if you come without resistance."

"What do you want with me?"

One of the men began descending on iron rungs. Pippa hadn't noticed the built-in ladder was even there before. He stepped down and approached her. He was blond and big. He could be a model on the cover of GQ—just the right amount of beard scruff—and a stylish haircut she guessed wasn't a Saturday morning *Super Cuts* special. His masculine-scented body spray reached her before he did. It was a pleasant scent, and she found herself breathing it in. Dressed in a business suit and tieless, the top two buttons of his fitted dress shirt were undone, revealing a muscular hairless chest. This man put in some serious gym time.

"You can call me Mr. Taffy."

"Like the candy?"

He didn't answer.

She watched him appraise her, his eyes first taking in her face and then wandering up and down the entirety of her body. But she didn't get any hunger vibes from the scrutiny—nothing sexual. Mister metro-sexual had a job to do and she was being appraised, not unlike a rancher assessing the sale of a Jersey cow at a county fair. After pulling a knife out from somewhere, he cut the quick-tie binding on her wrists. Gratefully, Pippa rubbed at the raw skin there.

Taffy gestured with his flashlight toward the ladder. "Mr. Loren has a gun pointed at you. Please climb the rungs."

Pippa moved in the direction of the ladder, suddenly self-conscious of the wetness of her backside. She was wearing off-white skinny jeans and she wondered what lying in the sewer had … she cut her own thoughts short. *Who gives a shit what my pants look like?*

The truth was she had never met a more perfect-looking man in her life, as if he were created in a laboratory. *Weird.* She climbed the rungs and waited next to Loren. In the dim light, he looked to be in his early forties, dark and brooding—almost *gangster-like.*

"What do you want with me?" she asked, as Taffy finished his climb up.

"Shut your mouth or I'll put a sock in it," Mr. Loren said.

While Taffy exuded all the emotion of an ant, Loren fumed with pent-up rage. She could see it in his eyes—a powder keg ready to blow at the smallest provocation. Taffy assumed the lead, then Pippa, with angry Loren following in the rear. She felt his eyes on her backside.

They walked along the concrete catwalk for what seemed ten minutes before they came to a nondescript metal door—a door without a handle. Taffy stood still, his body perfectly erect at the door, and looked up. Then she saw it too, a small black box … a camera. She heard a buzz and the door unlatched. Taffy pulled the door open and walked through. Pippa felt a not-so-gentle shove at the small of her back and took the cue to follow. They entered into some kind of transportation terminal—like a subway station—but there weren't any trains or subways here. The station was immaculately clean. Her eyes took in the polished concrete floors and intricately tiled walls and recognized lots of money had been spent here. Like the earlier concrete sewer pipes, they now approached another kind of pipe: just as big, but totally clear. No, not perfectly clear—it was filled with water. In a blur, a giant pill—like a huge white Tylenol—whisked by.

The scream was high and piercing. "Pippa!"

Pippa spun around, fists clenched, prepared for whatever was coming. To her surprise, it was a woman running toward her. Arms stretched wide, it was Heidi Goertz, wearing a dazzlingly bright smile and designer everything, right down to her red Jimmy Choos. Heidi, tan and fit, her yellow-blonde hair pulled back into a tight ponytail, looked like a million bucks.

Pippa didn't resist the quickly coming embrace, as Heidi's arms enfolded her, pulling her in tight. Heidi then stood back, holding Pippa at arms' length, and appraised her. "Oh … I love the blonde look."

Pippa remembered the last time she'd seen the WZZ leader, in Baden-Baden, Germany. At that time Pippa's looks had been altered for cover—her blonde hair dyed almost black—and there were other cosmetic changes as well—including her cup-size.

Heidi spun Pippa sideways and looked down at her water-stained jeans. Her English was near perfect, only the slightest hint of German as she spoke: "We need to get you out of these wet things. I'm so sorry for the dramatics … you must have a thousand questions." She glanced disapprovingly at silent Loren.

Pippa used the back of her hands to pry Heidi's hands off her shoulders. "Just one, actually. What the hell do you want with me?"

"Oh, come, come … you can't still be mad at me?"

"You mean, after you drained out my blood and had a roomful of neo-Nazis drinking it from a bucket?"

"I got caught up in the moment. We all make mistakes, Pippa. But now is now, and we have so much to talk about." Her smile faded as soon as she turned toward Taffy and Loren. What came next was nothing short of shocking. Heidi moved with the speed of a wild panther. Her right foot swung up and, like a pile driver, extended out into a forward thrust. The bottom sole of her shoe, more precisely where the four-inch spiked heel protruded from it, struck Loren in the solar plexus, directly below his sternum. Startled, he stared wide-eyed and unmoving for at least five seconds. When he eventually toppled over onto his back, clearly dead, Heidi's right-footed Jimmy Choo was still imbedded in his mid-section.

"Fetch me my shoe, will you, Mr. Taffy?"

Pippa's eyes moved from the shoe to Heidi, standing with one bare foot raised off the floor. Heidi giggled and shrugged. "You shouldn't have been so mistreated … that was not my intention." Her eyes next flashed toward Taffy. Pippa was pretty sure he got her not-so-subtle message, as well.

Taffy retrieved Heidi's shoe, pulled a folded handkerchief from an inside jacket pocket, and wiped away all traces of Loren's blood. He handed the shoe back to Heidi. "It won't happen again, Mrs. Goertz."

Another huge *Tylenol-like* pill was approaching. This time, it stopped at their terminal and a segment of the pipe separated and rotated upward. Dual streams of escaped water splashed down onto the tile floor, as double doors on the big pill slid apart.

"What is this place … and what is that?"

"Simply a means to an end, my dear Pippa. Subterranean-travel that goes unfettered and unnoticed. There's so much you don't know … few do … including much of your own government. With deeply buried tubes like these, now transecting the United States and most of Europe, and terminals like this one operating in most key cities, our organization today has the amazing capability to move great distances in a fraction of the time it would take to fly."

They left Loren where he lay and moved into the pod-like car. The best way to describe the interior was plush. Pippa thought it made Calloway's G550 look like a covered wagon in comparison. Everything was done in a soft, cream-colored leather—the wide bucket seats, the walls and ceiling, and even the floor seemed to be covered in leather. A straight line of six porthole windows, positioned halfway up on both sides of the pod car, provided views into the station on one side and more polished concrete walls on the other.

Heidi sat and patted the seat across from her. "Sit here, Pippa. I need to talk to you about something important … something wonderful."

Pippa sat, keeping her expression neutral. She watched as Taffy continued on forward, waiting for the next hatch to slide open, then sitting down next to the pod's driver. The hatch slid silently shut.

The pod car began to move and Pippa felt herself being tugged snugly into her seatback. She didn't need to look out the closest porthole to know they were traveling at high speed.

"Where are we going, Heidi?"

"Eventually, Denver, but first we need to make a quick stop in New York—the Chrysler Building, to be exact. We need to pick up Leon." Heidi rolled her eyes at her own mention of Leon, then looked Pippa up and down and pursed her lips. "I think I have just the thing for you to wear in my closet."

Pippa remembered that Leon, Heidi's husband, had purchased one of the world's most recognizable New York high-rises, for Heidi's birthday. She didn't think, after their plans for dominating the world's financial markets were squelched, that the purchase still could be finalized. Heidi and her husband, as well as anyone else associated with the WZZ, were currently being hunted by virtually every covert agency around the world.

Nothing was even remotely discernible out the porthole now. "How fast are we moving?" Pippa asked.

"This little thing moves along at hundreds of miles an hour, once it gets going. This one, of course, is our own private hydro-pod; most pods are quite utilitarian-looking, but still capable of traveling the same rapid speed."

"Where are we? Still in Kingman?"

Heidi smiled at that. "No, my dear … little Kingman doesn't have a terminal; how silly of you. Actually, you haven't been in Arizona for quite some time now. You were brought to me unconscious and were kept that way for quite some time."

Pippa wanted to ask just how long that had been, but Heidi continued on:

"Right now … we're leaving Washington, D.C. We should be in New York in less than an hour."

Washington … New York … Denver? Things are happening so quickly! "Then what?" Pippa asked, surprised by Heidi's willingness to share information.

"Get you freshened up, for one thing. Out of those dirty, damp clothes."

Pippa, doing her best to look nonchalant, waited for her to continue.

"Just know, I will be keeping you close to me." Heidi's expression changed to one of concern. She leaned forward, bringing her face in close. She reached up and with the back of her hand gently stroked Pippa's cheek. "Dear … try to escape, or contact SIFTR … and I'll be forced to kill you. Plus, I have another surprise for you before I'd do that—something that will make you wish I had killed you first."

Chapter 5

It was late afternoon before Gustavo drove us back in the electric garden cart to the Lockkeeper's House.

"Get the tools."

"Okay," I said, hopping out of the cart. I collected both shovels and a five-gallon bucket full of hand tools, while Gustavo unlocked the front door to the house. He swung the door inward and held it open for me. It was dark inside and smelled just like you'd expect a garden shack to smell—soil; weed-eater-type chemicals; manure. The space was now open, but probably wasn't like this back in the 1800s. At least eight metal support beams were strategically placed to prop up thick wooden crossbeams along the span of the ceiling. The entire space was virtually filled—two wheelbarrows; a pallet of stacked potting soil; mowers; grass-edgers; trimmers; and every other kind of garden tool imaginable. At opposite ends of the space, brick fireplaces were positioned—each blackened from years of soot accumulation.

Gustavo took the shovels from me, hanging them up on a rack on the wall that also held a collection of other long-handled tools. It was then, when his back was turned away, that I needled him. Courtesy of Baltimore, I injected a tiny, but potent amount of narcotics into the nape of his exposed neck. My injection delivery method was via a small thimble-like sleeve worn over my forefinger. He staggered, struggling to reach around his neck with his hand, but dropped mid-motion. I caught him as he fell and lowered him to the floor. I had about ten minutes before he'd start to reawaken.

I wasn't exactly sure what I'd find here that the other agent hadn't. There seemed to be nothing unusual around. It seemed logical that there must be some kind of access panel leading down below. I moved the two wheelbarrows aside—nothing there. I pushed against the stack of potting soil but the pallet didn't budge. I next hurried to the fireplace on the right—pushed and pulled at virtually every brick. I crossed the open space and repeated the same procedure on the other fireplace. Gustavo's leg twitched.

I scanned the space one more time, looking for the one thing I might have missed. Gustavo's other leg moved. Out of desperation I gazed up at the ceiling. *There!* A trapdoor. I saw a cord hanging down, and in three strides I was beneath the door and pulling on the cord. Similar to an attic access panel in a home, the trapdoor opened, partially lowering an attached, expandable ladder. I inspected the mechanism and unlatched the bottom part of the ladder—sliding it the rest of the way down to the floor. Gustavo coughed and turned onto his side.

Up the ladder I went and was surprised to discover an upper area set up as an office. Three ancient-looking wooden desks and chairs, plus several file cabinets placed along the back wall, occupied the whole second floor. I didn't linger—I knew exactly where I needed to go. Across to the bricked fireplace wall on the right, I found the nearly imperceptible seam—a space not more than a sixteenth of an inch gap, where the brick chimney met the brick wall. I followed the seam upward and found where it continued on, running within the mortar and across the chimney, about a foot over my head. I pulled on the chimney—it held steadfast. I stood back and looked at the bricks for something out of the ordinary. Low, and along the left side, was a discolored darker red brick. I knelt down, and as I gave it a push, it receded inward. I heard an audible click and a seven-foot-by-four-foot chimney section swung open on internal hinges. Pulling it ajar, just wide enough to peer inside, I could see metal ladder rungs leading downward. I stepped back and used both hands to push the chimney section back into place. The one recessed brick popped back out.

By the time I reached Gustavo, he was trying to sit up. I placed a hand on his shoulder and held him steady. "Hold on there, man. You took a bit of a fall."

Gustavo's eyes cleared and he looked up at me. "I don't know what happened … I was putting the tools—"

"It's all right. Probably only a mild heatstroke." I handed him an opened water bottle. "Drink some of this … hydrate."

He drank up and was soon looking better. "We need to empty the rest of the cart." He tried to stand.

"No … you need to go on home, Gustavo. Take it easy. I can finish up here. I've already emptied the rest of the tools and pipes out of the cart. I'll put it all away. Take the cart."

"No. You're not authorized. You don't have keys."

I knew Gustavo was feeling pretty sick—nauseous—a temporary effect of the drug. Soon, he'd be dealing with relentless diarrhea. He suddenly passed gas and his eyes opened wide.

"Perhaps you're right. I don't feel so good." He put a hand on his stomach and slowly got to his feet. "I need to go. Okay … here, take these. Lock up as soon as you're done. Be here six in the morning, along with my keys." He half-walked, half-shuffled to the entrance. He murmured, "Shit shit shit …"

I heard the little electric motor on his cart turn over, then soon fade away into the distance.

I spent the next few minutes bringing in the rest of the garden tools and sections of PVC pipe. I closed and locked the Lockkeeper's House front door from the inside. At some point, someone outside watching might notice I hadn't come back out. How long I'd be in here depended on what I'd find at the bottom of the metal rung ladder.

Within thirty seconds, I was climbing up the trapdoor ladder and heading toward the brick chimney wall. I used the toe on my boot to depress the brick. The mechanism clicked and I swung the chimney section out and away. Moving inside the wall, I saw a swaying string hanging from somewhere above me. I gave it a tug and an exposed lightbulb came alive. Dim light illuminated a thousand cobwebs all around the narrow space. I descended several rungs, then spotted a brass handle; pulling the chimney section inward, I closed it. Something small and crawly dropped onto my cheek and I brushed it away. Down the rungs I went—soon I was passing what looked to be a roughly chiseled out section of foundation. The vertical shaft I was descending was also made of brick, but moist and blackened with decades of mold. At forty feet down, the single bulb's light, hanging high above, was barely reaching me. Feeling cool air rising up from below, I looked down but could see nothing but blackness. In the ten seconds I'd hesitated, four large spiders settled onto the back of my left hand, then three on my right. *Hacklemesh Weavers*—sometimes called *Black Lace Weavers*—they like crawling around in dark, moist places, in most upper east coast states. I figured there was a nest of the damn things close by me. I blew them off my hands and continued climbing downward.

* * *

I had to slow down my descent as complete darkness enveloped me. Nagging concerns for Pippa's welfare were heavily intruding into my thoughts. This new venture was taking far too long—I was giving it too much energy and time. Whoever had Pippa could be torturing her this very second. Hell, she might already be dead.

I probably missed a light switch to a second light source somewhere along the way down. By the time I reached the bottom of the narrow shaft, I figured I'd descended about one hundred and fifty feet. Maybe even more. Several times I'd debated if I should re-ascend, go back into the house above, and look for a flashlight. But now, somewhere below me, there was a light source—I could just make out dimmed lighting coming off from my left and right. Soon, I was standing on worn cobblestones, in an area I figured was constructed several centuries earlier.

In the dim light I noticed movement off to my left—a shape—roughly the size of a loaf of bread; a loaf of bread with a head and four legs. Bar none, it was the largest rat I'd ever seen—King Kong of rats. It lumbered forward within the passageway as I headed off in the opposite direction. The passageway was roughly ten feet wide by ten feet high. The cobblestones were now submerged, lying beneath several inches of water; my leather boots were drenched as I slogged forward. The good news was the light ahead made for much better visibility. I slowed my pace as I approached what looked to be some kind of expansive construction zone. Then everything opened up—into a cavern of sorts—beneath bright construction spotlights. Several large dump trucks, along with other mining-type vehicles, sat idle. I stayed low and walked between the vehicles, noticing the ground was now solid rock beneath my soggy boots. A wall of rock loomed in front of me. Sitting half-in half-out of the wall was a spectacular, immense, twenty-five-foot-tall boring machine. I climbed up onto a nearby ten-foot mound of rock and dirt, and looked around me. There were tunnels in the distance … a whole network of tunnels were down here. A single-wide construction trailer sat nearby, its single door wide open. Dressed in khakis, a button-down shirt, with a hardhat on his head, a man's silhouetted, backlit-form filled the open doorway. In his hand was a gun—one that was pointed directly at me.

"Move … twitch … and you're dead."

Chapter 6

Before answering, I began probing his mind. He'd been warned earlier this morning to stay alert. They'd gone to great lengths to make this underground site, and others like it, inaccessible to outsiders. He'd been armed and told to stay vigilant for anyone showing up not authorized to be there. He was some kind of Civil Engineer—and by the guttural inflections in his speech, German. I continued to read the myriad of images flashing through his consciousness and was surprised to see that Heidi Goertz was one of them.

"Are you deaf? Get down from there … slowly."

"Ich bin hier um Sie zu warnen," *I'm here to warn you,* I said, hoping my German was convincing.

"Worüber redest du?" *What are you talking about?* he asked.

I switched over to English: "I'm the man watching up top … the National Mall."

"I don't know anything about that," he replied back, speaking English.

"Then you can call Mrs. Goertz … I'm sure she won't mind if you disturb her during her busy day."

He hesitated. I'd struck a chord using her name. He was seriously afraid of that woman. "What is it you want? Why are you here?"

"Lower the gun. There's been a sighting … a man seen entering the sewer system. Where's your security? Don't tell me you're the only one here?"

His gun lowered to his side. Looking around, realizing now he was the only one still at the site, he said, "We don't work on Sundays ... you should know that. What did you say your name was?"

"I meant your security. Are you daft? Of course I know things are shut down on Sundays ... but trespassers don't give a shit what day it is."

"Security is making their rounds. They just left ..." he looked at his watch, "twenty minutes ago."

I mentally suggested to him that he put his gun away. He hesitated, then raised it up again. "Why not just contact me by radio? Why come all the way down here?"

I let out a long breath, looking annoyed. "Do I look like I have a radio on me? You think I carry it around for everyone to see? I'm a fucking gardener." I was now getting more useful information from his mind. He definitely didn't trust me—suspected something amiss—and mentally was running through all the access points I could have used. This underground system, whatever it was, was vast. Something referred to as the *Hydrospan*.

"Let me take a look at your engineering drawings. I'll show you where the—"

"Stay right there!"

Halfway down the mound I stopped and held up my hands. My mind flashed to Pippa. I didn't have time for delays.

"Shoot me, then. Just be prepared for what Heidi will do to you." I put my arms down, walked the rest of the way off the mound, up the steps, and onto the platform he was standing on. I moved past him and entered the construction office. In his mind, his thoughts noted I smelled like shit.

The confined office space was taken up with a desk. A

large computer was running, its screen displaying multi-colored CAD-type drawings. A close-by drafting table was littered with giant, schematic-type engineering drawings. Countless other paper rolls were piled around the office.

"Show me … where are we here?" I asked, standing at the table.

I noticed the gun was now tucked into the back of his pants as he moved to my side. He used a marker to circle one small section on the plans. What I was looking at was the largest civil engineering feat in the history of the United States … perhaps the world. Billions … maybe trillions of dollars of investment must have been requisitioned for this kind of enterprise to succeed. More importantly, its magnitude and scope could not have gone unnoticed. At a minimum, city water and electrical utilities would be alerted to such a vast undertaking. Even though the construction site was a hundred fifty to two hundred feet down, this underground venture couldn't have gone undetected, which meant high-placed government officials had some kind of involvement.

"Wie heißt du?" *What is your name*, I asked.

"Moritz. Zeigen Sie mir, wo er entdeckt wurde." *Show me where he was spotted.*

I tried to make heads or tails of the plans in front of me—thousands of intricate lines and symbols, which, for the most part, made no sense. The tiny text was written in German. Then I spotted FDR Gedenkstätte, the *FDR Memorial.*

"Right here … near the FDR Memorial."

"Ahh … yes, there is an access point there." He used his marker to draw a line, starting at the memorial, then straight down into what looked to be a sewer line. Through a series of right and left turns, the line finally ended right here, at this deep, subterranean level.

Moritz continued to look at the plans but his mind was racing. He no longer believed my story. He knew, beyond any doubt, that it was me who shouldn't be there. The truth was, my story was weak. I was surprised he'd bought into it as long as he had. In the end, though, he was an engineer, not an operative. In a fraction of a second, I pulled the gun from the back of his pants and pointed it at his head. "Okay, Moritz, we have a lot to discuss. Take a seat."

* * *

Apparently, the armed, five-man security team was on rounds, covering several construction sites like this one, and scheduled to return within the hour—maybe sooner. It took me close to thirty minutes to get any meaningful information from Moritz. I'd ask a question and he'd refuse to answer it. That was fine—I silently retrieved the answers from his mind anyway—at least to the extent that he mentally was in possession of the right answers to my questions. His range of knowledge, basically, was limited to his particular engineering duties. What I did glean was that an army, in the thousands, had been assembled over the last few years. Composed of scores of men and women—of Germanic origin, mostly, although not entirely. As suspected, U.S. government officials were indeed involved. Who they were, Moritz did not know. What I did learn was that Washington D.C. was not the hub, or central command point, for the operation. That was in Denver. Interestingly, its location was beneath DIA—Denver International Airport.

I continued with the questioning: "Why? Specifically, what's the main purpose of ... Hydrospan?"

He shook his head, just like he'd done throughout the long list of questions I'd asked. But reading his mind, the answer to my last question came across clearly … *rapid deployment of military assets.* When the time was right, the organization he worked for would strike … and One World Government would take charge. The result promised an end to future wars and global suffering; international, ego-driven, geo-politics would come to an end. One thing was certain: the scope of this operation extended all the way up, to the highest levels of the U.S. government. I thought about that. Not knowing how close their full operation was to completion, SIFTR would need to tread carefully. Hell, it might already be too late. Then something else struck me … *how could SIFTR—Calloway—not be aware of this?*

There were noises coming from outside the trailer. I held the gun up to Moritz's temple. "Go to the door and wave … let them know everything is fine. Remember, you'll have a gun pointed at the back of your head."

Moritz stood and went to the open doorway. Stepping onto the platform, he waved. I stayed out of sight, but still delved into his mind and I could see what he was seeing. There were five men—dressed in black combat fatigues and armed with M4 Carbines—standard U.S. Army infantry issue. With its shortened barrel and collapsible stock, I could see how the M4 would be ideal for potential close-quarter combat down here. *So who in hell was supplying them with standard Army-issue weapons?*

The security team spread out, slowly inspecting the construction site. Periodically, each man spoke into his shoulder mic, declaring an area *clear*. Again, Moritz waved and I saw the men head off in the direction of a distant bored-out tunnel.

Now I had to deal with Moritz. It was most important that my presence here remain undetected. Unfortunately, that meant Moritz had to go. I had one more injection thimble left in my pocket. This one would deliver a lethal compound, triggering an instant heart attack, and be completely undetectable in an autopsy. It had been intended for Gustavo, if it had come to that.

"They'll be back very soon," Moritz said, still looking off in the direction of the tunnel.

I placed the small device on my forefinger and peeled back the tiny protective plastic sheath from the needle. Reaching over, I placed my hand and fingers around Moritz's neck. Before he knew what was happening, I heard a breathy *humph* sound escape from his lips, and his legs gave out. Right there to catch him, I dragged his lifeless body over to a chair in front of the small desk and eased him into it. Tilting his upper body forward across the CAD monitor, I looked at my handiwork. He looked as if he'd died there … a massive heart attack in the midst of a busy day's work. I placed his right-hand fingers over the mouse. Then I remembered he had held the gun in his left hand—he was left-handed. I transferred the mouse into that hand. Now it was time to return to the Lockkeeper's House and contact Baltimore. I heard a sound—the subtlest of creaks, like the settling of weight on worn, tired floor joists. I looked up and saw a large man standing in the doorway. The muzzle of his Glock 19 was pointed directly at my head.

Chapter 7

Pippa sat quietly in her seat while keeping a leery eye on her captor, sitting across from her. Aside from Heidi's obvious sociopathic tendencies to kill those people she was displeased with, the woman clearly had other issues. She was constantly in motion—fussing with her hair, checking and rechecking her reflection in the nearby portal window, and she talked to distraction—always about herself.

"I think you and I should be friends ... best of friends, in fact."

Pippa stared back at her without answering.

"Oh, I know you're still upset with me. I don't blame you. I get caught up in the moment. That's what makes me ... what? So dynamic."

"If we're going to be friends, a good start would be to let me off this train."

"Hydro-pod," Heidi corrected. She waved Pippa's comment away as if she were swatting a fly. "What I will do is give you something ... something special. Hmm! What shall it be? Ten million dollars placed into your bank account? No ... too pedestrian. I have it! I'll share with you something only a handful of people know about. Not even your own president. You'll learn that knowledge is power. Power is worth far more than money. Money is easy to come by ... but power is earned and it's what elevates one to greatness."

Pippa gave her a perfunctory nod. *So Heidi has elevated herself to greatness. Is there no end to this woman's vanity?*

"You've never had power, Pippa. Not really. So you don't know what I'm talking about. You can't know what you don't know. You don't know the sheer visceral thrill of it."

"I guess I don't. Oh well …"

Heidi scowled at her and then, just as suddenly, was again smiling mischievously. She looked up, raising her chin, as she peered toward the back of the pod. "Taffy!"

The big man approached from behind Pippa's seat and stood before Heidi, who let one of her Jimmy Choos fall to the floor.

"There's still blood on my toes," she said, rocking one bare foot with her legs still crossed.

Taffy looked down at her perfectly clean-looking foot and shrugged. Brows raised, Heidi continued to move her bare foot back and forth, like a fast-moving metronome. Taffy gave a hesitant glance toward Pippa.

"Lick my toes, Taffy. Make sure each and every toe is thoroughly clean. Do a good job now, Mr. Taffy, and I'll reward you later."

Again, Taffy glanced over to Pippa. Face flushed, he pulled at the fabric over his knees, slightly hiking up his slacks, then lowered himself down onto the floor. Heidi's waving foot became still, as Taffy took her foot in one hand and brought it up to his chest. Heidi tilted her head forward and let out an impatient breath.

Pippa felt the man's humiliation. She wanted to say something … hell, she wanted to drive her own foot into the woman's surgically altered, perfect face. But she knew it would be the last thing she'd ever live to do. Heidi was undoubtedly prepared for Pippa to do something. This ruse, of course, was a test.

Taffy brought the woman's toes up to his mouth and slowly, starting with her biggest one, began to lick.

Heidi's eyes were not on her foot, nor even on Mr. Taffy. They were now locked onto Pippa, her mischievous smile still in place. "Take off your shoes, Pippa."

Taffy hesitated, but soon was back at work, licking her two baby toes.

"No."

"No?" Heidi repeated, seeming surprised—as though she hadn't heard that word before.

"You want to kill me for keeping my shoes on, have at it. But I'll leave torturing this poor man all to you."

Heidi laughed out loud. "Do you hear that, Mr. Taffy? She feels sorry for you. Mr. Taffy … my poor mistreated homicidal bodyguard. That's fine, Taffy. Run along now."

Taffy reached for the lone shoe on the floor.

"Just leave it!" she barked, her face suddenly twisted into a hateful glare. The man stood, brushed off his knees, and silently moved away behind Pippa.

"Is that the kind of power you're talking about?" Pippa asked.

"Sure. It's all a matter of degrees, though. Maybe it's time I tell you why you're here. What you're going to do for me."

"I'm not going to lick your toes."

Again, Heidi laughed. "No … I wouldn't make you do that … unless you wanted to," she said, making a naughty expression. "You're going to deliver to me a certain person. A very important person, Pippa."

"I'm just a mid-level government agent, Mrs. Goertz. I couldn't deliver you the UPS man unless he was delivering a package." Pippa felt the pod decelerating. Looking out the porthole she saw they were entering another station, of sorts.

"Oh, please. You have proven yourself to be far more

than a simple agent. Pippa. You, and that Agent Chandler of yours, were the first to have bested me, and my organization. Although to be honest, it was only a temporary setback. Agent Chandler has capabilities far beyond those listed inside his SIFTR personnel file."

Heidi must have noticed Pippa's sudden uneasiness.

"I don't know how he does what he does, but you'll tell me in time. What I do know is that he has the ability to alter the playing field. Perhaps it's a genius, even savant-level IQ. Like I said, I don't know. What I do know is that he, and you, will soon be working for me."

Pippa did her best to look nonchalant. "I don't even know where the man is. We're no longer together, so I can't help you."

"Uh huh. You need to understand that we have infiltrated the SIFTR organization. Rob is currently in Washington, D.C."

Pippa shrugged. "So?"

"So you need to tell him to stop what he's doing and come to you."

"I don't know what he's doing. He does what he wants."

"So be it," she said, looking as if she had just come to some kind of decision. Heidi began fishing in the small purse that matched her shoes. She found her iPhone and brought it out in front of her. "The video-capture capabilities of these new phones today are truly amazing. We're talking 1080 resolution, you know."

Pippa watched Heidi with mild interest. With a furrowed brow, Heidi tapped at the phone's screen. "Ah!" She held up the iPhone and pointed it toward Pippa. "Oh, come on … can't you give me a little smile, hon?"

Bewildered, Pippa shook her head, flipping both Heidi and her iPhone the bird, then offered up a condescending smile.

Pippa felt the slightest shifting of air behind her seat. At some level she was aware of the presence of Mr. Taffy. What came next happened so fast—so suddenly—she didn't have time to react or, more importantly, catch her breath. An arm moved in front of her and next, something was around her neck. A garrote. She knew instantly that Taffy had gotten the thin wire wrapped around her neck, and was in the process of pulling both handled ends of the wire weapon taut. Reflexively, both her hands reached for her throat, only to find it impossible to get her fingers in between the garrote and her flesh. She felt warm oozing moisture—her own blood. She kicked out wildly with one foot, and then with the other, desperate to connect with something solid—something she could get a footing on. Anything substantial enough to gain purchase on, and maybe, swing back around on her attacker. Her head felt as though it was going to explode; her eyes—already nearly popping from their sockets—saw Heidi across from her, her iPhone still raised. Heidi's face was frozen in a sick voyeuristic expression. Pippa, now straining desperately to breathe—unable to scream out—or make even the slightest of sounds, watched as her vision closed in, as if she were looking through a long tunnel there would be no escaping through. Briefly, she thought of Rob … *is all this for him?* Of course it was … he would watch her die in 1080 resolution. *I'm sorry, Rob. I love you …*

Chapter 8

Rob recognized the man holding the gun. He was one of the two men in Calloway's photographs, carrying the body bag—Pippa's body bag. Tall and broad-shouldered—thick on top, with an ample belly—his hips and legs were, in relation to them, relatively slender, giving him a cartoon character-type appearance. But it was the man's face that held my attention. Of Latin descent, perhaps Italian, his thick, black, combed-back hair began about an inch and a half above his bushy eyebrows and gave the impression he virtually had no forehead. That feature, unfortunately, gave him a somewhat Neanderthal countenance. In stark conflict was the manner in which he was dressed. He wore an impeccably tailored dark gray suit.

He glanced at the dead body of Moritz—leaning over the CAD monitor and then back to me. "Mr. Chandler, would you please step away from the desk and raise both hands."

I did what the large man asked. The barrel of the Glock followed my movements. I peeked into his head and found a mind that was orderly and highly intelligent, giving credence to the fact that you really can't judge a book by its cover.

"My name is Alberto T. Boccaccio. My friends call me Albo. May I call you Rob?" His baritone words came out with a heavy Brooklyn accent.

"Sure … call me whatever you'd like."

"That's good. We're starting off on the right foot, Rob … that's very good."

Mind-reading is invasive at an unparalleled level. For the most part, I tend to skim someone's mental playbacks—I'm not interested in someone's darker compulsions or addictions. To be honest, I don't want some other folks' shit taking up residency in my own mind. Like flipping through the pages of a book, I often let the images flash by so quickly that much of what I see is nothing more than a blur. That is, until something catches my attention at a subconscious level. And that's what just happened: My heart had begun to race, my breath catching in my chest before I knew why.

"Did you hear me, Mr. Chandler? You'll be coming along with me. You don't want to try anything. There is far more at stake here than your own life, I can assure you."

I tried to swallow. I tried to speak. *What did I see inside his head?* I backed out of his mind, no longer wanting to look into anyone's thoughts ever again. *What the hell did I see?*

Albo stepped further into the small office, and two men—both heavily armed and dressed in black—took his place at the doorway. Albo transferred his gun to his other hand and reached into his inside breast jacket pocket. An iPhone, one of the near tablet-sized models, appeared in his big fleshy hand.

"I have something to share with you, Rob. It's important that we start our relationship with everything placed on the table. There should be no secrets … no hidden agendas, between friends, Rob."

What did I see? Suddenly, I felt sick. The office was spinning around me—I reached a hand out to steady myself. The two men at the entrance raised their automatic weapons.

Albo was at my side now—aftershave and garlic filled my nostrils. I felt his hand on my shoulder. "Are you all right,

Rob? Do you need some water?"

His face showed real concern, which was surprising in light of … *in light of what?*

I shook my head. My eyes were on the screen of his iPhone, which was now held out in front of me, as if a friend were showing me pictures of his family; or perhaps, vacation pics, maybe someplace warm and humid, like Cancun or Tahiti. *I don't want to see his vacation pics.*

"Rob … prepare yourself. I apologize in advance for what you are about to see. It's startling, to say the least, but again necessary …" He let his words trail off—maybe, at this point, realizing the futility in saying anything more. He pressed the video play button and the black screen suddenly filled with a familiar scene. A scene I'd glanced at only seconds earlier, inside Albo's organized mind.

Pippa, dressed in white skinny jeans and a light blue button-down blouse, was sitting in what had first appeared to be an airplane cabin, but these surroundings now showing on the screen looked more like a plush train car—but, then again, round, porthole-type windows could be seen, off to the side. Pippa was staring back at whoever was holding the camera. She looked tired, her hair somewhat disheveled, but she was also beautiful, and did seem fine, perfectly healthy. *See … all that worrying for nothing!* I found myself smiling as Pippa, a sardonic expression on her face, flipped the bird at the photographer. *That's my girl.* I heard a familiar laugh and then the camera was flipped around to show the one holding it: Heidi Goertz. She waved and nodded, and then flipped the camera back around to show Pippa.

Again, I felt sick. *I don't want to watch this anymore.* I turned my face away, only to feel strong hands on my head and chin. One of the armed men at the door was now inside the office and standing by my side. *When did that happen?*

How could I have missed that?

The video continued to play and I watched Pippa adjust herself in her seat, move her blonde hair away from her face. Movement. It came in from behind her in a blur. An arm … no, two arms crossed, reaching around in front of her. It all happened within a second. The garrote was over her head and then around her neck. *I don't want to watch this!* Pippa's fingers were prying at her neck, her face already turning red. Legs kicked out—she was flailing hopelessly now. A dark stain spread at her crotch as she wet herself. Blood covered her fingers.

I no longer tried to look away. In fact, I wanted to watch every second … I wanted to remember this scene for the rest of my life. The attacker's face briefly appeared behind Pippa—handsome and relaxed; to him, this was just business. I burned his features into my memory, vowing never … ever … to forget his face.

The garrote came away from her neck nearly as quickly as it had been placed there. Pippa lay still, slouched forward. I hadn't seen this part of the video yet … hadn't made it this far, looking within Albo's mind. I no longer felt sick—the room was no longer spinning around me. All that had been replaced with a steely determination: to make them all pay. I was going to kill Heidi Goertz, and I knew exactly how I was going to do it.

The hands on my face remained, but I glanced away. I'd seen enough.

Movement.

Pippa swayed. Perhaps it was just a shifting … a relaxing of the dead, as I'd seen some bodies do more than once in the past. But the dead don't move their arms and sit up.

Her hands were at her throat and her eyes remained closed, but she was definitely alive. Someone was handing her a cup of water—the same man who had nearly killed her. The same man I was going to enjoy sending straight to hell. Pippa slapped the cup away—sending it flying out of view.

The camera was pointing now at Heidi, her expression serious. "Hello, Rob. That must have been very upsetting to watch. Disturbing. I'm sorry for that, truly I am. But you now know the seriousness of the situation. The importance of following my instructions to the T. There will be no second chance for Pippa—no last-second reprieve, allowing her to live. Do what you're told and you will see your beautiful Pippa again. Don't, and you'll watch another video … with a completely different outcome. Mr. Boccaccio has all the information—everything necessary for you to accomplish your next mission. Welcome to the WZZ, Rob. I'm excited at the possibility of having someone with your unique capabilities working for me."

The video stopped playing: her face, frozen—her cold, psychopathic, emotionless eyes stared back at me. Sometime, soon, she'd be wearing a different expression. I was going to make damn sure of that.

Chapter 9

"Take a breath and let me tell you what is needed from you," Albo said.

I said nothing but evidently the expression on my face said tons.

"Hate me all you want … I understand. I've been in your shoes. What you, as I, too—and many others—have come to realize is the futility in fighting this. The organization always wins … always prevails."

"The organization? You're talking about the WZZ?"

Albo looked confused, then shook his head. "No … the WZZ is but a flea, riding on the back of a much, much larger animal. What I'm talking about is the Order: a multi-national consortium of the fucking super rich. The Order is the real power behind everything … behind mega-corporations, behind world commerce, and behind super-power governments. The Order is the great Oz behind the curtain, man."

I shrugged. "That's nothing new to me … to most anyone. Yes, big money players have a lot of control that transcends geographical borders. So what? That doesn't mean there is only one huge, united, Empire-like organization running world governments. I think you're exaggerating."

Albo plopped his bulk down onto the armless chair in front of the drafting table. He made a motion with his chin and the armed man in black left the cramped office. Moments later, I heard both men descend the stairs out of our sight.

Albo continued, "I'm not only not exaggerating, it's been like this for over a hundred years. The power brokers began wielding their influence in the late eighteen hundreds … the turn of the century. You've heard of Tesla? The socially awkward genius who discovered AC electricity; not to mention things like the radio … even lasers. Did you know both Tesla and Edison were vying for patent approval for dispersing electricity … light … to the masses? Both had their own unique concepts. Edison advocated for direct current, DC, while Tesla fought for alternating current, AC. Here's the kicker … Tesla's methodology was far superior, a much more elegant and efficient approach. He also got his paperwork into the patent office before Edison."

"I know all that. Tesla was screwed; ended up dying in obscurity—a broken man." I was still reeling from what I'd seen Pippa go through and was having a hard time concentrating on anything else. It occurred to me that Albo was yammering on to settle me down.

"Yes, but why? He had the far better technology … I'll tell you why," he continued on, "Tesla wanted to give electricity away to the masses … for free. Was adamant that electricity was a natural phenomenon that could no more be regulated than the very air we breathe."

I nodded my head; I'd heard all this before.

"Keep in mind, Edison was backed by J. P. Morgan, the wealthy investor; Tesla was backed by George Westinghouse. Now, J. P. Morgan was an interesting character and perhaps that is where things first went awry. Did you know that Morgan escaped military service, during the Civil War, by paying a few hundred bucks for a stand in to take his place …

to fight for him? Then, during the same war, he purchased thousands of rifles for $3.50 each and sold the lot of them for $22 apiece? Here's the kicker … the rifles were defective. Hell, some shot off the thumbs of the soldiers firing them! Some time later, a congressional committee convened on the matter, but a bought-off federal judge upheld the deal and Morgan was totally exonerated. That should tell you the type of person that young titan of industry was, and it was only the beginning. Ingeniously, Morgan backed Edison, using Tesla's AC electricity to power a new-fangled, corporal punishment device—called the electric chair. Only it didn't quite operate as intended, and the poor, death row son of a bitch was slowly roasted alive. His head caught on fire in front of a crowd of onlookers. It was a well-staged spectacle that ended up being front-page news across the country. The populace was aghast—immediately afraid of Tesla's alternating current application. That was that … the end of Tesla's AC, and free electricity for the masses. Edison, and his multi-million-dollar backers, prevailed; but something more important arose from all that: the early beginnings of a consortium. Having experienced, first hand, how easily they could manipulate both business and public perception to their own needs, this consortium of power brokers went underground, at least, partially. And that was the beginning of the Order. It exists today and is far more powerful than any one government. It is the great manipulator, behind all things on planet Earth."

"That's all very interesting, but I don't care about any of it. What is it you want from me? What do I need to do to get Pippa back?"

"You join them. You don't resist the inevitable, and just *maybe* the two of you will be allowed to live."

"Live to serve the Order?"

"Yes."

"And what is it that the Order holds over you, Albo?" I glimpsed into his mind and saw fire. I didn't understand what I was viewing for several moments—what I was witnessing was too up-close. Flames and smoke and sounds of someone, presumably Albo himself, frantically calling out to someone. But then I saw these same images from a different angle and knew it was a car on fire, and I also knew that it was Albo's brother who had gone up in flames, from a planted car bomb, more than ten years earlier.

"Let's just say I have a large family and the Order will stop at nothing, have a hold on anyone important to you, as a looming threat for you to comply. Mr. Chandler, no one is safe … no one is beyond the reach of the Order, if they want something from you."

Albo was doing his best, unsuccessfully, to not think about his wife and three children. He feared for their lives and had done terrible things to ensure their ongoing safety—their very survival.

"What you viewed … with Miss Rosette was more than a threat to you and her; it was also an initiation, of sorts, for the Goertzes. Heidi and Leon have been trying to win the Order's favor for years. To merge the WZZ into the far larger, and more influential, Order consortium."

"So this has all been orchestrated by the Order?" I asked.

"Of course it has. With few exceptions, clandestine agencies, from nearly all governments—the CIA, FBI, the SVR, in Russia; the DGSE, in France … are all pawn players at the beckoning of the Order's latest directives. If it suits them, if it gains them profits or power, or both, you've witnessed firsthand the lengths they'll go to—from manipulation, on a personal level—to full-out war between countries, on a global level."

"Why me … why Pippa?"

Albo smiled, but his eyes showed no humor. "Come on, Rob. Do I need to spoon-feed you here?"

I thought about it and knew why: "SIFTR?"

Albo let out a breath: "SIFTR—a miniscule, pathetic really, organization, compared to its sister and counterpart agencies—has become somewhat of a problem."

I thought about my boss, Calloway, and suddenly I felt a new respect for the man. Without a doubt, he was well aware of the Order, but he had resisted their manipulations. I wondered at what cost to himself … to his family?

Chapter 10

Albo shrugged and raised his bushy brows. "Thus far, Calloway's been impossible to get close enough to … to … take out. Recently, we've even taken down one of his SIFTR G5s, only to discover he wasn't actually on board."

"And what if I am willing to sacrifice Pippa? Not go along with you … with the Order?"

For the first time, I saw real compassion in Albo's eyes. "I'd certainly admire your convictions. A part of me would love to see it happen. Let's see … well, first of all, I'd be terminated for failing to make good on the Order's directives. The same would go for some, or most, of my family members. The Order always makes good on their threats. But you won't do that, Rob. I saw your reaction to the video. Your horror, then your overwhelming relief at seeing your dear Pippa was still alive. They own you now, just as they own me, and many thousands of others."

"What's to stop me from killing you right now?"

"You can try. You might even be able to avoid getting yourself killed by the highly-trained special ops team surrounding this trailer, but to what end?"

He had a point there. I'd be on the run for the rest of my life, always looking over my shoulder and waiting for a bullet. And doing that, Pippa would still end up dead.

"There are time restraints, Rob. You have to make a decision … today. Right now, would be preferable, or face the consequences."

I rolled my eyes at that but saw Albo wasn't exaggerating. "You're serious? I'm supposed to abandon all loyalty ties to my country … the people I work with?"

"That sizes it up nicely. The Order has a problem that only you can address."

"Uh huh. Let's say I do this thing for them. Then what? Pippa will be allowed to live happily ever after?"

"You're a big boy, Rob. I think you know there's no fairy-tale ending here. Pippa and you will survive. That is the one guarantee."

Pippa and I will survive … but live out our lives in servitude to the Order. Terrific. "Since you're being so forthcoming, Albo, who's driving the bus … who's in charge?"

"It's a consortium, man. I thought you understood that."

"I know what a consortium is. Who's the person sitting at the head of the table? There's always a top man or woman."

"I'm not cleared to talk about such things," Albo replied.

Albo was fairly certain it was a man named Palmolive. Rudy Palmolive. I saw a glimpse of a little, bird-like man, garbed in a black suit. I briefly wondered if he was familially-tied to the dish soap people?

Albo said, "I have no idea who … sorry."

I slowly nodded my head and pursed my lips. I don't make a practice of getting into people's heads and causing them pain. It takes its toll on me too. Not to the same extent, but it's no fun.

Albo was looking at me, waiting for any other questions I might ask. He blinked and widened his eyes several times, as if he were momentarily trying to clear his head. I spoke slowly, in a lowered voice. "Lying to me is a mistake, Albo."

He looked confused. He reached a hand up and massaged his right temple.

"Ever have one of those Seven Eleven Slurpee drinks,

Albo? I'm betting you have. They're wonderful." I stepped in closer and brought my face down to his. "Right now, your gray matter, which is a combination of nerve cells and something called glial cells, has the consistency of tofu. Oh, and just so you know, the brain is seventy-five percent water. So it's water and tofu, which is, unfortunately for you … rapidly undergoing a transition. You feel it, don't you? Soon, that big oversized brain of yours will be nothing more than a Seven Eleven Big Gulp."

He wavered and I took the gun from his hand and placed it in my overalls pocket. I then put all my concentration into giving Albo the worst headache in the history of all headaches. I picked a location, right behind his eyes, and envisioned a drill bit, spinning and churning out bits and pieces of his brain. From prior experience—doing this same thing to someone else—I knew the effect was devastating. Albo slid from his seat, right down onto the floor. I followed him down, keeping my face close to his while he swayed precariously on hands and knees. I increased the size of my imaginary drill bit. Now, with his head buried in his hands, tears filled his eyes and he moaned continuously.

"Albo. Do you want the pain to stop?"

He stopped moaning just long enough to say, "Sweet Jesus, yes!"

"Do you believe I can make the pain worse?"

"Yes … I guess so." He was whimpering now.

"Do you want me to show you?"

"No! I believe you. I believe you!"

"That's good, Albo. But I want you to remember I can start it up again. At any time or place. Here or three thousand miles away from here," I said—lying. The truth was, this intrusion, like my mind-reading capabilities, was pretty much a line-of-sight type of thing. But I needed him to believe I could bring him literally to his knees at any time.

I stopped the mental drill bit suggestion and put a comforting hand on Albo's back. He opened his eyes and, as if waiting for the pain to return, turned his head to look at me.

"What the hell did you do to me?"

"Hurts like a son of a bitch, doesn't it?" My own head was also starting to hurt quite badly; I'd just escalated the timeframe when I'd need to tap in by a big factor. Soon, I'd be feeling the effects—withdrawals.

"Listen to me, Albo. That could have been much worse for you. I could have killed you, if I'd wanted to." I might have exaggerated some on that point, but he didn't know it.

"How did you …"

"How is not important."

"What do you want? You know they'll still kill Pippa—"

"No, they won't, because you're going to tell them I'm on board. You're going to tell them I'll do whatever they want."

Albo stayed crumpled where he lay, gazing at the floor only inches from his face. "My family. They'll kill my family."

"Not if they believe you're still the same loyal criminal you've been all along. Come on … let me help you up." I propelled him back onto his seat, where he quickly wiped at his wet cheeks with one hand.

"What were your orders, once you'd given me the ultimatum?"

"To send you back to SIFTR HQ. Your task was to immediately terminate Calloway. Today, if possible."

"And you? What were you to do next?"

Albo shook his head. "Move on to the next one. This time, convince a successful entrepreneur that he needs to close down operations."

"And why is that?"

"Because fossil fuels bring in billions of dollars to the

Order, and the young tech genius has discovered a new engine, fuel-injection, technology that quadruples automobile mileage." Albo looked at me. "You cannot go up against the Order. You'd have more success moving a mountain."

"So maybe I'll make the mountain come to me. Tell me how to get back in touch with you?"

Albo reached into his jacket and came out with a black business card. There was no name on it—only a phone number printed in small white numerals. "This will route you through to my cell. Just know, they'll expect news on Calloway—his certain death—within the next week or two, at the most. If you don't comply, Pippa will be terminated."

"Then I guess I'll need to work fast, won't I?"

"What makes you think I won't tell my superiors about …"

I cut him off: "That I got the best of you? That I was given the name of the man at the very top of the Order by simply giving you a little headache? Tell me, how do you think that will go over, Albo? Do you think … maybe … they'll consider you a liability at that point? Perhaps they'll take out their revenge, starting with your family. No. You won't mention any of this. You can only hope and pray that I find a way to bring down the Order, freeing you from the crushing weight you carry around with you day to day."

I watched Albo, sitting there slumped, looking back at me. He had a lot to consider. Finally he said, gesturing to the business card in my hand, "Don't use that number. All incoming calls are monitored." He picked up a pencil off the desk and scribbled a phone number onto the top sheet of a note pad.

He tore off the sheet, folded it, and handed it to me. "Leave a message and I'll get back to you as soon as I'm able."

I nodded and handed Albo back his gun.

Chapter 11

The Order's same two black-clad military men were back at the entrance to the office. Both had their weapons up and pointing toward me. Albo gave them a confident nod and said, "Let him pass. He understands what he has to do."

I moved toward the doorway and squeezed past them without looking back at Albo. At the bottom of the stairs, another ten or so similarly outfitted armed men were fanned out in a semicircle around the construction trailer. I heard a faint sound of static coming from one of the men's radios. I assumed he was being told to let me pass. I moved around them, heading straight for one of the larger, bored-out tunnel openings off to my left. I wouldn't be returning to the Lockkeeper's House chimney, as I doubted I had the stamina, at this point, to climb the hundreds of metal rungs. I recalled the basic layout of the plans and the underground tunnel construction. The closest egress from this subterranean maze was through a hidden panel above me, near the FDR monument. I entered the tunnel and headed off into the semi-darkness.

I couldn't get the image of Pippa's horrific attack out of my mind. Her suffering, how close she was to being killed—her vulnerability. My heart ached and all I wanted to do was rush to her side. I was tempted to comply with anything

Heidi and the Order asked of me to ensure her future safety. But after years of doing what I do, I've learned one can't give in to that kind of manipulation. In the end, both her and my suffering would never end. The chance of Pippa being allowed to live long-term, at the hands of her captors, was pretty much non-existent anyway. No, I needed to rescue her.

* * *

Going directly to Calloway wouldn't be an option. That's what handlers were for, and Curt Baltimore was mine. I called him as soon as I emerged from the subterranean tunnels into a tall grove of boxwood shrubs on the outskirts of the FDR Monument. Baltimore told me to sit tight and wait for him. Ten minutes later he showed up, driving a nondescript Ford sedan. He pulled over to the curb on busy Ohio Drive, where I quickly got in as he pulled into traffic.

He scowled at me, "You reek."

"Thank you … nice to see you, too. I need to talk to Calloway."

"You can speak to me." He continued to stare at me. "What's wrong with you? Your hands are shaking."

"I'm fine. Where do you have me staying?"

"Where you asked to stay… The Jefferson. But you need to be debriefed first."

"No, I need a shower … give me an hour or two."

"Pippa?" he asked, his tone more amiable.

"I'll tell you everything during the debrief. Just give me some time."

It took another seven or eight minutes to reach the hotel. Baltimore drove into its small circular drive and stopped at the hotel's entrance, keeping the engine running. "Be back here in two hours."

A young, sandy-haired porter opened my car door. Seeing me sitting there, dressed in dirty gardener overalls, and getting a good whiff of me, he immediately stepped back, while keeping one hand on the car door. As I exited, he took another step back. Baltimore leaned over the passenger seat and looked up at me. "You're registered as Mr. Drew Gallop … keys at the counter."

I watched Baltimore pull away, aware of the fact I hadn't disclosed crucial information. Pippa's life lay in the balance and I needed to think things through first. The porter rushed ahead of me and opened the big brass door at the hotel's entrance. "Enjoy your stay here, sir."

* * *

Room key in hand, I made my way to the small inset alcove off of the lobby where two polished brass elevator doors sat unmoving. I pushed the call button and the door on the right immediately opened. A sturdy, elderly woman wearing a blue bonnet-style hat briskly moved past me, leaving a heavily perfumed car interior in her wake. I was tempted to press the button for the seventh floor, where my room was located, but honestly didn't think I could hold out any longer. From my frequent trips to Washington, and regularly staying at this two-hundred-year-old establishment, I had my tapping-in routine down pat. The hotel's high-voltage lines came in through the sub-basement. I pressed the B button and waited for the door to close. Alone, I leaned back and closed my eyes, finding Pippa waiting for me there—her legs flailing outward and her face contorted—fear in her eyes. The car came to a jerky stop and the door slid open.

Where the rest of the hotel was elegant, catering to

highbrow millionaire businessmen and high-up government officials, its basement was no different in appearance than that of any other D.C. commercial building. Dimly lit and damp, even above my own stink, there was an earthy, mold-like tinge to the air. The shaking in my hands had spread to the rest of my body. I wrapped my arms around myself and, hunched over, made my way into the bowels of the hotel's underground.

"You can't be down here."

With his back to me, I'd spotted the black maintenance man, working at a small workbench off to my left. I was fairly sure he hadn't noticed me, but I was wrong. Normally, talking my way out of this kind of situation, or inserting a perfectly placed suggestion into someone's mind, wouldn't be a problem. But my brain faculties were completely muddled and my mental powers almost toast.

I hurried along the slump stone passage without slowing my pace.

"Hey! I'm talking to you, man. Stop!"

I heard his footfalls quickening behind me so I ran as best I could manage, heading for an obscure metal door up ahead, marked *Panels*. A tall wooden crate partially blocked the passage, and I had to turn sideways to move past it. Holding up behind it, I leaned against the wall and watched the man's approach by looking through a narrow gap between the crate and the wall.

I tried hard to think of something … some reason for being down here. Nothing came to me. I momentarily pictured myself being bailed out of jail … perhaps by Baltimore. In the silence of the basement passageway, I saw him slow—looking for me. He hadn't spotted me yet. Once again, I tried to enter his mind. This time I was successful. *There's an emergency on the fifth floor. Toilets overflowing … shit's all over the place … hurry!*

I looked again and found no one over there. The passageway was empty.

I hurried to the door marked Panels and, as expected, it was locked. I knew where the key was kept from previous visits to the hotel's *Panel* room. I retraced my steps, back to the small work area and workbench. I found the rusted old Sanka coffee can on a shelf and riffled through the collection of door keys that were secured to a metal ring. Once back at the *Panel* door I unlocked it and let myself in. The room was no different than a hundred other electrical rooms I'd found myself in over the last few months. The incoming high-voltage line was located in a pipe, painted red, emerging from the stoned wall three feet off the concrete floor. The enclosed room, seeming more like a vault, was easily ten degrees cooler than the rest of the basement. I found myself shaking even more uncontrollably than I had seconds earlier. I really needed to find a better way to tap in.

I knelt down and leaned my head against the hard, cold pipe. Instead of the typical, blissful tapping-in process I had grown accustomed to … I was immediately aware of something odd, something new. As if being physically pulled, manhandled, by strong hands—I was transported past the place where I'd typically spend my mental tapping-in process. I became aware of others—the same beings I had never looked directly at, ensuring they'd stay faceless and leave me alone. Now, heads turned and dark-shaped bodies scurried out of our way. I tried to pull away—to free myself from the being's grasp. We moved faster as an increasing warble sound pulsed around us; there was a red glow somewhere ahead of us. I reached a hand out in front of myself and felt something thick and viscous, as if we were moving through molasses, and more dark shapes began converging there. And then, suddenly, I no longer noticed others around me here in these blurry surroundings. I realized the pair of tightly gripping hands were now gone. Something in front of me moved—it was getting closer to me. It looked human … no … maybe not human.

Help me, Rob … oh God … help me!

What do you want? What do you want from me?

Look at me.

I am looking at you.

LOOK at me! Really look at me … you must look at me!

He was in my mind … or was it *my own mind speaking?* My heart continued to race. *Why am I so afraid?* I wanted to leave this place—get away from this … this being. I turned my eyes away from the approaching dark shape. Instinctively, I knew not to look into his eyes. *How do I know that?*

I have waited so long for this, Rob.

What do you want?

You know.

Who are you?

You know who I am … I am Darwin.

You want your freedom … you want to leave this place? I questioned.

Yes … will you help me?

The shape, now mere inches in front of me, shifted position. For a fleeting moment I saw enough detail through the viscous surroundings to make out something: it was an eye. I looked away.

You cannot deny what you already know, Rob.

Stop! Get out of my mind.

It's only a matter of time, Rob … for the transference. You'll find someone, just as I found you. It is the way. It is time.

No! My thoughts flashed to Pippa, near death, desperately struggling for life. Suddenly, anger rose up in me; fury consumed me. I felt my hands tighten into fists and I stood up tall. I no longer feared this being, this thing that wanted to trade places with me. I would die fighting anyone, or anything, that kept me from rescuing Pippa.

Clarity. The viscous surroundings were taking shape. The being before me was taking shape. I no longer struggled to turn away. I glared at him, my eyes wide open. I moved closer, towering over him. The being looked left and right, and then stepped back.

It is my turn, Rob.

Find someone else.

I have tried … I cannot—

I reached for the being that was not human. I wanted to tear its strangely shaped head from its strangely shaped body. I wanted to kill it.

It is my turn, Rob.

I awoke out of breath, my fingers still wrapped around the red-painted metal pipe. Anger still seethed in me.

Chapter 12

I was in my seventh floor hotel room, overlooking Sixteenth Street NW and busy Washington, D.C. beyond. I showered, shaved, and dressed in the starched white shirt I saw hanging in the closet, and a dark gray suit. Polished shoes had been lying side by side beneath. Everything was impeccably tailored to my build. I checked the inside jacket label but didn't recognize the Italian designer's logo. Apparently, the powers that be at SIFTR had other plans for me today … above and beyond using a leaf blower and digging trenches. I decided on an old-fashioned Windsor knot and adjusted the light blue and yellow striped tie beneath my collar. Looking in the mirror, my eyes held fast on my forehead. *Who … or what is in there*? Something from my past, or perhaps something looming in my future … was wrangling for my very existence. Would I have to confront this entity every time I tapped in? Would it even be *me* emerging the next time?

There was a brown paper bundle, lying on the vestibule, with a blank envelope affixed to it. I opened it and read the enclosed card:

Rob: Inside you will find a wallet, holding credit cards and one thousand dollars cash. You have a license and passport included as well. You'll be traveling so don't forget to grab the suitcase in the closet.

Meet me in the Quill.

Baltimore.

I glanced into the partially opened closet and saw an upright case waiting there.

* * *

I dragged the rolling suitcase behind me and left it with a porter in the Jefferson's lobby. I backtracked, climbed three steps, and headed down an adjacent hallway—airy, with bright-white painted walls and high-up crown moldings. I passed by the small library, with its collections of hundreds of hardbound books, and overstuffed chairs and couches, and entered the *Quill.*

There are few places that provide such an immediate impact. To me, this is the quintessential man cave—with its indirect lighting, dark wood flooring, mahogany bar and tables—the lounge exudes comfort and luxury. I spotted Baltimore at the far side of the room, sitting at a small table by a window.

I sat across from him, noticing he too was business-dressed in suit and tie.

"You smell better."

"I'm having the overalls sent to your home as a special gift."

He ignored my comment, only looking up from his laptop to acknowledge an approaching waitress.

I pointed to Baltimore's glass. "Same as his."

She did an about-face and headed off toward the bar.

"I need to talk to you," I said.

He nodded and finally brought his attention across to me. "Look, I suspect you have more questions. Maybe you feel we haven't been completely honest—"

I cut him off and leaned in: "Just shut the fuck up."

He looked at me, startled. "What … what's wrong?"

"Earlier today, I watched a video clip—watched as Pippa was nearly decapitated. Let me ask you, Baltimore, have you ever watched someone you cared about being garroted from behind? Watched their eyes bug out, blood seep from between their fingertips as the flesh of their throat rips apart?"

His face grimaced. There was true concern in his eyes. "Oh my god. Is she …"

"Dead? No … I don't think so. It was a demonstration meant for my benefit."

The waitress returned with my drink and a replacement one for Baltimore's empty tumbler. I took a sip of the aged whiskey, slowly swallowing the smoky alcohol, which delightfully burned all the way down my throat.

I continued, "Pippa has been taken hostage by Heidi Goertz."

"As in Leon and Heidi Goertz?"

"Don't play dumb. This is where you start leveling with me … or so help me—"

Baltimore held up a palm in mock surrender. "Hey, no need for threats. I suspected you'd have questions at this point. I'll tell you what I can, but first you need to tell me everything that happened. Start at the beginning."

I sat back and let out a breath. "I need to speak to Calloway. This all revolves around Calloway."

"That's not going to happen. He's … let's just say he's dealing with his own set of problems. He's gone to ground."

That jived with what Alberto Boccaccio spoke of. Calloway was being hunted.

"You knew that WZZ was back in the picture?"

He nodded.

"You knew about this Order? This power-broker consortium?"

Baltimore's expression alone said I was stating the obvious. He pursed his lips and seemed to be weighing what he was about to say. "What you're calling the Order is referred to by ten or twenty other names, as well. It's not talked about openly. Not if you want to keep breathing."

"Seriously?"

"The problem is, you never know who it is you are really talking to. Perhaps you're being tested by someone within the organization itself."

"So what if you are?"

"I don't know what you were told, Rob. But now that you are aware of this ... this ... *Order* ... you are at risk. We're talking about a group so powerful, so influential, that having you—or anyone else—sanctioned is a very simple matter for them. Only a little blip in the organization's everyday operations."

"I was told they control government agencies—"

Baltimore's agitation was clearly growing and he cut me off: "You're not getting it. They, quite often, *are* those agencies. It's not like they are a separate, definable group of people. The Order is a conglomerate of highly influential men and women, from all around the globe—from government officials to corporate CEOs to organized crime bosses to ..."

"I get it," I said. "How does one join?"

"It's by invitation only. One can petition the Order for inclusion, but rarely does someone get in that way. Truth is, most individuals are invited, and even that's more of a mandate. They want the influence or services you can wield, and they don't take no for an answer. They can be very persuasive."

I looked at Baltimore. In light of what I'd told him about Pippa, he quickly realized I already knew about that. "The president ... he's a part of this group?"

"Sure. All presidents are. Comes with that high level of position, on a global scale. But that doesn't mean James C.

Morrison is one hundred percent in their clutches either."

"And Calloway?"

Baltimore took a sip of his drink. "SIFTR, as you know, is about as obscure and hidden an agency as they come. It was put into play by the president. And Calloway's not an actual member of the Order, although the invitation has been offered to him. They—the Order, of course—are now well aware of SIFTR. And, furthermore, the lack of influence they hold over that covert agency makes them nervous."

"So, then is it both the president and Calloway's intention to bring down the Order?"

Baltimore laughed out loud at that, and then glanced around the bar to make sure he hadn't brought too much attention to himself. "That would be impossible. The Order's too entrenched within the global infrastructure. But like any other high-powered organization, who's at the helm counts ... and the leadership sometimes changes."

"And has that changed recently?"

"Most definitely. How do you think the Goertzes were accepted? For years, the Order was controlled by moderates—something called the Council of Five. Nobody knows who the five are, only that they are among the wealthiest, most influential people on earth. We do know there's been a shakeup, and several new members have supplanted others. There are new additions within the council too, so I'm not sure if it's now called the Council of Seven, or Eight, but these new members are tied more to the typical criminal element than, say, to the corporate or government members. A far darker influence, I might add. The president and, subsequently, our leader, Calloway, would like to restore balance—influence events back to the way they were."

"Is that even possible, considering the level of secrecy involved?"

"Like I said, we don't know for sure who the members—"

I cut him off, "Rudy Palmolive."

Baltimore's jaw dropped. He leaned forward, looking profoundly interested. "How do you know this name?"

I started at the beginning and recounted everything that had happened to me, from finding the hidden chimney trap door in the Lockkeeper's House, which led to the underground tunnels; to Moritz, the engineer; to Alberto T. Boccaccio, and his relationship to the CIA; Pippa's horrific near-death experience; and the still-looming threat over me of termination, if I didn't comply. I also spoke of my own invitation into the Order and, subsequently, the first assignment given to me—kill Calloway. Baltimore had me repeat everything twice when it came to describing the *bird-like man*, Rudy Palmolive.

"We knew of him but not that he was a member. Rob, this changes everything." He sat back and smiled. "Okay … your itinerary has just changed."

"That's fine, just as long as it includes rescuing Pippa."

Chapter 13

"Where am I?" Pippa croaked, immediately regretting speaking. She brought a hand up and probed at the bandage around her neck. Sitting up, she kept her eyes on Mr. Taffy. He sat on an identical-looking white leather couch, with his hands on his lap—fingers intertwined. She looked beneath the throw blanket, now draped over her shoulders, and saw that she was wearing different clothes than her own. She pulled the blanket up higher around herself.

"From New Zealand. The finest … softest Alpaca wool money can buy."

Pippa rose up and turned around. Heidi was sanding in front of two immense windows. It was dark out, but Manhattan's skyline lights were unmistakable.

"This isn't the Chrysler Building," Pippa said, zeroing in on several recognizable landmarks in the distance. Both the Empire State Building and, farther off—near the Hudson River—the new World Trade Center. Again, she touched her bandage.

Heidi scoffed, "Truth be told, that old building is a decrepit old pit. Everything's small—doorways, rooms, windows—why, it's almost a hundred years old, for God's sake. No, I'm sure Leon had good intentions and all, buying it for me, and the thing is spectacular to look at … but I'd much rather own it than live in it." She did a modified pirouette and pointed a well-toned sleeveless arm out. "There … that's the Chrysler Building."

Pippa recognized the familiar metal spire and nodded. "We're up so high."

"Well, that's what one hundred million dollars buys you on Park Avenue, dear. These condos start at ten million each."

Pippa stayed quiet. She was fairly certain the condo wasn't Heidi's—that she was only posturing, as usual.

"Don't you have something to say for yourself, Mr. Taffy?" Heidi said.

For the first time, Taffy moved. His chin tilted up several millimeters and his eyes found Pippa's.

"I'm very sorry, Ms. Rosette, for the discomfort I caused you."

"Discomfort? That's what we're calling it? You nearly killed me by decapitating me with a wire."

"You were in no danger of dying," he replied, matter-of-factly.

"Fine. You were only following orders, anyway. Isn't that right, Mr. Taffy?" Pippa was addressing Taffy, but her eyes were on Heidi.

"Now, now, Pippa, that's all over. Nothing like that ever has to happen again. We can go back to being friends … true BFFs," Heidi said, showing her a toothy smile.

"What now? What are you going to do with me? Do I remain a captive indefinitely?"

"Captive? Hardly." Heidi came around the couch and sat down next to Taffy, across from Pippa. "You are free to go. In fact, my personal jet will deliver you anywhere you desire, even back to Kingman, if that's what you want." She'd said the word Kingman in an exaggerated, disgusted, tone.

"Uh huh."

Heidi leaned forward, resting an elbow on her knee, her

small fist beneath her chin. Her silk chemise blouse, with its two thin spaghetti straps, was draped open just enough to expose the tops of her two perfectly proportioned breasts. "I'm being honest with you. But then again, I believe that once you fully understand the situation, Pippa, you'll prefer to stay here … with me."

Pippa raised a brow and gave a half smile.

Heidi sat back and nodded to Taffy. He reached forward, grabbing ahold of a manila file folder from the marble coffee table between them. Pippa could see that it was packed full of eight-by-ten photographs. He stretched the folder out across the table to her, holding it there.

"It's for you," Heidi said. "Go on, take it."

Pippa did as told and seized the folder from Taffy's grasp. She brought the folder down to her lap and opened it. She gasped, "No … please no!"

"She looks so happy, doesn't she? If I didn't know better, I'd swear I was looking at photographs of you … maybe ten years ago?"

"She's innocent. Don't do this, Heidi. Even for you, this is over the top—so diabolical." Pippa glared at Heidi, but soon couldn't keep her eyes from straying down to the photographs on her lap. Arlington, *Arly*, was her niece. Her sister's only child, and the most precious relationship Pippa had with anyone, with the exception, perhaps, of Rob. And Heidi was right; Arly looked more like Pippa than she did her own mother. She had the same long blonde hair; was tall with an athletic build, and her Nordic features, down to the same, slightly turned-up nose, made them look more like twins than aunt and niece. Arly loved her too, and to her parents' chagrin, she wanted to follow in Pippa's footsteps and become an FBI agent.

Pippa flipped through the glossy color photographs of

Arly. Each one captured her in a different location at different times of the day. One photo of her was in Central Park, sitting on the grass with friends. They were all laughing, enjoying a casual summer afternoon. Another one caught Arly in the evening; she appeared dressed in a miniskirt, entering a nightclub. Another showed her sitting at a small desk, a stack of books placed off to the side, studying. The photo was grainy, shot from a telephoto lens somewhere below, but Pippa recognized Arly's small Brooklyn apartment. There were many more photos, but Pippa closed the file.

"I want you to look at them again, Pippa. Only this time notice the man positioned nearby."

Pippa let the folder fall open and arbitrarily lifted one photo out. It was the Central Park scene. She brought the photo closer and scanned the image. Off to the right was a dark-haired man, wearing a white windbreaker and sitting on a blanket, looking directly into the camera lens. Now that she noticed him, he indeed looked out of place. She chose another photo and held it up close to her face. This was one she hadn't seen before. It looked to be early morning and showed Arly jogging in the city somewhere. It took Pippa several seconds to spot him, but there he was in the distance, standing in a storefront doorway. It was the same man, wearing the same white windbreaker. She grabbed up another photo and saw it was a companion image to the one of Arly sitting at her desk, only a wider view. This one showed several adjacent apartment windows, sited to the left and the right of Arly's own. Pippa brought the image closer, nearly touching it to her nose. There, to the right, she spotted Arly's next-door neighbor; he was pulling the curtains apart, and again, it was the same man, still wearing a white windbreaker.

"He has only one job in life. He's been well paid … over a million dollars."

"To do what, exactly?"

"To never … ever … let her out of his sight. He knows where she is at all times. She, Pippa, is his life. And with one call, her life ends."

Pippa was doing everything she could to keep her breathing rate steady. She wanted to jump from her seat and beat Heidi to death with her bare hands. "What do you want from me? What will it take for you to leave her alone?"

"In time, Mr. Chandler will come for you. Of course, he will! He and Mr. Baltimore—we want both of them, along with you, to join our organization. We need to garner far more influence within the ranks of SIFTR. It's really as simple as that."

Pippa shook her head. "So much trouble. Why go to such lengths? I mean, we're simply agents …"

"More will become apparent to you in time, Pippa," Heidi said. "Let's just say for now that there are certain monumental occurrences, coming soon—well planned and synchronized. We're talking global-level here, Pippa. It's exciting and, well, a bit scary too, to be honest. There can be no hiccups. There can be no surprises. SIFTR is but one of several unknown entities we're addressing. Chandler and Baltimore, and your boss, Calloway, are unpredictable loose ends. So now, let me speak to you about the Order. Just like I recently have done, you too will pledge your allegiance. We will become sisters, Pippa."

Pippa continued to stare at Heidi, even more certain now that the woman was bat-shit crazy. But she needed to learn more about their Order organization, and the people who ran it. It was time she started thinking strategically and taking control of her situation. She'd play along, do everything she could to keep Arly safe, but she wouldn't be their puppet, either.

She glanced at Taffy and considered him for a moment. The man was more than a simple henchman—a robot-like thug—at Heidi's beck and call. He gazed back at her and then looked away. Maybe it was something Pippa saw in his eyes. At some level, he cared. At some level, he regretted hurting her.

Pippa knew Heidi was right. Rob and Baltimore would come for her. And this Order would set up a well-planned trap, so it was up to her to keep things slightly off-kilter—inject the unexpected.

Pippa stealthily unbuttoned a button, and then another one at the top of her blouse. She didn't quite match in size Heidi's ample bust, but she, too, had enough cleavage to catch a man's eye. Pippa let the luxurious Alpaca wool throw fall from her shoulders, as she leaned forward to replace the file folder full of photographs onto the coffee table. In her periphery vision, she could see Taffy's attention on her ... taking in the view.

Chapter 14

We were back in Baltimore's Ford sedan, driving roughly in the direction of the Pentagon and the nearby SIFTR agency.

"What is it?" I asked. I hadn't seen Baltimore like this before. He was totally immersed in thought and something was needling him. I was in the process of probing his mind when he said:

"We'll talk later, once we're below ground."

We slowed and pulled up to a nondescript guard station. In addition to the man inside, there were four armed guards situated outside—two on each side of the black-striped metal gate. Baltimore was handed an electronic tablet, which he held up before his face. I saw a mirror image of his face on the tablet screen, as facial recognition software confirmed Baltimore's identity. Next, a zoomed-in image of one of his eyes, a retinal scan, completed the security check. Baltimore passed the tablet over to me and I followed the same procedure.

"Heightened security?" I asked.

Baltimore didn't answer. The armed men relaxed and the gate came up. It took another minute to reach the brick single story SIFTR building. I'd been here numerous times now, and still found it so architecturally unremarkable I almost didn't give it notice, which was the whole point.

Entering the lobby, here, too, were added upgraded security measures. In the past, rarely was anyone stationed here, letting the building's electronics and hidden armament measures handle security. But today, there were several armed guards, holding on to automatic weapons. Again, we went through the same rigmarole with the tablet before we were allowed to progress to the elevator.

Baltimore waited for the elevator door to slide shut and begin its descent below ground before he spoke. "You need to understand something, Chandler—we're *it*." He gestured with an open hand to nothing in particular around him. "SIFTR … us … we're the only *clean* agency left."

"Clean?"

"Autonomous. No one from the Order works within our ranks."

"How could you possibly know that for sure?" I asked. Before Baltimore could answer, I continued, "It's the nature of our business. Even if an operative can't be bought, he or she can still be manipulated in any number of ways."

"I'm well aware of all that. But SIFTR's security measures have been doubled—sometimes tripled. Our field agents' activities are scrupulously tracked, and they can no longer access our agency network without jumping through rigorous hoops. With very few exceptions, even those here at headquarters who've undergone baseline verification are still not permitted to leave."

"Baseline verification? What the hell is that?"

The car slowed, coming to a halt, and the elevator door slid open. "Come this way, you're about to find out." We made our way through glass-paned double doors into the agency's lab and continued past several ultra-clean-looking glass-partitioned compartments. I noticed there were far fewer technicians milling about than usual.

"Here I am!"

Both Baltimore and I stopped and turned, seeing Bridgett Bigalow, SIFTR's quartermaster—our own version of James Bond's Q—carrying an armful of clothes, and other objects piled up high.

Ms. Bigalow, in her early thirties, wore thick-lensed glasses, no makeup, and dark hair pulled back into a tight ponytail. She smiled at me as she joined us.

"Hi Rob, really good to see you again."

I'd always suspected the nerdy, but refreshingly real scientist had something of a crush on me. Now, seeing her schoolgirl-nervous blush—I suspected my hunch was confirmed.

"Good to see you too, Bridgett. Doing some last-minute laundry?"

Her confused eyes looked enormous and distorted behind her glasses. Then she looked down at the stack of items she held and laughed out loud. "You're so funny. We'll talk about the stuff I'm holding as soon as you're done with baseline."

She brushed by us and strode off without looking back. Baltimore gestured with his chin for me to follow her. We turned down one corridor and then the next, into an area I hadn't visited before. Bridgett was gone. I stopped and looked behind me, seeing Baltimore several paces back.

"In here … you walked right by me," sounded Bridgett's voice in the near-distance.

I retraced my steps and entered a room, dimly lit, surrounded by floor-to-ceiling equipment panels. High tech was everywhere. I could see the top of Bridgett's head, moving on the far side of a console at the back of the room. When she emerged, she said, "Take a seat, Rob. This won't take long."

An open, reclined dentist-type chair was waiting for me, and I settled into it. Baltimore remained standing, but moved back into the shadows.

Bridgett sat on a stool and scooted in close to me. "Listen to me, Rob. This is a totally non-evasive procedure. There are hundreds of censure guns pointed at your body."

"Guns?"

She shrugged. "It's what they're called. They measure every aspect of both your mental state and physiological responses. Please keep your hands on the armrests and stay as still as possible. I'm going to ask you some questions; you just need to answer them as honestly as possible. Do not think before answering—I'm looking for natural responses—what first comes to mind. I'll need to ask you a few obvious yes or no questions in order to create a baseline."

"Wait … this is a lie detector?"

She glanced around the room and wobbled her head back and forth. "I guess you could call it that, but this newer technology is incredibly advanced. It all but reads your mind, Rob." She smiled. "So best keep all those dirty thoughts about me hidden away." She laughed out loud again, far too loudly, then scooted back away. She gave a nod to Baltimore as she again disappeared behind the console at the back of the room.

I was suddenly uneasy. How much of what she'd just said was actually true? Could this newer technology detect my mind-reading abilities? I immediately discounted that as being almost impossible.

I heard an amplified voice come from a speaker above me. "Rob, okay … we're ready to start. Are you comfortable?"

"I'm good."

"Yes or no, Rob."

"Sorry … yes."

"Rob, do you currently reside in Kingman, Arizona?"

"Yes."

"Rob, do you have blue hair?"

"No."

"Rob, did you arrive here today with Curt Baltimore?"

"Yes."

"That's good, Rob. We'll get started now."

"Rob, have you had any direct contact with an agent, or with any personnel associated with the organization commonly known as the Order?"

I hesitated before answering. "Yes."

"Other than Alberto T. Boccaccio, have you had any other contact with the Order?"

"Yes."

I saw movement in the shadow, where Baltimore was standing.

"Whom, specifically, have you been in contact with?"

"I was shown a video clip intended for me … from Heidi Goertz."

"Anyone else?"

"No."

"Rob, are you working, even indirectly, willingly or unwillingly, for the Order?"

"No."

"Rob, have your loyalties to SIFTR been compromised in any way?"

"No."

"That's enough," Baltimore said, stepping back into the light. "We're under a bit of a time crunch here. He's clean."

A moment later Bridgett emerged. "Um … I have more questions. Some of the readings are …"

Perhaps she detected my uneasiness about divulging my mind-reading capabilities. Baltimore shook his head. "Next time. If you tell me he's answered honestly, we need to move on."

"He answered honestly. I detected no deception taking place."

Baltimore stepped over to the door. "Meet us in lab conference room 5."

* * *

Less than ten minutes later, Bridgett Bigalow, again carrying the same stack of clothes, entered lab conference room 5. She placed the stack on the glass table and sat down across from Baltimore and me.

"Okay, here are the clothes you'll be wearing at the ranch. We were in a bit of a rush, but everything has been triple-checked." Bridgett took the first clothing items from the top of the pile, placing five folded plaid shirts before me. Each was obviously Western-style wear, having pearly-white, snap-type buttons down the front, as well as on the collars. "Cowboy garb?"

"Yeah. Now listen … you'll need to wear one of these five shirts at all times. It's the only way we'll be able to track your location. Now pay attention: sewn into the sleeve snap buttons, one on each sleeve, are alternating, high-frequency signal generators—unlikely to be detected by anyone but us. We'll be able to track your GPS position anywhere on the planet—even nine thousand feet up, in the high mountains of Colorado. As a safety measure the trackers are activated only when snaps are snapped closed. If someone comes near you with a wand … checks you for electronics, unsnap your cuffs … just to be safe." Bridgett then pointed to the two collar snaps. "These work the opposite way. Unsnap both top collar buttons and a distress signal is immediately generated. It's your way of telling us to send in the cavalry."

Baltimore added, "Be damn certain you're ready for that, because it will be the end of the mission."

"Uh huh," I mumbled. I noticed the brown holster and pearl-handled six-shooter, previously hidden by the shirts, now lying exposed at the top of the stack in front of Bridget.

"This is a very special weapon—a Colt, single action .45 Army … sometimes referred to as the Peacemaker."

"Wait … just stop for a minute!"

Both Bridget and Baltimore looked over at me.

"What the hell is this stuff? What's going on here?"

The corners of Baltimore's mouth turned up. "Let me back-step a bit. That tidbit of information you dropped on me earlier—the name Rudy Palmolive—well, it changes everything. Knowing now the name of one of the Council members is a monumental game changer. What's more, we suspect he's the newest member—undoubtedly criminally-connected—who could even be seated at the head of the table."

"Okay, so what's with all this Roy Rogers shit?"

Bridgett laughed and Baltimore rolled his eyes. "This is serious, Chandler. Serious as a heart attack, so you need to dial-back the smart-ass attitude."

I didn't think I was being particularly smart-ass, but I nodded my assent just the same.

"Rudy Palmolive is one of the wealthiest people in the world. He's also dying. Terminal something or other."

"Knowing that, he still joined this Council of Five?"

"Yes, he's got a few years left; more, if he stops smoking. Anyway, in addition to whatever he's doing as part of the Council, he's now living life to the fullest."

"Livin' la vida loca!" Bridgett added with enthusiasm.

"Given what time he has left, he's become a devout family man. He'll go to any length for his wife and two young sons—young boys, who live and breathe the Old West … cowboys and Indians. Your Roy Rogers remark, actually, was not far off the mark. They'll be vacationing for the week at a billionaire's dude ranch. Everything there is totally authentic—down to the clothes you'll wear, the trained ranch horses you'll ride, to the O.K. Corral shootouts."

"It's a vacation destination?"

"Our intel is limited. We suspect there are some family-friendly aspects to this place, as well as a sectioned-off area not intended for wives and kiddies. There's something in the works here … something big. The Order is in a monumental growth phase. There are indications that this place maybe some kind of proving ground … perhaps a way to vet new members." Baltimore patted the butt of the six-shooter, nestled now into his holster. "Of course, the family living quarters are far beyond luxurious. This is a dude ranch on a whole different scale. Getting you an invitation was difficult; also cost the agency five million dollars."

"So what's the plan? What will I be doing?"

"Your mission is to get close to Palmolive: befriend him, and from there, glean whatever information you can from him. I understand he has a weakness for aged Scottish whiskey. Once you've determined you've gotten all you can then … end him."

Chapter 15

"The dude ranch opens for business in three days," Baltimore said, getting to his feet. He fetched the holstered six-shooter off the table and secured the belt around his hips. He wore the pistol low, on his right side—to me, he looked fairly badass.

"We'll need every bit of that time to get you into shape."

"Into shape?"

Baltimore drew the pistol, twirled it twice around on his index finger, then returned it to his holster so fast my eyes barely registered the movement.

Bridgett gleefully clapped her hands. "I've been waiting to see this."

Baltimore drew the pistol again, this time pulling the trigger, then returned the unloaded gun into his holster in less than a second. He looked at me. "You have three days to get better at this than I am."

I scoffed. "You're dreaming. There's no way—"

Baltimore cut me off, in no mood for an argument. "You will, if you want to get Pippa back in one piece." He undid the buckle on his belt and placed the re-holstered gun down on the table. "Two weeks ago I couldn't do any of this. We have somebody in-house here who will be working with you. He's a bit rough around the edges, but you'll get used to him," Baltimore ended, sitting back down.

"Why? I mean isn't the place just a dude ranch … a vacation place?"

"Again, I'm not sure how the place is configured. There will be numerous others staying there, as many as one hundred, or more: Vacationing families, ranch help, and Palmolive's security people. From what I understand, his people will keep out of sight, mostly blending in with the existing ranch personnel. Anyway, you'll have very little time to make an impression on Palmolive—so it has to be something out of the ordinary. We figure your Wild Bill Hickok skills will be a good start. Remember, he and his kids are Wild West fanatics. You'll also be disguised as a prominent multi-millionaire—a corporate tycoon named Troy McAlister."

"Why does that name sound familiar to me?" I asked.

"Because he's been on the covers of Inc., Fast Company, and Forbes this past year. He's the Elon Musk of personal transportation devices. Think the Segway, on steroids. You'll be briefed on all that as well."

Bridgett got up and left the conference room.

I changed subjects: "What's the latest on Pippa? Do we know where she is?"

"We know that she was in New York." Baltimore then said, "Look, she is a trained operative. The truth is, she's exactly where we want her to be, as difficult as that may be to hear. She'll find a way to contact us and convey needed intel. Something's happening, Chandler … something very big. I've heard the word *cataclysmic* batted about in the field. Whatever the Order is planning, we need to get in front of it. The best way to do that is to let Pippa do her job and for you to get chummy with Palmolive. Now can we get back to your mission?"

I nodded.

"The real Troy McAlister has been briefed and is actually

on vacation in South America, at an undisclosed location. You'll be made up to look like him, using the same cosmetic procedures we used for the Baden-Baden mission."

As if on cue, Bridgett stuck her head in the door. "Is he ready for me?" She held up a glass beaker, half-filled with a clear liquid, and smiled at me. "Time for me to change the color of your hair—all over."

* * *

Over the next three hours, my brown hair was dyed a dirty-blond color—thanks to Bridgett's magic liquid. My features were altered, too, through a series of precise facial injections—enough for me to closely resemble the real Troy McAlister. Baltimore gave me a glossy, multi-page brochure to look over, describing Morning Hawk Ranch. Other than indicating the ranch resided at a high elevation—somewhere in the Colorado Rockies—no specific location was provided. I had to admit, the dude ranch looked like a lot of fun. Something about it reminded me of the old Yul Brynner movie *Westworld*.

Baltimore found me waiting in one of Bridgett's lab compartments. I remarked, "This is an experiential, family-type environment. I'll stick out like a sore thumb, going in there on my own."

"You're not going in alone. Carmen is going with you … as your wife."

"Carmen?"

Baltimore used the conference room intercom to page her. Less than a minute later, a husky woman, with round, rosy cheeks entered the conference room. I'd seen Carmen before—though her face looked different.

"Seriously? She's not a trained field agent. It's far too dangerous."

"Look around, Chandler … it's slim pickings around here. Remember, SIFTR is virtually in lockdown. Anyway, she's been made up to look like Loretta McAlister; she'll be fine."

"See, you didn't even recognize me," Carmen said, her hands on her ample hips.

"Uh huh. Well, okay," I said, taking in her poofed-up chignon—reminiscent of hairstyles back in the sixties.

"I know, I look like a chubby Tammy Wynette."

* * *

I'd stayed at SIFTR in the past, on another level, where the dorms are located. Although not optimal, tapping in was not a monumental issue. AC wall outlets provided both 110 and 220 volts—all over the facility—even in the dorm. I did have to carefully pick and choose the proper time to sit on the floor, my head resting against the wall, to avoid being noticed. So far, I'd always managed to schedule it just fine.

True to Baltimore's word, my six-shooter coach was indeed a bit rough around the edges, and he looked ancient. His long white beard and old overalls made him look more like Elmer Fudd than Billy the Kid, but he knew old-West quick-draw routines like no one I'd ever come across. For three days, I worked with Howard Pleck, starting with the basics. In no time at all, I was pulling my holstered pistol as quickly as Baltimore had done. A quarter of our time was spent at the SIFTR indoor range. I found it one thing to simply draw fast, like a gunslinger, but it was altogether different to also actually hit what I was shooting at. Already a pretty good shot, I soon mastered that aspect as well. I was ready—as prepared as I was going to get in the brief time-frame of three days.

Chapter 16

I had to give the people at Morning Hawk Ranch their proper due—for providing us as realistic a means of transportation to the ranch as possible. After an hour on the old dirt road, and a driver intent on rolling both into and over each and every pothole, my sore ass could attest to its true authenticity, derived from traveling on a one hundred-and-fifty-year-old stagecoach.

The two wooden bench seats sat across from one another—each was wide enough to sit three adults. Our coach had four adults and three young'uns. Carmen sat directly across from me; Mr. and Mrs. Jacobson sat next to Carmen; while their three kids, ranging in years from about five to ten, sat next to me—sometimes on me.

Keeping to their promise of high-security all the way, Carmen and I earlier flew, via a private jet, to an unlisted private airport somewhere in Colorado's mountains. Once we landed, we were scanned for electronic devices. Our watches and jewelry, once removed, were placed into secured lockers. I'd already opened the appropriate snaps on my Western shirt … just in case, ensuring there wouldn't be the slightest chance of any signals being generated or detected.

Our luggage was not only scanned, but also unpacked and inspected. Obviously, the airport's personnel were going to great lengths to ensure that the anonymity of the ranch's actual location stayed hidden. At the small, nondescript airport I also got my first look at some of the others we'd be spending the next few days with.

"So ... where did you two come in from?" asked the woman, sitting beside Carmen. The same woman who'd yet to tell her three bundles of joy to settle down and shut up.

"Freeport, Maine," Carmen replied cordially. "It's a pretty town ... most people haven't ever heard of it."

The husband, who looked even more uncomfortable than me, scowled, "I've heard of it. Freeze your balls off there in the wintertime."

The wife backhanded her husband's kneecap. "I've told you, you need to watch your language around the kids, Fred."

We'd done the introduction thing earlier, at the get-go of our long trek up the mountain. They were Fred and Alice Jacobson. She was mid-forties and tired-looking; he was pot-bellied, about the same age, and had a bad comb-over.

I asked, "First time at the ranch?" I'd thrown in something of a Western drawl, which surprised even me.

Fred's scowl returned. "Of course, it's our first time here. This is opening weekend for the ranch."

"But the brochure, the pictures of the happy families ..."

"All marketing bullshit."

Again came the slap to his kneecap.

Carmen added, "Well, it should be loads of fun just the same, don't you think?"

Neither Fred nor Alice had the chance to answer as the coach came to an abrupt stop. Someone outside yelled, "Welcome to Guffy ... ten-minute stop. Best you take advantage of it."

The coach door was opened and the three kids clambered out together. I held out an open palm, indicating that Fred and Alice should exit next. Once Carmen and I were alone, I said, "It's good they took my pistol away at the airport, holding it there for me."

"Come on, they're not that bad. I think the kids are adorable."

"Uh huh. Well, as the man said, best we take advantage of the stop." Again, I held out my hand, inviting Carmen to climb down before me.

Stepping onto Guffy's Main Street was not what I expected at all. I expected to see a true *Old West* town, like those you see in the movies. This place definitely was not that: There was a scattering of maybe ten, or twelve small, roughly-hewn, cabins; erected low to the ground, they appeared as old as the stagecoach we just stepped out from. There was also a wide array of junk scattered about in front of the cabins—mostly the skeletal remains of old automobiles, dating from the nineteen forties and 'fifties. I never saw such an accumulation of rust in my life.

"So much for that Dodge City ambiance," I said.

"I'm going inside to use the little girls' room. All that jostling!" Carmen headed off toward the closest of the cabins—the one with the sign on its roof that spelled out General Store. The letters looked like rusted-out auto exhaust pipes.

Standing on Main Street and taking in the town, I noticed a number of locals had come outside their small abodes. I waved to a bearded man wearing soiled clothes, standing across the road from me, but he simply glared back. His expression read: You have five minutes to get the hell out of Dodge. It quickly became apparent—Guffy was not only incredibly remote from the rest of the world, it was also terribly impoverished.

Something wet and brown flew by my left shoulder, landing in front of me in the dirt. I turned to see an elderly man who looked identical to the bearded man across the street.

He smelled of old sweat and chewing tobacco as he came to a halt next to me.

"Town's small, but we watch out for one another here."

I nodded, turning away, not knowing how to respond to that.

"Don't look like much, but we have everything any bigger town has. I'm Corki, the sheriff here … elected fair and square every six years."

I turned back, noticing Corki had a Glock secured into a leather shoulder holster, beneath the dark-stained armpit of his crumpled shirt.

"Is crime a big factor in Guffy, Sheriff?" I asked. "What do you have here, maybe fifty … a hundred … residents?"

"Seventy-five. But considering the bulk of them are men, needing to get away from the rest of the world … 'cause a lot are ex-cons—yeah, there's a bit of mischief I need to contend with on a regular basis."

I reassessed the townsfolk, milling around in front of us. "You have a jail?"

He laughed at that. "Of sorts. Justice system here is unique. Our mayor is a cat. Our prosecutor does double-duty as Sheriff. I'm also the undertaker and the barkeep." He pointed toward a slightly larger log cabin structure, farther on down the road. On its roof sat a sign, reading *BAR,* and by its appearance, it was made from old beer bottles.

"What do you think of the … um … dude ranch traffic?" I asked him, gesturing toward the idling stagecoach and four horses.

"We'll see. Could bring a bit of cash into Guffy … that certainly wouldn't hurt. There again, not sure I'd want to open up a dude ranch this close to the kind of folks who live around here. There's no shortage of perverts and degenerates within a stone's throw of where we're standing."

"This close?"

Corki spit again and nodded. Without turning around to look, he pointed a thumb over his shoulder: "Right back there ... over yonder. See it?"

I spun around and took in the distant landscape. We were in somewhat of a valley, between golden, grassy hills. Behind us, the highest ridge peaked several miles away; perched on its crest was a sprawling structure made of stone and logs. Sunlight was reflecting off its oversized, pane-glass windows.

"That it? Morning Hawk Ranch?"

"Three hundred and thirty acres of prime mountain land. I suggest you stay within the fence at night."

I didn't notice it at first, but there it was: A rusted-out chain-link fence encircling the portion of property I could see from this distance. I could also see visible gaps and breaks in the fence. Scanning the distant property, I suspected much of the three hundred-and-thirty acres were actually out of sight, on the far side of the ridge.

I heard the familiar sounds of fast-moving horses and the clattering of rigging and spotted another stagecoach, approaching down Main Street. More dude ranch guests in transit, I guessed.

"All aboard!" bellowed our driver, as he pulled himself up and onto the top seat of the waiting stagecoach.

I saw Carmen as she made her way toward the stagecoach. She waved me to join her. The sheriff touched my arm. "Listen, I don't know you ... but you seem like a nice enough guy. Watch yourself up there. Things may not be what they seem ... just a sayin'."

He had no idea. Or maybe he did? "I will, thanks." I ambled off toward the stagecoach, dodging a stampede of five- to ten-year-olds in the process.

Chapter 17

Heidi, wearing oversized white-framed designer sunglasses, plucked a pink silk blouse from a nearby rack, held it out at arm's length, and appraised it with a squint. Turning toward Pippa, she tucked the hanger under her chin, letting the garment cover her torso. "Is this me?"

"Sure. Why wouldn't a five-hundred-dollar blouse be you?"

Heidi stuffed the hanger back onto the rack, letting the blouse fall to the floor in the process. "It's time you called your boyfriend again."

Pippa tugged on the oversized turtleneck she wore—a loaner sweater from Heidi. Beneath the bandage, her neck was starting to itch. She'd gotten more than a few puzzled glances for wearing such a heavy garment in the middle of summer. "I told you, he doesn't think of me that way … not anymore. We broke up." Even as Pippa said the words, she knew they were false. She could only imagine the pain Rob felt, seeing her garroted on that video. She also knew SIFTR was well aware now of the recent merging of the WZZ and the thing called the Order. The truth was, she was still alive, feeling relatively capable, and where she needed to be. Being rescued at this time would actually be counter-productive to her gaining important intel. She needed to stay alive long enough to be of some use. What she wanted now was to find a way to contact the agency—away from the constant scrutiny of Heidi and Taffy.

Pippa looked over her shoulder and found Taffy standing nearby, holding an armful of dresses, blouses, slacks, and shoes—at least half of them, she knew, were intended for her.

"Go ahead, Mr. Taffy, and check those items out. All I'm seeing here are last year's rags," Heidi instructed.

The small clerk, standing at the swank Manhattan Gucci counter, raised his nose at her comment, but quickly became enamored with handsome Taffy.

Heidi guided Pippa out the front door and onto the busy Madison Avenue sidewalk. "Call your superiors at the agency now," she ordered, holding out her iPhone.

"Here … in public?"

"Yes. Do it now!"

That was new. Twice earlier, Pippa had been instructed to call Rob's cell phone directly, but got only his voice mail. She dialed SIFTR's direct line, heard it ring once, and a voice said, "Provide code."

She spoke the ten digit alphanumeric code and waited. After thirty seconds of intermittent clicking and dead air, she heard a familiar voice.

"Pippa?"

"Baltimore? Yes, it's me—"

Suddenly, the phone Pippa was holding was no longer pressed to her ear, as Heidi snatched it away and began speaking in a hushed tone. "Mr. Baltimore … it's Heidi Goertz. I'm sure you remember me."

Although Pippa could only hear one side of the conversation, she was fairly certain what Curt would be saying to Heidi.

"Mr. Baltimore, let me put this to you as simply as possible. Do you want to see your agent again … alive? Or should I finish the job that was started and just send you her head?"

"Well, your actions are contradicting that statement. Was my video message unclear?" Heidi asked him.

There was a significant pause and then Heidi fired back, "I certainly am accessible! Are you telling me a covert organization such as yours doesn't have the basic resources to find me? Well, that hardly speaks well of SIFTR's capabilities, does it?"

There was another pause. "As you just heard, she's alive and well. But if you don't care enough to get her back, I can remedy that here and now."

"No … my demands have not changed. Bring me Mr. Chandler and yourself. The exchange must happen today … right away."

Taffy emerged from Gucci's entrance, carrying no fewer than eight large shopping bags. Heidi spun around, raising a waving arm into the air.

Fifty yards away, a black Range Rover accelerated, dodged a VW Beetle, and inbounded toward the nearby curb.

The driver gave a perfunctory nod as Heidi reached for the rear door handle. Taffy sprang forward. "Wait!"

Heidi rolled her eyes as she unlatched the back door. "Thanks for the chivalry, Mr. Taffy, but you'd need a free hand to …"

Pippa watched as Heidi stood frozen, looking inside the rear of the Land Rover.

The voice was hushed but unmistakable: "Get in. You first, Mrs. Goertz, then Pippa. I want pretty boy out there to hop into the front passenger seat."

Out of view, Baltimore had managed to remain obscure in the back seat. He was holding a gun, now pointed straight at Heidi. Pippa couldn't hold back the smile from her face.

Heidi continued to look indignant, not making a move. "You wouldn't, not here in public."

The words had no sooner left her lips than a gunshot rang out and the SUV's rear window disintegrated. A startled woman, walking nearby on the sidewalk, screamed, but was uninjured.

Baltimore said in a calm voice, "The next bullet will take one of your ears off."

"I'd do what he says, Heidi. I've practiced with him at the firing range. He's a shitty shot and I'm betting he's aiming at the middle of your face, just to be safe." Pippa smirked at her.

Heidi huffed but did as told, disappearing into the back of the SUV. Pippa opened the front passenger door and said, "Get in."

Taffy stood there, looking as if he were contemplating his next move. He raised both hands, clutching multiple Gucci bag handles. "And these?" he asked.

"Hold on," she said, relieving him of the holstered pistol hidden at the back of his pants, then said, "Okay, give them to me. Make one false move and he'll kill her. I hope you know that." Pippa waited while Taffy placed all the bags into her outstretched arms, before sliding into the front seat. Pippa leaned down and looked at the driver. "Pop the back hatch."

With their day's shopping secured in the rear compartment, Pippa squeezed in next to Heidi and closed the door. She gave Baltimore an appreciative smile. In the distance the approaching sound of a siren could be heard.

Baltimore kept his weapon trained on Heidi's ribcage as she sat beside him. He caught the driver's eyes, staring back at him in the rearview mirror. "Drive, asshole."

Doing as instructed, the driver accelerated into the busy Manhattan traffic. "Where to?"

"Stay on Madison for now," Baltimore said.

Heidi was fuming. "How did you find me? My phone is totally secure … invisible. So is Taffy's."

"Facial recognition … there's no shortage of security cameras in this part of the city."

"No … our faces are well-covered with oversized sunglasses … there's no way." She, Pippa, and Taffy were all wearing ridiculously large sunglasses.

"You had Pippa try on some clothes."

"Yeah … so?"

"So I guess you didn't realize that hidden security cameras are placed out of sight in some of the dressing rooms. Pippa took off her glasses when trying on clothes."

"You watched me getting undressed?" Pippa asked, not really liking the idea, but grateful to him just the same.

He shrugged. "The things we have to do for love of country."

"It doesn't matter," Heidi said, "there's no place you'll be able to hide. The Order is everywhere … every police station will be putting out … what do they call them? APBs?"

"You said it yourself, Heidi; you and Fabio there were pretty unrecognizable. Nobody's looking for you, although this car is definitely a problem after that gunshot. Make a left on East Sixty-fifth."

The driver made the next left.

"Turn right on Second … then get on the Queensboro Bridge. From there, head on to JFK. Don't forget, there's a gun in my hand."

The driver nodded, looking back through the rearview mirror. "I don't want any trouble. I'll do what you say."

"You can't bring weapons onto commercial airlines," Heidi said.

"Yeah … well, we won't be flying commercial. Just sit back and enjoy the ride." Pippa sat back too, now only seeing the back of Taffy's head.

Baltimore leaned forward, looking past Heidi. "Pippa … can you check his pockets?"

She scooted forward, bringing her hands around Taffy's chest, and retrieved a handgun from an inside holster under his jacket. "Huh … U.S. made Beretta. Nice. Thought you'd have a German weapon, maybe a Glock." She placed the weapon under her right butt cheek and continued searching through his pockets. "Ah … here we go! Your little garrote toy." Pippa leaned in even farther, putting her lips next to his left ear, and whispered, "You know, I am going to kill you. Should I do it now? It would be so easy." She held the wire's two wooden handles out so he could see the garrote. "Do you think a thin little wire such as this can actually cut someone's head clean off? I mean, I'm not nearly as strong as you are. I'd probably make a mess of it … sever only halfway through, and have to give up … let your big fucking head droop and flop around on your neck for a while … half on, half off." Pippa sat back and looked over to Baltimore. "He's clean."

Chapter 18

Three people entered the six-sided hexagon from three different entrances. The first, Colby Brighton, who'd waited the longest, watched as the middle-aged woman, dressed in a smart-looking gray suit, sat down at the glass table, which mimicked the hexagon shape of the room.

"Mrs. Gulliver."

"Mr. Brighton," she answered back, with a slight nod of her head.

They both watched as the third person, Leon Goertz, tan—far too energetic-looking for such an ungodly time of early morning—joined them at the table.

"Mrs. Gulliver, Mr. Brighton," Goertz said.

Brighton gave a perfunctory nod and Anne Gulliver said, "Good morning, Mr. Goertz." She waited for Leon to get seated before asking, "And where is Mrs. Goertz? We were expecting both of you."

Leon shifted in his chair, maintaining a casual smile. "I'm sure it's simply a matter of a traffic snarl in New York City, or perhaps she missed her wakeup call at—"

Anne Gulliver interrupted his speculations. "You're not in touch with her? You haven't spoken to her? She's your damn wife, Leon!" Two men, both in suits, entered the ultra-modern conference room and made their way to seats at their table.

Leon, who'd rehearsed the same general conversation with himself several times on his way over, knew the importance of keeping his cool—of maintaining a professional demeanor. The truth was, he had no idea where his fucking wife was. Granted, they lived more or less autonomously these days, but it was highly unlike her to pull something like this. Hell, for years this was what they'd worked toward; this was the golden ring! There was no greater honor than to be a part of something so monumental … so impactful … so powerful. The Council of Five, soon to become the Council of Seven, was the culmination of both his and Heidi's life work: seats, literally, at the BIG table.

Leon looked back at the Council of Five, minus one. Their newly appointed leader, Rudy Palmolive, was also absent—taking some kind of personal time off. The little asshole, supposedly, was on the fast track to the Pearly Gates. Why they'd elected that little weasel as the head council member, when he only had two or three years left on his ticket, eluded Leon. *I'd have been a far better choice*, he mused. Then again, every pitcher on the mound has another pitcher warming up in the bullpen. Inwardly, Leon thought it interesting that he'd used a truly American sports analogy, when he was from the Fatherland … *Germany*. Had he been in the States so overly long that he'd lost touch with his first true allegiance?

"Mr. Goertz, I'm speaking to you," Anne Gulliver said.

"Yes, of course, we keep in constant communication. These are busy times and I'm positive Heidi will be here momentarily."

The two most recent arrivals joining the meeting looked over at Leon with disdain. He gave them both a confident nod. "Mr. Berg … Mr. Chang …"

Anne continued, "I have Mr. Palmolive's endorsement to begin these proceedings. Do you have any idea to what lengths we've gone to bring the four of us together? From Europe, parts of the U.S., and the Far East?" Her eyes flashed over to Mr. Chang. "Why don't you try her on her cell phone—" she said, cutting herself short.

Leon gave a half-hearted nod—one that said, *well, that's a problem now, isn't it?* At present, they were two hundred and eighty-five feet below ground. No cell phone on Earth could receive a signal down here. It was the most secret, most protected, location on Earth. Leon gave the hexagonal conference room a quick glance. It was beautiful, with its granite-like walls and high ceilings. Just sitting there, he felt the impregnability of the place. Most people surmised Washington, D.C. to be the hub of power for the free world, but they were wrong. Purposely misled. Here, hundreds of feet below ground, below DIA—Denver International Airport—was where everything, the ultimate world order, would stem from. He'd heard the nutty rumors; watched many *conspiracy theory* YouTube videos with skepticism. But, in this case, the conspiracy was an actually true fact. A multi-billion-dollar below-ground facility did exist beneath DIA. Skyscrapers built below ground: a new city that could survive a mass uprising or even the next world war. And there were clues to be seen—elaborate, wall-sized murals were strategically placed throughout the airport up above: Bizarre, out-of-place renderings of an Armageddon-like world. Leon contemptuously thought of the thousands of travelers who passed by them daily unaware—another indication of the masses' cluelessness.

"The President of the United States is in transit: Air Force One's ETA, to land at DIA, is an hour from now. He's been granted access to this room so he can meet with other Order, mid-level, members. I suppose we can break now ..." Anne Gulliver looked at her watch. "We can convene back at 2:00." She looked at Leon with disdain. "Don't make us regret the trust we've placed in you, Mr. Goertz. The most significant event in history is imminent—mankind's evolution—away from warring egos and religious-based conflict. It's all about to end—one nation under God becomes, instead, One World under God. Do you want to be a part of that, Mr. Goertz?"

"I most certainly do, Mrs. Gulliver, and fellow council members. Together, we will change history." Leon thought for a second. "Perhaps my wife is close; is there a way to communicate with her hydro-pod?"

Mr. Berg answered, "Yes, of course, but Mrs. Goertz is not in transit, at least not via her hydro-pod. It's sitting back in New York City and that is a growing concern for us."

It was to Leon as well. Currently, an ever-expanding network—tens of thousands of newly bored subterranean tunnels—crisscrossed the United States, as well as in Europe and the Far East. Massive amounts of military equipment were being repositioned; the same with the Order's Armed Forces. Not so different, really, than what President Eisenhower initiated back in 1956: a 41,000 mile U.S. Interstate Highway System, making life simpler for travelers and commuters to jaunt across the country. Actually, the Interstate's primary function would allow the Defense Department to quickly move its military assets around, in case of enemy invasion. Years later, the Order initiated the same system, but went a step further—constructing an elaborate subterranean combination of roads and hydro-passages between the country's major cities. Above ground roads can be bombed—destroyed. What the Order successfully accomplished underground was ingenious. There was no stopping them now.

Leon briefly wondered if Heidi had taken another pod. If so, perhaps the thing was having mechanical problems? But he quickly discounted the thought, since there really wasn't much mechanics involved. She wouldn't be caught dead in a maintenance pod, anyway, preferring to take her private jet.

"I'm sure Mrs. Goertz will be here by two and we can continue. Thank you for your patience," Leon said, looking at each member with the most confident expression he could muster.

Anne Gulliver held back as the others hurried from the room. "Hold on, Leon."

She waited until she heard all the doors close in the distance. "Is there a problem? If so, tell me now, don't wait till we reconvene. The others will be far less tolerant. You're not a member yet. You don't have the protection that comes with being a full member." Stooping, she picked up her leather satchel by her feet then clutched it to her. "In just a matter of days, the order to attack will come from Palmolive. You and your wife do not want to be loose ends. Clear her absence up today, or face the wrath of the council." She strode away without waiting for Leon to answer.

He heard the door swing closed behind her. "Shit!" He pulled his cell phone from his breast pocket and looked at it, then gazed around at the surrounding granite walls. "Shit! Shit! Shit!" There had to be some way to get in touch with Heidi. He scrolled through his contact list and found Taffy's number. *Fucking pretty boy.* He hated the man … was sure he was screwing Heidi on a daily basis. But, really, so what—he too was having his own indiscretions, in spades.

Leon hurried off toward the exit. He needed to get aboveground fast.

Chapter 19

I gave Carmen a sympathetic smile. She closed her eyes and leaned her head back. Between the smell from the horses, the constant dust swirling about, and the long, ever-winding dirt road we were on, she looked close to throwing up.

"We're almost there," I said encouragingly.

"Just stop talking."

The sibling trio of our fellow passengers stood together at the stagecoach's right side windows. "Look … there it is," the oldest of the three boys said, pointing.

I wasn't sure what to expect, as the brochure hadn't actually shown the front of the property. It was impressive. The dirt road had given way to a graveled, circular drive that U-turned around the front entrance of the largest log and natural stone structure I'd ever seen. Perched atop a ridgeline, which offered up magnificent views of the distant mountains and the valley below, from here it was easy to find the messy little town of Guffy—a far-off clump of dark-looking structures and tired automobiles that looked more like dead ants from this distance. Perched atop the ridge line, the lodge and two smaller, ancillary, structures looked like they had been there for decades, if not longer, which I knew was not the case. In the distance was a timber gazebo. Inside, a man and woman could be seen, silhouetted against the midday sun, embracing and kissing.

Two other stagecoach rigs, horseless, rested on the property. We weren't the first to arrive. When our coach door swung open the kids jumped out first. Fred and Alice Jacobson, both looking excited, followed behind them, leaving the two of us alone.

"Better?"

"Somewhat. Just help me get the hell out of this damn thing."

I took Carmen's arm and guided her to the door.

"I've got it from here," she said.

The thing that struck me first was the abundance of people milling around—all dressed in Western attire. Carmen joined the Jacobsons, now being greeted by a tall, sixtyish man, wearing a black cowboy hat, a six-shooter on each hip, dark leather chaps, and well-worn boots with spurs—Western-attired the whole nine yards. I joined the huddle and nodded to the black-hatted gentleman.

"Good … so you've decided to join us, Mr. Holliday."

As part of the earlier registration process, all guests were issued alternate names—mostly some name derived from a real-life, Old West character. No one was to know anyone's legal name, the one they used in the real world. It was both a means of adding realness to the overall experience, as well as protecting the actual identities of those lodging here. Carmen and I were named the Hollidays, after the infamous Doc Holliday, I presumed, from the Wyatt Earp storied legend.

"My name is John—John Wayne, and I run this little shindig."

It took me every ounce of willpower not to roll my eyes. "Glad to meet you, John," I said, taking his outstretched hand. I found his grip somewhat disappointing, especially for someone calling himself John Wayne. He was of medium height and slightly built. Beneath his Stetson I spotted white hair at the temples, clear blue eyes, and two enormous ears. John said, "Did you know that Wyatt Earp in his elder years, when he lived in Los Angeles, was actually a technical advisor on a cowboy movie? One of the early talkies. He took up friendship with one of the young actors … a guy named Marion Morrison. Do you know who that was?"

I shook my head but Carmen quickly responded, "John Wayne!" probably louder than she intended.

"That's right. The Duke claimed many of his portrayals of cowboys and Old West lawmen were based on tales told to him by Wyatt Earp."

John turned toward the crowd now amassing: "I'd like to talk about the rules and regulations. Following them will make your stay here far more enjoyable and safe."

I was having a hard time following John's introductory chat, due to some kind of scuffle going on between two hired hands attending to our stagecoach horses. I saw one man shove the other, and the quick reciprocal shove back. That's all it took for an all-out fisticuffs to break out. Soon others—other ranch workers, I presumed—were also going toe to toe with each other. It was mayhem. I felt Carmen move closer to me. "Is this for real?"

I flinched my shoulders, unsure at first. I know what it looks like when someone is struck in the face with bare knuckles, as opposed to a fake, Hollywood-type punch. The punches thrown now were real time, and real blood dripped from the corners of more than one fighting man's mouth. I probed the minds of the closest ones. There was real anger there—borderline hatred.

John Wayne moved with surprising agility for a man his age. In five strides he put himself in the middle of the ruckus, pulled one of his pistols out, and fired off two rounds into the air.

"That's enough! What kind of impression do you think

you're making for our guests? Now get back to work. The next man throwing a punch will be spending the night behind bars." John waited for the ranch hands to disperse before holstering his weapon and rejoining our group.

Alice Jacobson said, "Was that part of the show, Mr. Wayne?"

"No." He looked at her as if she had three heads. "Let me make something perfectly clear here, right from the get-go: this is not Disneyland … Magic Mountain … or goddamn Knott's Berry Farm. You people paid for authenticity. Paid an unimaginable amount of money for it. Though we take the utmost care to protect all the little ones, folks do … and will … get hurt here. You can take that to the bank, missy."

John next turned his attention to Fred, then to me. "Now I suggest you both go get your side arms. This is not the kind of place you want to walk around unprotected." With that said, he strode off in the direction of another arriving stagecoach.

Alice, pulling her three boys closer to her, said, "He has to be joking … right? It's all part of the Old West atmosphere they're trying to provide here, right?"

I gave her the best look of reassurance I could muster up. "Yes, I'm sure it's all part of the experience, Alice."

"Millie," Fred said.

I looked at him.

"Our names. I'm Sam Bass, the famous train robber. She's Millie—my wife."

"Fine. Millie, I'm sure this is all part of the show, but I'd keep a close eye on your kids, anyway. At least, until we know the lay of the land." My words seemed to soothe her ruffled feathers somewhat.

"Come this way."

We all turned in unison toward a young black man,

dressed in stained trousers and a torn, long-sleeved, linen shirt. "I'll be *showin'* you your rooms."

The first thing that occurred to me was this had to be the worst show of political incorrectness I'd ever witnessed. The handsome young fellow appeared to be a servant of some kind.

"I'm Matt. I'll be *fetchin'* your bags and things later. Please come along." He smiled and hurried toward the main entrance of the dude ranch resort. I held back and let the others go first, while watching the last passengers exit the other coach. Two women, dressed in long dresses and bonnets, emerged first. Then came a tall man, wearing wire-rimmed spectacles and a bowler hat, followed by a smaller man, dressed similarly to myself. He was pale, and moved with quick, bird-like, movements. Rudy Palmolive.

* * *

Even from the back of the group, I could smell Matt's sour body odor. If authenticity was what the Morning Hawk people were striving for, they were right on target. He told the Bass family to wait in the expansive entranceway, and gestured for Carmen and me to follow him upstairs.

Everything was made of roughly hewn, light-colored timber logs—walls, stair treads, and banisters—which certainly provided a rustic Western ambiance. At the top of the staircase, Matt made a left turn, ushering us past three closed doors. He stopped at the end of the corridor and opened a far door, motioning for us to go inside.

Carmen smiled and nodded at Matt, and I did the same. Once inside, we found ourselves in a sunny room that overlooked the front drive, and provided a spectacular view toward the mountains.

Matt too moved inside and walked over to another door. Opening it, he said, "Here's the toilet. You've got a tub, shower, and two sinks in there." He then pointed to a row of closet doors. "You can put your clothes and stuff in there. Supper's at 4:00, in the main dining hall. No hats in the dining hall. Hats worn at supper upset Mr. Wayne."

I was only partially listening to Matt. My attention was on two wall-mounted lanterns on either side of the king-sized brass bed. They seemed to be old-fashioned, oil-type lamps. I pointed to one of them. "Oil lamps?"

He looked confused at first, then said, "Oh … yeah … no electricity here. More realistic."

I nodded appreciatively. That news could definitely pose a problem for me.

I reached into my pocket and brought out a few bills. Matt held up his palms: "Oh no—no one's allowed to take a gratuity. It's not allowed here." He left, closing the door behind him.

Carmen moved over to the bed, sat down, and gave it a few good bounces. "Comfy!" she remarked, and gave me a toothy sideways glance. "Which side of the bed do you want?"

There was a knock at the door and I hurried to open it. Two men that I recognized from the brawl out front were holding our suitcases. One of them had my holstered six-shooter hung over his shoulder.

"I'm Jude. This is Jordan. Matt tell you about supper?"

"Yes," I said, noticing Jude had a pretty nasty scar running down the left side of his face. Both men were rugged—as genuine-looking as two legend cowboys as I could imagine. They were shorter than average and walked somewhat bowlegged. Jordan, the friendlier-looking of the two, had large white teeth. One, an incisor, was slightly off-color—a false tooth.

"Um … is there any electricity here? You know, to use my electric shaver?"

Jordan shook his head. "No need to shave here, if you don't want to."

"Fine. Is there electricity …"

"No, man … this isn't the Hyatt. Have to get used to it." He put my suitcase in the closet as Jordan placed Carmen's on a folding luggage rack in the corner. Jordan handed my holstered gun over. "Let me know if you need me to show you how to use it."

"Thanks, but I think I'm okay."

Chapter 20

We took turns using the shower. When I emerged from the bathroom, a towel wrapped around my waist, Carmen was already dressed in fresh clothes and sitting on the bed. Although I didn't know her particularly well, I could tell something was up and needling her.

"Funny how we both took nice hot showers yet the place has no electricity. That must be some campfire they have … boiling water somewhere," I said.

She tilted her head and inspected the toe of one extended boot—but said nothing.

"Okay, what is it? What's bothering you, Carmen?"

"I'm not stupid, you know."

"I know that."

"I'm also not oblivious to your … quirks."

I had to smile at that. "I have quirks?"

"Did you know that SIFTR dorms have 24/7 surveillance? Cameras that see perfectly fine in the dark?"

I proceeded to pick through my suitcase, keeping my expression neutral. "That sounds a little stalker-ish. Did you enjoy watching me sleep?"

"Knock it off, Chandler. You and I both know you spent a significant amount of time on the floor, your head up against an electrical outlet. And there's been other weirdness—all dealing with high-voltage, which I'll not go into now—culminating in your most recent obsession with electricity at this ranch."

I straightened, holding on to the clothes I'd selected from the suitcase. "Mind if I get dressed before we talk—"

"Whatever. Go," she said, gesturing toward the bathroom.

I smiled and headed toward the door, all the while probing her mind for what she'd really figured out. What I found was disturbing. She'd had suspicions about me for some time now, ever since the Baden-Baden mission. Apparently, too many aspects were left unexplained in my field report; there were too may coincidences and suspected outright lies. She was right: I did use my mind-reading powers to intrude mentally into others' thoughts, implanting suggestions favorable to myself numerous times. While getting dressed, I weighed what I should do next: Tell her everything—try to convince her not to share the information with her superiors and SIFTR—or come up with some quick elaborate explanation. Could I manage that? I knew I could make up stories with the best of them, but Carmen was no fool.

I opened the bathroom door, finding her right where I'd left her. She raised her brows.

"I'll agree to tell you … tell you everything, if you agree to keep it to yourself. Not tell Baltimore or Calloway. No one."

She looked at me and chewed the inside of her lip, coming to some kind of determination. "Agreed, unless you're some kind of crazy freak who needs professional help." She was quite nervous, inclined to the point of calling off the mission.

I sat down next to her on the bed. "We're going to be late for supper … maybe—"

She cut me off. "Rob!"

"You know I was in a car wreck and nearly died. It put

me in the hospital."

"Yes, I know the whole story. It wasn't an accident … it was Harland Platt; he staged the whole hit on you."

"Well, what you don't know, only Pippa knows, is that I was changed—physiologically—in that wreck. Had something to do with a high-voltage line hanging over my head for so many hours. Um … I came away from all that with the ability to read minds. Not only that—with some I can actually influence their thoughts."

Carmen continued to study me with a furrowed brow. "You're full of shit. Why can't you just answer my question, without making up such a stupid … ridiculous … story?"

I returned her stare with mild amusement. "Fine. You're going to make me jump through hoops, so here goes: Think of something—it doesn't matter what."

I waited then said, "No, I don't snore."

The smile on her face evaporated. "Think of something else."

She wanted to know if I routinely read her mind. "No, not to say I never have, but I don't make a practice of breaching the minds of people I care about." That response wasn't entirely true. Pippa could attest to that.

"That's amazing! I mean totally, F-ing, amazing!" She scratched her nose, then scratched it again.

I smiled at her.

She looked at her hand. "You didn't just make me …"

"I did. But here's the thing: There's a flip side to all this."

"You periodically need to be near something with high-voltage, right?"

"That's right. No less than ten minutes, every twenty-four hours. The higher the voltage, the better."

"What happens if you … you know, don't—"

"I call it tapping in. If I don't tap in within twenty-four

hours, I go into withdrawals, which are as bad, or worse, than a heroine addict's. It isn't pretty. I also lose my mind-reading abilities."

She shook her head. "So how long before you need to … do your tapping in?"

"I have about four hours before I'll start feeling the negative effects. So is my secret safe? Can you keep this to yourself?"

She nodded. "No worries there. You'd be little more than a lab rat for them the rest of your life. That and other things." She cut herself off. "Your secret's safe with me."

I stood, grabbed up my gun and holster, and secured it around my hips. I gestured toward the door. "Shall we?"

* * *

We found the great room on the first floor by following the sounds of people talking and laughing and chairs being dragged across hardwood floors. In one corner stood a rock fireplace, large enough for five men to stand upright in. Forty feet above us was a massive timber beam, running the length of the expansive room. Across from the fireplace, floor-to-ceiling windows looked out on a setting sun, off to the west. Before us, six long plank tables with bench seats on either side were arranged. Husbands and wives, and a scattering of kids, were taking seats. Dressed all in black, John Wayne stood near the fireplace on an old wooden milk crate, waiting for something.

I felt an elbow in my ribs and turned to see Carmen staring off to our right. Rudy Palmolive, his wife, and their two sons were just getting seated midway down one of the long tables. Carmen moved quickly so she could grab seats on the bench opposite them. I followed, sitting down in the seat she patted.

Once down, I began probing Palmolive's mind. Immediately, I knew he was a man of remarkable intelligence. He was in the process of sizing up everyone around him: assessing and cataloging their characteristics, strengths and weaknesses. He kept an inner running monologue going on, too. Strangely, it was a voice not his own. *Wait!* It was a deep and accented voice, like James Earl Jones—like Darth Vader's voice. *Really weird.*

Carmen was talking to me.

"I'm sorry, what did you say?" I asked her.

She smiled, "I said, this is Carolina McCarty."

I stood and reached across the wide table, taking ahold of the delicate hand of the woman sitting next to Rudy Palmolive. Her dark hair had long, natural-flowing waves. She was petite and had a face that literally took my breath away. She smiled, looking somewhat embarrassed. One peek into her mind told me she thought this dude ranch vacation thing was stupid. She also had no choice in the matter. Like most other things in her life, it made her feel a captive. She was miserable. Her eyes flashed toward her husband. He didn't like her touching other men or looking at other men.

Carmen said, "I'm Claire and this is Doc … Doc Holliday."

I was still standing when Palmolive looked up at me, as if seeing me for the first time. He was aware who I was—Troy McAlister, the wealthy entrepreneur. I'd forgotten about my altered appearance.

"Ah … Mr. Holliday, I'm Henry McCarty, better known as Billy the Kid." He seemed to take pleasure playing that notoriously ruthless gunslinger. His two young sons stopped what they were doing and looked up at their father. Younger versions of the stern-looking man, both were small, had dark beady eyes, and a preponderance of small black moles dotting their faces, just like their dad.

One of the sons pointed an outstretched finger at me. "I know who you are … you're Wyatt Earp's friend." The other boy added, "You were at the O.K. Corral … in Tombstone."

"Very good! You both seem to know the Old West gunfighters."

"There's very little they don't know about the Old West, Mr. Holliday. May I call you Doc? You can call me Billy."

This was getting stupider by the minute. "Sure, why not?"

Preparing to sit back down, Billy the Kid's son said, "Are you as fast as they say you are? Do you think you could beat my dad? Billy the Kid's fast—he's the fastest …"

I drew my gun, twirled it twice, just like Baltimore and I'd practiced for almost three days straight, and just as quickly holstered it again. I was impressed with myself for not dropping the thing and making a complete fool of myself. I sat back down next to the proud-looking Mrs. Holliday.

"Wowie!" said the boys simultaneously. They looked up at their father expectantly, but his eyes remained on me, the smile on his face wavering. Reading his thoughts, I inwardly heard the same deep unmistakable voice—*Keep it up, asshole … maybe I'll shove that gun …*

With that, I pulled out of his mind. At least I'd gotten his attention. It was a start. I hadn't forgotten why we were here … not for a second. He was my connection to finding Pippa—not to mention bringing down the WZZ and, perhaps, the Order too.

Chapter 21

"Listen up, everyone. Grub's on the way … be leaving the kitchen in a minute. We're having chili with black bean and Angus steak. There's also Mrs. Wayne's home-baked cornbread; hot, right outta the oven." John Wayne looked around the room, hands on hips, trying to embody the Duke's infamous off-kilter stance.

I glanced in Mrs. Palmolive's direction and saw her stifle a yawn.

John Wayne continued, "Tomorrow is a big day. Moms, you'll be taking your young ones down to the stables. Everyone gets a horse to call their own during their stay here. Right after breakfast, we're forming a posse. Seems there's been a jailbreak. John Wesley Hardin, notorious gunfighter, is on the run and we need to catch him. I want horses saddled and moms and their kids ready to move out by nine a.m."

Carmen leaned into me and whispered, "I really hate horses. Maybe I can pass on this whole posse thing?"

"Men, we've got bigger problems right here in town. You've all been warned. Some of the meanest, most notorious criminals are among us. You may see them on the road into Tombstone—our own little town on the east side of the property. Or sitting right in front of you at a poker table, or in the process of robbing the Tombstone Bank. You don't want to be caught around these parts unarmed. Listen to me now: I want you all to draw your weapons."

John Wayne drew one of his own single-action Colts and held it up. He flipped it around, then pointed to the butt of the pistol. "See this green sticker? Well, you should have the same sticker on your own six-shooters."

Every man in the room looked at his gun. And sure enough, I saw a green sticker on the butt of my Colt.

"If your gun doesn't have a green sticker on it, come see either me or Jude right away. Remember, all ammunition must strictly come from the Morning Hawk Ranch armory. Is that perfectly understood?"

I flipped open the gun's cylinder and examined my six chambered rounds. Each bullet had the telltale red tip—they were blanks. I saw the other men in the room doing the same. There were more than a few nods of relief.

A blonde, middle-aged woman stood, two tables over. She wore a matching leather jacket and pants—both fringed in copious amounts. Like John Wayne, she too had six-shooters holstered on both hips.

"Calamity Jane … you have a question?"

"Two things: First, just because I'm a woman I hope you don't expect me to be joining the kids' morning ride."

"I'd expect you to pass on that, Jane," John Wayne said. "Second?"

"So you've swapped out all our ammunition … to blanks, right?"

From his stern expression, John Wayne obviously didn't like Calamity Jane discussing such information in public.

"My question is this: If there is an … altercation … a gunfight, how's it determined who's the winner?"

With a peek at Calamity Jane's thoughts, I discovered I was wrong. Her question was prearranged. She was a plant—she worked for the Morning Hawk Ranch. Then I noticed

Jude standing off to the side, surveying the crowd. The other cowhand, Jordan, joined him and whispered in his ear. I could inwardly hear their conversation, as easily as if I were standing beside them, but this time, I read Jordan's thoughts.

Jordan: *I checked through their luggage … all their stuff.*

Jude: *What did you find?*

Jordan: *Nothing. Oh, and he doesn't have an electric razor. I thought that was weird.*

John Wayne spoke up again: "Thank you for your questions, Ms. Jane. Altercations, as you put it, can happen in a place like this. It's the way of things, in the old Wild West. I want you all to take a good look around the room, around the perimeter. See those men?"

Sure enough, there were now quite a few, maybe fifteen, ranch hands surrounding our tables. They looked serious and surprisingly dangerous. Arbitrarily, I read a few of their minds and came to the quick determination that all was not good—not good at all. In an attempt to employ local help, these men were hired almost entirely from Guffy—the local town's worst gene pool. Some of them were the same men Sheriff Corki warned me about. Maybe Corki exaggerated and they weren't all perverts and degenerates, but from what I was seeing and hearing, I wasn't particularly optimistic.

The Duke continued: "These men will be watching … always around. They're trained and know what to look and listen for. A determination will be made as to which man drew down first and if his, or her, aim appeared dead on. They will determine who is the winner."

"What happens to the loser?" a colossal-sized, rosy-faced man in the front of the room asked. He was sporting a silver belt buckle the size of a butter plate. Even from a distance I could make out a pair of small gold pistols, their muzzles crossed, affixed to the buckle's center. I recognized him as a

U.S. congressman, from one of the southern states. Maybe Georgia or West Virginia.

"Well, then he's dead, Butch," he replied, with a deadpan expression.

The room went quiet in anticipation of some further explanation.

John Wayne smiled and further said, "He or she will be taken into custody and placed into our jail for a period of no less than five hours. Being slow on the draw in these parts has certain repercussions."

The Guffy ranch hand nearest me was close enough for me to see his holstered Colt. Instead of a green sticker on its butt, there was a red one. I stood and caught John's attention.

"Mr. Holliday?"

"I … um … noticed that your ranch hands all have red stickers on their pistols instead of green. Should we take that to mean they'll be firing live rounds?"

"I was wondering when someone would notice that. As I've said, these men are specially trained and are doing double-duty as our ranch security. We've an important bunch of folks here, so high security is essential at Morning Hawk Ranch." John smiled and dug into his front pocket. "For being the first one to figure that out, you win the prize. Please come on up and retrieve your award."

All heads turned in my direction. With the exception of the servers, bringing in trays loaded with Angus chili and Mrs. Wayne's hot cornbread, the room was quiet. I hitched up my shoulders in mock confusion, and made my way between the tables to join John Wayne.

Stepping down from his milk-carton perch, he held up a large metal star, showing it off to the crowd. "I hereby appoint you, Doc Holliday, sheriff of Dodge City." He pinned the star over my heart and stepped back—appraising his handiwork. He turned me to face the room of onlookers, then clapped his hands. Within seconds, everyone likewise was applauding.

I held up a waving hand in appreciation and made my way back to my seat. This could complicate things. I wondered how it would impact my getting close to Rudy Palmolive and finding Pippa.

I sat down and saw the look of consternation on Carmen's face—she wasn't happy. Mrs. Palmolive, on the other hand, looked more than a little intrigued.

"Are you going to kill my daddy?"

I looked at the boy, sitting to the right of his father—Billy the Kid. "Well … that could happen."

Chapter 22

The man next door prepared for the day much the same way he had for the past fifteen days. Up at 5:30 a.m. sharp, he opened his laptop and checked on the status of the girl. Video feeds from all her rooms were operational. He clicked on the window for her bedroom and it filled the screen: *Ah, she's still asleep.* He hurried off to the bathroom to do the three *S*s: shit, shower, and shave. After dressing, he checked on the girl again and found her waking up. He watched as she reached a thin bare arm into the air and stretched, her long blonde hair partially covering her face. She sat up, letting the covers fall down to her lap. The man observing her noticed the top of her white panties—she was naked from the waist up. With both arms extended behind her, supporting her, she looked toward the window.

The man looked at his watch: Three hundred and sixty hours and thirty-four minutes. He liked a steady routine. At rare times, he allowed himself to ponder certain possibilities, though he never overly-invested himself emotionally either way. With that said, to deny a preference for certain outcomes would be lying to himself.

* * *

He grabbed up his white windbreaker from the clothes tree, standing to the right of his apartment's front door, and put it on. He stood still, patiently waiting. His eyes took in the surface of the off-white front door, less than a foot from his face. Chips of paint were missing along the top edge, revealing multiple undercoats of old paint jobs—pea green, pinkish tan, and even pale blue. Paint was also missing from around the small brass peephole, positioned nearly-perfectly at eye level. He tilted his head slightly, hearing sounds from next door. The girl was preparing to leave. She coughed and cleared her throat—her cold seemed better but not quite gone. He heard the metallic rattle of the chain, first sliding then dropping away. She slid the deadbolt and turned the doorknob. The man remained perfectly still, taking slow, even breaths. The girl used her key to lock the door behind her, and hurried down the corridor. Her tennis shoes made little sound on the scuffed hardwood floors. He gave her another few seconds before unlocking and opening his own door. Standing on the threshold, he checked his watch again. It was now 6:32 a.m.—two minutes late. Mrs. Goertz never deviated from that timetable. Not once, for that was their agreement. Check-in time was 6:30 a.m., sharp.

The man in the white windbreaker hurried down the stairs, taking them two and three at a time. He needed to keep Arlington in sight. He slowed when he heard her distant footfalls on the linoleum below. She'd reached the foyer. The sound of a door swishing open confirmed she'd left the apartment building. He hurried down the last few steps, sprinting for the door. He knew her routine: she would turn west, go up Colonial Way two blocks, and enter the Starbucks on the corner of Colonial and Brighton. Outside, he forced himself to slow his pace—not bring attention to himself. Up ahead, he saw her walking on the sidewalk. She was hurrying along, pulling her hair back into a high ponytail. She'd chosen a short black skirt and a gray top to wear. He'd seen both garments on her before, but not together. *She has good fashion sense,* he thought. Today of all days it mattered what she wore, for she would never wear something different—today's outfit was the outfit she would die in.

* * *

It was no mistake … no mindless miscalculation of time. Mrs. Goertz hadn't checked in. Twenty minutes was a long enough deviation from a set routine. The girl had to be terminated—this morning. Now.

Arlington entered Shasta Park, carrying a tall latte in one hand and the straps of her small backpack in the other. The man stayed with her, never letting her completely move from view. She stopped at a waist-high iron fence and watched a mother swan with several small chicks paddle by in the park's largest pond. Twenty yards away, he removed his jacket and draped it over the fence. He watched as Arlington suddenly reached into a front pocket of her pack and retrieved her cell phone. Her face brightened and she laughed at something the caller'd said. The man patted his front right pocket, feeling the contours of the box cutter inside. He had no real preference for one means of killing over another, but if left strictly to him to decide, knives and box cutters would be his first weapons of choice. And today, the choice was his to make. The victim deserved that much.

An elderly woman approached behind him, startling the man. She had a plastic grocery bag in one hand, with the remnants of a loaf of bread inside. She'd obviously come to feed the swans. She approached the fence and leaned over the railing, her left hand accidentally brushing his jacket. He didn't like his things touched. She looked up at him smiling, but seeing his face—his outrage—she quickly scurried off.

The man retrieved his jacket and put it back on. Casually, he looked around the park. *Perfect.* No one else was around, just Arlington and himself. He withdrew the box cutter from his pocket, keeping it hidden in his palm. He used his thumb to slide the small protruding switch forward, till he felt the extended razor blade catch. He stayed on the path that ran alongside the fence, and walked toward Arlington. She was still on the phone—nodding at something the caller said. She was lovely, and this was an appropriate place for her demise. She deserved a pretty place. He made final determinations on how the next few seconds would unfold: Her death would be very, very quick. He would walk right past her—perhaps she would look up and smile in his direction. Once he was within arm's length, he would lash out, catch her on the left side of her neck, and cut her carotid artery. It would all happen in a blur, and he'd be gone before she hit the ground.

Ten feet away, Arlington, leaning on the fence, was turned away from the pond—she noticed the man approaching her.

* * *

21 hours earlier ...

The airport would have to wait until the following day, since Pippa insisted things go down a certain way—her way.

Heidi was anything but forthcoming about the man wearing the white windbreaker. Other than the fact he would kill Arli, once their scheduled check-in call was missed, even by several minutes. Sitting pinned between Pippa and Baltimore, Heidi clammed up—smiling contemptuously—as if she hadn't a care in the world. Pippa knew immediately how to deal with her.

"Break her nose, Baltimore," Pippa said matter-of-factly.

The driver of the Range Rover stole a quick glance over

his shoulder toward the back seat.

"Do it so even the finest plastic surgeon in Beverly Hills has a hard time making it look right. Make her ugly."

"I can do that," Baltimore said. Shifting in his seat, he looked at Heidi—appraising how best to go about striking her in the face. He brought his left arm up: Keeping his palm open, he positioned the heel of his hand forward, as his fingers slowly curled inward. His hand now an effective martial-arts weapon in itself.

Heidi's eyes were like saucers. Taffy, in the front passenger seat, was looking back at her, his expression tense.

"Wait! Let's talk about this," Heidi piped.

Pippa brought her face closer to Heidi's. "What's your check-in routine with the guy watching Arli? Tell me now or I'll have Baltimore rearrange your features. Children will run away, screaming at your hideousness. Lie to me even once …"

"Fine … no need for all the dramatics. I check in with him three times daily: Five-thirty in the morning, at noon, and eleven at night. Happy?"

Pippa checked the clock on the dashboard. "You made the noon check-in?"

"Yes."

Pippa gave Baltimore a subtle nod and he lowered his hand. Heidi glared at him, then at Pippa.

"Turn into the next motel, driver. We need to work things out for tomorrow morning. We're also going to need another agent or two."

* * *

Present time.

Pippa laughed into the cell phone, doing her best, at least

partially, to obstruct her face. The man wearing the white windbreaker was standing off to the side. Nearby, an elderly lady looked ready to feed a few swans. Earlier, Pippa hadn't a problem fitting into Arli's youthful outfit. She was a bit surprised how perfectly the little black skirt fit around her waist. Suspecting Arli's apartment to be monitored, they'd worked out the switch—to take place inside Starbucks, in the bathroom. Once inside there, they quickly hugged and proceeded to exchange clothes.

Now … in the park, so far so good: If the man following her suspected anything, Pippa couldn't tell. Holding her phone to her ear, she turned around, leaning her backside onto the railing. Baltimore was seventy-five yards away—on the other side of the pond—holding binoculars. He was on the other end of the call, relaying the exact movements of Arli's pursuer, and now hers.

"Okay … grandma just rushed off in a huff. Be ready," Baltimore said.

"You know, I loved that movie too! The ending … oh my god …"

"He's moving now. He's reaching into his right front pocket. Can't see what he has there yet. Be ready!"

"You really are silly. No, I wasn't drunk, I'm not a big drinker." Pippa had no idea what she was saying—pretty much just talking gibberish—trying to look like a relaxed young woman ten years her junior. She could see his face clearly now for the first time. He was pleasant looking, with a nice, almost peaceful, expression—a man out for an early morning walk in the park.

"Be ready … whatever is in his hand—"

Pippa never heard the rest of Baltimore's sentence.

Chapter 23

I was awakened at 5:30 the next morning by the sound of a diesel engine revving somewhere nearby outside our window.

"What the hell is that noise?" Carmen asked, draping an arm over her face. "Don't look at me," she said, pulling the blanket up over her head. "Oh God, you're used to perfect little Pippa. I must be a frightening sight to you."

"Oh come on, that's nonsense." I got up and went to the window and peered out through the curtains. "Looks like John Wayne is maneuvering a tractor rig into the circular drive below. He's pulling a flatbed trailer ... stacked with bales of hay. Your ride's here."

When I turned back she was already scurrying into the bathroom. "Not a morning person, huh?" I remarked, suddenly needing to sit back down.

"Just find me some coffee." A moment later, though, she peered around the door. "Hello? You okay?"

I was seated back on the bed. I'd planned on getting up hours earlier, two or three in the morning, but without my phone's alarm function, I'd slept through to daylight. "Not a hundred percent. Need to tap in ... I'm way overdue." I raised a hand and saw tremors starting up.

"And I was worried how I looked," she said, looking concerned. "Why don't you get in the shower first ... get dressed."

I nodded. "Okay."

* * *

Showered and dressed, I emerged from the steamy bathroom feeling somewhat better. Carmen greeted me, holding a large mug out. "Caffeine … stimulates the release of dopamine."

I took the hot mug from her. "Thanks." I gulped down several large swallows, and felt the hot liquid hit my stomach. "I need to find where the power panels are to this place."

"I'm a step ahead of you. The kitchen help is a yappy group." She looked at me with concern. "You know, if you had told me about this … this condition earlier, I could have made special arrangements. Come up with—"

I held up a hand. "Please … the panels?"

"Oh, sorry. Unfortunately, the incoming power feed and panels are located in a separate structure, adjacent to the main lodge here."

A knock on the door was followed by a woman's voice. "Breakfast in the main hall. Ten minutes."

It was John Wayne's ditsy wife, Harriet. A moment later, we heard tapping on the door next to ours. "Breakfast in the main hall in ten minutes."

I said, "Finish up getting ready, and I'll go and get the lay of the land outside. I'm used to this routine."

* * *

Guests were already milling around downstairs, and there seemed to be more kids than I remembered seeing at supper. The front double-doors were open and I could see John outside, still trying to maneuver the big, brand new-looking tractor rig around. Either Jude, or Jordan, was standing behind him, signaling with his hands as John slowly backed up, but his angling was wrong. It was evident the Duke hadn't a clue how to drive a tractor, let alone one pulling a large flatbed trailer behind it. Fortunately for me, a significant crowd had formed outside, around the front of the lodge. Men, accustomed to being in positions of power, barked off suggestions and outright commands. By the look on John Wayne's reddening face, he was about ready to tell them all to shut the hell up.

I took a left at the bottom of the stairs that led into a wide corridor. I passed by the busy kitchen, preparing for the breakfast service, and found a series of sliding-glass doors leading out to the back, east-facing, yard. Twenty paces further on was the start of an Aspen grove of trees—mostly saplings. I stopped and wavered some as the shakes hit me full-force; the scenery around me was spinning.

"Hey, you all right, man?"

"Fine … must be the altitude," I said. At first, I thought the man standing before me was part of John Wayne's security team from Guffy, but he was no local mountain dude, carrying a six-shooter. The man was highly trained—most likely a special-ops soldier. It takes one to know one. I had wondered how Rudy Palmolive was handling his own security—now I knew. Leaving things to the likes of Jude, Jordan, and the others wouldn't have sufficed. Although this man, like me, was dressed in Western garb, he carried a shoulder-slung automatic rifle, and wore a holstered Beretta side arm on his upper thigh. Three men, similarly outfitted, were also moving around, patrolling off in the distance.

"Take care of yourself," he said. I noticed a small comms device in one ear as he moved away. Looking to my right, down a path, I noticed an open-sided wooden gazebo. Off to the left, north, was a large garage structure of sorts, and twenty yards beyond that—a low-profiled building with a facade covering of grayish river rock. *Bingo.* I started walking in that direction.

I could see only a single entrance into the structure, located on its far side, with cement steps leading down to a nondescript metal door. It looked profoundly strong, impregnable for someone in my shaky state. I followed the steps down, as if I'd done so a hundred times before—acting like I belonged there. Reaching for the doorknob, it suddenly swung out, and a woman wearing all white, a stained apron tied around her waist, abruptly rushed out. I jumped back out of the way and gave her an impatient glare. "You best watch what you're doing next time, young lady." Clutching a large sack of potatoes in both arms, she offered an apologetic cringe as she hurried past me and up the stairs.

I wasted no time entering the rock structure. Immediately feeling the difference in temperature—cool and musky—I found myself standing in a large slump-stone room. Off to the right were heavy metal shelves, holding food stores—commercial-sized boxes of cereal, instant potatoes, and premixed cornbread. Directly in front of me was a large black cylindrical tank, holding Propane, I guessed, and beyond that were the electrical panels.

* * *

Thirteen minutes later, I found Carmen, seated in the main dining hall.

"I ordered for you," she said, gesturing to the stack of pancakes, bacon, and scrambled eggs sitting on the table right before me. She was halfway through her own meal. "There's more of Harriet's home-made cornbread, I hear …

if you want any."

My mind flashed to the stores of dry goods I'd just seen—the boxes of instant potatoes and pre-mixed cornbread. "No … that's okay." Famished, I dug into my eggs.

By the time I finished eating, the hall was practically empty. I found Carmen out front, waiting for me. John was rounding the distant bend, behind the wheel of the tractor.

"Feel better?"

"Much … thanks."

"We're in the last group. Everyone's required to go on the hayride, this is how we get to the stables."

I remembered John mentioning that everyone got a horse to ride. I thought about us, the last two to mosey on down to the stables. Could be only slim pickens left—old nags or obstinate fillies. I noticed two small boys, giggling, as they were boosted up onto the tractor's wide fenders. Jude assisted them on one side, Jordan on the other. Things were looking up. Rudy Palmolive, aka Billy the Kid, was among our group, as was his demure wife.

"Ready?" Carmen asked, heading toward the back of the trailer.

"Save me a seat … I'll just be a second."

Billy the Kid and Carolina were already seated atop high-stacked hay bales on the flatbed, closest to the wide rear fenders of the tractor pulling them, where their two sons now perched. John Wayne, who must have made this same trek three or four times already, looked impatient to leave. I gave him a friendly nod and looked up at Carolina.

"Good morning, Doc," she said, brightening at my approach.

"Good morning. Hey … I don't mean to be a damper here, but your boys …" I gestured to them both, seated on the rear fenders next to John. "Take a good look at those big smooth fenders. You know what they look like to me?"

She looked somewhat confused and Rudy had lost his smile.

"They look like kiddie slides. You know, the plastic-coated slides you see at playgrounds all over? Those tractor wheels are seven feet high, a foot and a half wide. How easy do you think it could be for one, or both, of your boys to slip forward—down onto the road—and get run over? Just one good jostle …"

Her hands rose to her mouth. Simultaneously, Billy the Kid jumped to his feet, reaching out first for one boy, then for the other. They protested but were soon seated securely beside their mother.

Carolina said, "Thank you! Oh my God, I can't believe I let them sit up there like that, so unsecured."

Rudy nodded at me then quickly turned his attention on the back of John Wayne's hatted head. Standing, he struck at John's black Stetson with his fist, sending it flying into the air before it settled on the gravel drive below.

John quickly began to swing around, his hand reaching for his Colt. Rudy, though small in stature, suddenly looked much, much bigger. He moved fast, grabbing a fistful of John's collar, jerking him awkwardly backward. In the distance, I heard the telltale sound of a round being chambered into an automatic weapon: Rudy's security team. "Jeopardize the safety of my family again like that and I'll kill you. You understand me?"

John, still half-turned backward, didn't answer.

"Don't forget who you're working for. Now drive this thing and try not to kill anyone in the process."

As I made my way to the rear of the trailer bed, I peered into both Rudy's and John's minds. John was going to make me pay for this. He'd killed men before … more than a few.

Somehow, some way, I was to become the victim of a fatal accident during my stay at Morning Hawk Ranch. Rudy, on the other hand, although inwardly fuming, was thankful for my intervention. Just maybe, I'd made a new friend. As I stumbled, moving between hay bales and scooting close to Carmen, I thought of Pippa. Was I wasting precious time here while she suffered at the hands of Heidi and Leon Goertz? Was she still alive? I needed to ratchet-up the timetable. The tractor got underway. We passed a group of ranch hands—one was Jude—his leveled gaze held steady on mine.

Chapter 24

I finally convinced Carmen, who was quite reluctant, to stay close to Carolina and join the posse in tracking down John Wesley Hardin, the notorious gunfighter.

I stood at the corral railing, next to Billy the Kid. We were both told to hurry up and select a ride. From what I'd heard one of the ranch hands say, there'd been fifty horses earlier this morning to choose from. Now, there were only six. The only other person standing at the railing was the robust, pink-cheeked U.S. congressman who represented either Georgia or West Virginia.

The lot of them—the few nags left—looked fairly pathetic. One was, in my guesstimation, not a horse at all but a boney pony. I patted my chest and felt the pinned-on metal star. As the newly appointed sheriff, it hardly seemed appropriate for me to go riding into town with my feet dragging on the ground.

"I don't think we've been properly introduced," the congressman said, holding out a beefy hand. "I'm Butch ... Butch Cassidy."

I shook his hand. "Doc Holliday."

"He's Sheriff Doc Holliday," Billy the Kid added, his eyes studying the six horses. One was down on the ground, lying on her side. I quickly verified that she was only sleeping by a quick look-see into the horse's mind.

"That at least makes the selection process somewhat easier," Butch said, gesturing toward the prone horse. "The small one's out for me … I'm too damn big. Probably you are too … huh, Sheriff?" Butch asked.

Billy turned on the congressman. "What are you saying? You implying something? That maybe I should take the fucking pony?"

Once again, I watched the leader of the Council of Five, perhaps the most powerful, influential man on the planet, go ballistic. I stayed out of it.

"I'm liking that chestnut," I said.

"No … that's the one I've been looking at. Pick another," Billy said, signaling to the closest ranch hand.

Gray horse is good.

I turned to see who had said that. It wasn't Butch and it wasn't Billy, already hurrying toward the corral's gate. Butch was busy, patting a small, somewhat mangy-looking dog on top of his head. He stooped to examine a hanging ident tag on the dog's collar. "Ol' Yeller 2." The dog was looking up at me.

Did you say that?

The gray is a fine horse. The others all have issues. Especially the chestnut … he bites.

I had to stifle a laugh with a fake cough. I signaled to the ranch hand: "I'll take the gray."

Jordan, the ranch hand, arrived at the corral as we were mounting up. He told us to follow the path heading east. "When it forks, stay to the left; it's a half-mile farther on from there. I'll be no more than ten minutes behind you." He dismounted from his own ride. "I need to deal with this matter first." Jordan pulled his Colt and entered the corral.

"Hold up there … um … Jordan," I said, watching him head toward the sleeping mare. "She's just sleeping … probably tired from—"

The shot rang out, echoing across the hills, then fading away into silence. Startled, my horse pulled against his reins. I continued to stare at the now-dead mare. There'd been nothing particularly wrong with the horse that I'd observed, only that she was old and tired.

* * *

The three of us—Billy the Kid on his chestnut, me on my gray, and Butch Cassidy on a pinto paint named Potts, rode side by side on the path heading east. Potts seemed to be a fine horse, like my gray, who went by the name Gunner. But Billy's chestnut, Ticker, true to what the dog had messaged me—spent a significant amount of time stretching his neck back, trying to nip at his rider with his large teeth.

"Fucking horse," Billy said, abruptly yanking the reins he was holding in the opposite direction. He leaned forward, bringing his face closer to Ticker's flinching ears: "There's another bullet … it has your name on it."

Butch and I exchanged a quick glance.

A Bad Man, the dog added, keeping pace with us. Now that he'd found someone who could understand his thoughts, he hadn't shut up since we'd left the stables. I tried not to encourage him—ignoring his chatty inner dialogue for the most part.

"This is beautiful countryside," the congressman remarked.

"It should be … for what it cost."

I looked at Billy. "What do you mean by that?"

"I meant just what I said. I own this land … the lodge … the town up ahead."

Again Butch and I exchanged a look.

"You did … all this … for your boys?" I asked, gesturing toward the horizon.

"They mean everything to me, those two." He shrugged. "But it's for me, too. I can afford it." He looked at me, the brim of his Stetson shading his face. "So tell me, Mr. McAlister, what makes you want to be a part of this?"

He'd overemphasized the name *McAlister*. I was immediately on guard. Was he aware of my true identity? He was an intelligent man, with unlimited resources, and I had no idea what he did, or didn't, know about me.

Slightly behind us—to both our left and right—were his mounted security team. They were attempting to stay out of sight in the flanking trees, but I knew they were there, and I knew more than one periodically had me in his crosshairs.

"I'm Troy McAlister … just a business man."

"That's not what I meant. You think I didn't have you vetted? Everyone here has seen your face on the cover of Forbes, plus other magazines, in recent months. You're on the rise … making a name for yourself."

"I don't know about that."

"We'll talk more later. I may be able to assist you. Significantly."

I looked at him without responding.

"Later. We'll talk later. Let's enjoy our nice ride; it's not the time to talk business."

* * *

We entered the town three abreast, beneath an arch that spanned the width of the rutty road. I looked up and saw freshly painted signage: *Welcome!* Not knowing what to expect, I found myself taking in what lay before me with a sense of wonder. Right here was what it was all about. Not the immense luxury lodge perched on the ridge behind us, or the distant stables, or the miles of open, untouched, landscape. No, it was this town. Even with a cursory first glance, I could see that everything was a hundred percent authentically constructed and meticulously conformed to the time period of the mid-to-late 1800s. Rough-hewn timber boardwalks, and the somewhat cloudy and misshapen glass windowpanes on the storefronts, went far beyond a Hollywood movie set, or a Western gimmicky amusement park.

We slowed our horses, continuing down the middle of the street. Butch whistled, obviously as captivated by what he was seeing as I was. With a quick glance back I saw Ol' Yeller 2 still tagging along behind us.

Folks here were dressed appropriately for the older time period, milling about from one location to the next, not giving us any special notice. I estimated the town's main thoroughfare was approximately a quarter mile long. Smaller structures, some attached, some detached, were at the far edges of the town. The closer we came to what I figured was the town's center, the bigger, and closer together, were the buildings. The women were wearing long dresses; some carried parasols and wore fashionable bonnets, while the men were either dressed formally, in business attire appropriate for the time—most with bowler hats on—or were dressed in real cowboy attire. We three, wearing today's blue jeans and brightly colored Roy Rogers-style shirts, didn't remotely fit in here.

What was so easy to forget was that none of this was real—none of it. The townspeople here were, in fact, actors—performing in a large-scale production. They didn't notice that we were dressed inappropriately, because they were paid not to. I remembered what Baltimore had told me earlier about the five-million-dollar admission charge; for that kind of money, everything sure better be authentic.

I glanced over at Butch. He'd sucked in his paunch and was smiling broadly at a pretty young woman in a frilly dress, standing in front of the town's General Store.

Billy the Kid was watching me—watching my reaction to everything. "Almost enough to make one truly believe it's really 1881, somewhere in Arizona. Perhaps Tombstone?"

"It's certainly something," I agreed.

Billy sat up higher in his saddle and, with a confident air, seemed to look down his nose at those scurrying around on the street. The elaborate town—the old-world Western setup he'd commissioned at some point in the recent past—was it simply on a whim? Barking off orders, like: *Build me an Old West town so real you forget what fucking year you're living in!* It was unfathomable to me the kind of wealth one would need to have something like this town commissioned. All the scenic acreage he'd acquired; the actual construction of the town; all the actors dressed appropriately in vogue, milling about? It was my guess Billy the Kid, aka Rudy Palmolive, hadn't given the venture that much thought once he'd barked off his initial orders. For he too was looking at the town as though he were seeing it for the first time, just as we were. What he'd probably set in motion, perhaps on a whim, had changed the lives of hundreds, maybe thousands, of people. It occurred to me right then that this elaborate staging was what he was all about; and on a small scale, what he got off on—transforming the world to suit his own desires. As the newly appointed leader, head of the table of the Council of Five, he was planning something far more sinister for the real world and on a much grander scale.

The short Napoleonic man smiled at me and gestured

toward what was clearly the largest building in town. "That is our destination." He gave Ticker a kick and moved out in front, veering off toward the two-story building. Its signage read Hotel and Saloon.

Butch reined up, close to me. "This is going to be fun … nice getting away from the kids and wife for a few days."

"I'm sorry?"

He chuckled. "You didn't know?" He gestured, using the brim of his Stetson. "Wives and kiddies are staying at the lodge; they'll do some nature hikes and fishing, and visit a wild wolf preserve. Nope … this town is no place for them."

As if on cue, a gunshot rang out by the swinging doors of the saloon. Butch and I pulled back on our horses' reins, trying to settle them down. A man lay still on the dusty road, about twenty feet in front of us; a splash of red was spreading across his chest.

Butch leaned in close and said with childish enthusiasm, "And let the show begin …"

But something didn't seem quite right about the way the man on the ground fell—the way one leg was drawn back, lying beneath him … unnaturally. There was also the red splash on his chest, now spreading outside his shirtfront and onto the dirt. Standing in front of two, still-swinging, saloon doors was Jude, a now-familiar ranch hand, whose six-shooter still pointed at the fallen, clearly dead man lying in the road.

Chapter 25

Deceiving, her face passive of expression, Pippa's eyes stayed locked on the man approaching her, wearing a white windbreaker. She took in his every movement. One thing was certain—he was coming for her.

Earlier, she'd heard Baltimore say into the phone, "I'm having Ackerman take him out." Ackerman and Moody, agents brought up from Washington the previous evening, were seasoned operatives. Both vetted—neither worked for the Order in any capacity. While Moody kept guard on Heidi and Taffy, sitting in a vehicle nearby, Ackerman waited a mere twenty yards from where Pippa was standing. He was ready to move in, pull his weapon, and shoot the would-be assassin at a moment's notice. But that option Pippa didn't elect to utilize; the mere thought of someone harming Arly, her dear niece, was too personal. She needed to handle it herself, or die trying.

At five feet out, he made his move. He lunged, his hand holding something—probably a knife—jutted forward with unbelievable speed. If she hadn't been ready and prepared for it—training for years in various forms of close quarters combat—it would have been all over for her.

Pippa had just enough time to bring her backpack up, blocking his initial strike. In a blur, she could see it wasn't a knife he held but a box cutter—the early morning sunshine reflecting for a moment off the small razor-like blade. The attacker, his face only inches from her own, showed momentary confusion when he realized she was not Arly—that he had been set up. He recovered quickly, stepping back just enough to spring forward again, this time using a left-to-right slashing movement with the razor, aiming toward her exposed neck. Pippa blocked his arm, using the proper knife-hand defense, and brought him up short with a precisely placed blow to his wrist. The blow, intended to send the box cutter flying, was unsuccessful. *This guy is good*, she thought, realizing she might have underestimated her opponent. Either that, or she'd overestimated her own abilities. Pippa then punched out with her left fist, connecting with nothing but air, and received a staggeringly hard punch to her left cheek. More from instinct than anything else, she brought her right arm up defensively to block the next inevitable strike.

She saw the spray of blood before she actually felt any pain. He'd sliced her forearm at an angle, from elbow to wrist. She quickly clenched her fingers, and was relieved to find she could still move them. *Good … no tendons were severed.*

Ackerman was halfway to her, bounding forward now and pulling his Glock from beneath his own windbreaker.

Pippa had discovered early on, when working for the CIA, that men routinely underestimated women's abilities—had underestimated hers. Instead of taking it personally, she learned to take advantage of it, requiring both patience and strategy. In the end, she'd used men's overconfidence or, as in this case, assumptions, against them. Men assumed women, even well-trained ones like herself, would never use a head-butt in a close-quarters combat—that it was something only a man would do. But Pippa didn't even have to think about it. His face, in that one instant, was aligned perfectly—not too close and not too far away. In a fast combination of thrusting forward and using a jerky bowing motion, she used the top of her forehead—where the skull bone was thickest—to spring forward with all the speed and momentum she could rally forth. She heard the gratifying sounds of cartilage and bone splintering and cracking. She knew she had crushed her opponent's nose. Warm blood sprayed into the air, then onto her cheeks and even into her mouth.

Ackerman was upon them, thrusting the muzzle of his 9mm pistol into the assailant's neck, directly below his chin.

"Move and I'll open a window at the top of your head, asshole."

With the man now subdued, Pippa stepped back and assessed her own injured arm. The nine-inch slice was still bleeding, but didn't seem particularly deep.

"That could use a few stitches," Baltimore said, out-of-breath after sprinting around the pond.

"I think it'll be fine." Pippa wrapped her arm in the sweatshirt she'd taken from Arly's backpack.

"You showed some nice moves there … and having him alive to interrogate is even better."

They heard sirens blaring off in the distance and a crowd of onlookers had formed around them. Since local NYPD, for the most part, had also come under the influence of the Order, they knew they needed to vacate the park quickly. "I think we better get moving," she said.

Baltimore took ahold of the man's left arm as Ackerman grabbed his right. They manhandled him toward the park entrance where, parked at the curb, a black Navigator idled. "I'm a step ahead of you. Our ride's there waiting for us."

Pippa followed closely behind them. Approaching the awaiting SUV, she saw Heidi sitting in the front passenger seat, Taffy sitting behind the wheel, and agent Moody perched on the rear seat, holding a gun pointed, undoubtedly, toward the back of Taffy's head.

* * *

Baltimore reclaimed the front passenger seat, so Heidi now sat alongside Pippa in the big vehicle's third-row seat. So far, Heidi hadn't even so much as acknowledged her injured employee.

Pippa asked, "What's his name, Heidi?"

Heidi continued to look forward toward the windshield. "He goes by Guntner, but it's an alias, I'm sure."

Pippa leaned back, her eyes on the back of Guntner's head.

"He'll be properly dealt with," Baltimore said from the front seat, "just as soon as he's interrogated."

Pippa nodded. "So what now? Where are we going?"

Baltimore didn't answer right away. "We have a unique opportunity: With Heidi's capture, we're in a position to infiltrate the Order as never before."

Pippa noticed they were approaching JFK International Airport. "We're taking them back to Washington … to the agency?" she asked.

Baltimore directed Taffy where to turn. Ahead was an airport guard station with VIP access to private jets; Pippa wondered if Baltimore's creds would still allow them access. How informed was the Order about their most recent actions?

Baltimore passed his government creds over, reaching past Taffy to the guard. He, surprisingly, with only scant scrutiny, passed them back and waved them through. Within two minutes, they pulled to a stop near a grouping of large private jets. Pippa recognized the SIFTR G6—the turbines on both its rear-mounted jet engines were spinning.

"Everyone out," Baltimore said.

Chapter 26

Pippa, the last one to enter the finely appointed G6 cabin, saw Guntner sitting on a leather couch, being treated by a medical professional. Baltimore had probably called ahead to enlist his aid. Moody sat to Guntner's left, his gun leveled on him. As Pippa passed by, the med-tech noticed her arm, under the bloodstained sweatshirt. He said, "Please, sit here … once I'm finished with him—"

Pippa cut him off: "No, just come find me when you're done with him."

Ackerman, his pistol drawn, selected a cluster of seats apart from the others. Heidi and Taffy, looking bored, sat across from him.

Pippa joined Baltimore, sitting to his left. She was surprised to see Calloway, seated across from them, next to the window. His briefcase was open, a stack of manila folders lying on the vacant seat next to him.

"Good morning, sir. I didn't expect to see you here."

"I've pretty much made this jet my home the past few days," he said. "Me and my security team, sitting back there."

She glanced beyond him and saw three men, dressed in suits, sitting together in the rear of the cabin. None looked familiar to her.

"You okay?" he asked, gesturing to her arm.

"I'm fine. Any word yet on Chandler? Is he …"

"According to his ever-changing GPS coordinates, he's alive. We're assuming he's still playing cowboys and Indians, in the mountains of Colorado."

"And Palmolive?"

"All indications are he's there too. Remember, there are no phones there, nor other means to make direct contact. We have to assume Chandler's making friends there and will be permitted entry into Palmolive's inner circle soon, where he can acquire crucial information."

"I'm sure he won't let you down, sir," Pippa said. The truth was, with Rob's mental abilities he didn't need to become Palmolive's BFF—he just needed to read the man's mind. "Can I ask you a question?"

Calloway nodded. "Of course."

"What's the end game here? I mean, from what I understand, the Order's organization has been around for nearly a hundred years, or more. Why now? Why decide now to seize control of the country—the world? Come out from behind their curtain?"

"First, you need to understand that the Order doesn't need to change its behind-the-scenes influence on governments and corporate interests. Think of them like the Mafia, at the height of their power, in New York, New Jersey, Chicago … and, of course, Las Vegas. Everyone played by their rules and, if you didn't get too greedy, you could lead a fairly normal life. From time to time you'd be asked to do them certain favors … sometimes, really big favors. You didn't say no to the mob. Well, the Order is much the same. Only those controlling, who are mostly white men, are amongst the most respected and wealthiest. It has never been in the Order's best interest to come out from behind the curtain, as you put it."

"So what's changed? Why construct a subterranean transit system? Is it for an imminent military coup?"

"Those hydro-passages, or underground Interstate highways, have been in the works for years, as a safeguard against a country attacking either the U.S. or Europe. Any country not completely under the Order's present day control, like North Korea, Iran, and even Russia, to some extent, haven't been playing by the rules. And when you have trillions of dollars at your disposal, why not create a safe haven for your interests; a way to ensure the long-term survival of the Order … even if some parts of America or Europe were to find themselves on the wrong end of a nuclear warhead."

"So the elite are covering their bets?"

"Yes."

"So again … why the coup? It doesn't make sense."

Pippa saw Calloway smile. "The WZZ, that's why."

"I thought they were small and insignificant, isn't that the word they used? Only recently were they allowed to merge—"

Calloway leaned forward. "And why do you think an all-powerful organization, such as the Order, even considered such a move? Allowing what they considered a fringe, neo-Nazi group of blood-sucking nut-balls anywhere near their operation?"

Pippa shook her head, her mind flashing back to when her own blood was being drained into a vat that Leon and Heidi Goertz, plus scores of others, hungrily drank from. Nut-balls was an understatement. "It doesn't make sense … not to me, anyway."

The smile vanished from Calloway's face. "We assumed the WZZ merged into the far larger, more powerful ranks of the Order. What we hadn't figured out, until recently, was that it actually was the other way around."

"How is that even possible? That makes no sense."

"Rudy Palmolive, along with his criminal contingent, has taken control of the Order."

"I know that," Pippa said.

"That, of itself, is not the problem. What *is* the problem is that thirteen months ago Rudy Palmolive fell head over heels in love with another woman. Someone other than his wife." He pointed a finger toward the front of the plane.

"No!"

"Oh, yes," Calloway said. "We're talking an all-consuming, lose all sense of reality, kind of love. Rudy, apparently, has gone over the deep end. Has to have her at any price."

"And the price was?" Pippa asked. Then answered her own question: "To head up the Order."

"Even more than that."

Pippa thought about that and smiled. "She wants to rule the world?"

Calloway nodded, not saying anything more.

"And that's the reason for the mobilization of the Order's military forces? That's simply crazy."

He nodded again.

"But we have her now. She's sitting right over there ... it's all over," Pippa said.

"The WZZ has already begun imbedding itself deeply into the organization. The only one who seems clueless about what's going on is Leon Goertz—who, we suspect, is not long for this world. No, our having Heidi, or even taking out Palmolive, simply isn't enough at this point. WZZ's infiltration, its control, is already too extensive. The intended coup might take place with or without them. There's too much at stake to take the chance."

Pippa waited for Calloway to continue—provide the answer to her original question—What's the end game here?

"We must help Palmolive see the error of his ways. Only he can avert a worldwide catastrophe at this point."

"Well, I'm here. I'll assist you any way I can," she said.

"I was hoping you would say that. We're now en route to Washington. Once back at SIFTR, you will be undergoing another transition, is that understood?"

"What transition? Did I miss something?"

"You, my dear, will be taking Heidi's place. You need to change Palmolive's mind back—away from initiating a coup. To do that, we need to physically alter your looks."

Pippa suddenly felt sick. The last time she'd undergone a series of facial and body injections to alter her appearance, it had taken months for the effects to wear off. Plus, there were other considerations—it was very painful and the physiological effects had been long lasting and terrible. They may have been the underlying cause of her and Rob's recent breakup. Added to those facts, she despised the woman. Pippa wasn't at all sure she could pull the ruse off.

Chapter 27

I didn't have to probe into the man's mind to know he was dead, but I tried anyway—nothing there.

Billy the Kid climbed down from his horse, loosely tying the reins to a nearby hitching post. "Put that gun away," he told Jude. "Who was he?"

I already knew the answer from peering into Jude's dark and menacing thoughts. He was Carl Holden, another wealthy businessman, who'd recently graced the covers of both Forbes and FastCompany.

Billy climbed up two planked steps, joining Jude outside the saloon's entrance. They spoke in low tones. Billy eventually turned back toward Butch and me, and said, "As you well know, guests staying here have paid a ridiculous amount of money. The tension you feel now in the pit of your stomachs … that's the real thing. Nowhere else can a more realistic, Old West experience be encountered, because there is the very real possibility here that you will be killed. Not so different from the way life actually was, back in 1881. Carl over there did not have to die. He drew down on someone who was a far superior gunslinger."

Butch looked like he was going to throw up. "But … but … his wife and little girl, they're both here, expecting to go home together at the end of the week."

Billy the Kid shrugged it off. "By the end of the week,

there will be other bodies lying in the street, or slumped over a poker table, a bullet in their foreheads, or even hanging from a rope. We'll provide an appropriate explanation to the wives. Perhaps a cave-in, at one of the many silver mines dotting the mountains around us—a convenient, completely inaccessible, mass grave-site. Let me be clear, Butch … you wanted this. You've also shown interest in joining a certain elite organization, correct? You survive to week's end then that becomes a very real possibility."

"No, I want to leave now," Butch said, his ruddy pink cheeks turning purple.

"There are highly proficient men, carrying automatic weapons, who patrol the surrounding landscape. If you make it past them, safely back to the lodge, then you and your family are free to leave. But, just so you know, two others earlier attempted just such a feat."

"Did they make it?" I asked.

Jude snickered. Billy the Kid shook his head, and said, "Unfortunately for them, no."

"So what do we do now?" I asked.

This time it was Jude who answered, saying, "I suggest, before entering the saloon, you first head across the street." I followed his stare and saw a small shop with a hand-painted sign above the door—*Guns and Ammo*.

"Shooting blanks is optional here, but not advised," he said.

* * *

As it turned out, the Guns and Ammo store had a wide assortment of other items also for sale: hats and gloves, gun belts, leather satchels, and saddlebags of varying size, as well as weapon cleaning and lubricating products. Butch stared at the shelves trancelike, still not taking Jude's menacing words well.

"Look, Butch, try to relax some. I'll be watching your back … you watch mine, okay? We're in this together."

"Um … yeah … okay. I just never thought it would be *this* kind of vacation."

I almost laughed out loud—but didn't. The congressman was already far outside his comfort zone. He'd shown an interest in something he should not have. Dealing with the devil has repercussions and I had some serious doubts Butch would last out the week.

I stood at the counter, now strewn with my stack of items ready for purchase. I'd chosen a brown leather saddlebag, a new black Stetson, four boxes of .45 ACP 230 gr., American Eagle ammo, and a cleaning kit for my gun.

"That's a lot of bullets, Mister, four hundred rounds. You realize each box holds one hundred rounds, don't you?" the clerk behind the counter asked me.

"Figured I'd get in some target practice later today."

"Can't argue with that," he said.

"How should I pay for all this," I asked.

"Compliments of Billy."

Before leaving the store, I reloaded my six-shooter with live bullets.

"I can take those blanks from you," the proprietor said, holding out an open palm.

I thought twice about it, then pocketed the blanks instead. "Nah … I'll hold on to them, thanks." I placed my purchases into the new saddlebags and draped them over one shoulder. On my head, I replaced my old cowboy hat with my new black Stetson—leaving the older worn one on the counter.

Butch began piling on the counter his selected items, apparently coming to terms with the no-win situation he was in, as I stepped out on the street. Somewhere off in the distance came a single gunshot. It sounded like a rifle report.

I noticed my horse and Butch's were both gone from the front of the saloon. I turned and looked up the street.

Horse back in barn.

It was the dog. I hadn't noticed him there, curled up on the walkway outside the saloon. Coming closer, I saw his eyes following me. "Thanks," I said aloud, as I pushed my way through the bar's swinging doors.

The saloon looked far larger on the inside than it had from the street. An older man, wearing a vest and straw hat, was playing an old tune on an upright piano in the far back corner of the room. I estimated there were an excess of twenty round tables, each encircled with men mostly playing cards, mostly smoking cigars, and mostly drinking what looked to be whisky. Some women were milling about … most were scantily dressed in low-cut, brightly colored, burlesque-type costumes. Directly in front of me was the bar of all bars. Easily thirty feet long—made of some kind of hardwood—its top was stained and lacquered to a near-black finish. Behind the bar were three busy barkeeps, pouring drinks for a lined-up bunch of cowpokes. They turned in unison to see who'd entered the premises. The piano player stopped playing and the room went quiet.

"Looks like there's a new sheriff in town."

And I thought things couldn't get any more clichéd. Billy the Kid, standing at the far end of the bar, made the comment, which produced a few laughs. Several men raised their shot glasses and said *Cheers* in my direction. Within seconds, the piano playing resumed and I was no longer of interest.

Billy threw back what was left in his glass and headed in my direction. As I noticed the patrons giving him a wide berth, it occurred to me that Billy the Kid might be highly experienced using the Colt he wore high up on his hip.

"You've got a new prisoner in the jail, Sheriff. Best you hear his side of the story before coming to any decision."

Decision? I followed Billy outside and quickly caught up to him. I was in his mind—observing his thoughts and the images playing there. He was a man who saw things either one way or another: Polarized—go or no go, advantageous or detrimental, kill or be killed. And there were strong emotions there, almost child-like, filled with resentment and suspicion—sometimes both. As Butch Cassidy now made his way across the street, carrying two armfuls of purchases from the Guns and Ammo store, I thought, *they are going to eat him alive here.*

Billy the Kid slowed and watched Butch too. His mind turned dark. He looked forward to shooting the man—actually relishing the thought of it.

"Here we go … the jailhouse."

It was a nondescript, single-story clapboard structure, painted white. In small letters above the door hung a board with the single, hand-lettered word: JAIL.

Upon entering the jail, I knew that things in here were just as authentic as everything else I'd experienced, everywhere in town. It was the pungent smell that took ahold of my senses first—shit and piss and bad body odor. Two iron-barred jail cells took up the back half of the room, while two old wooden desks were positioned close to the door, where we now stood. And that was about it for the jailhouse. My eyes were drawn to the wood-planked floor, heavily stained with dark patches of God only knew what—probably blood.

Something moved within one of the cells. A man, wearing a neatly trimmed beard, sat up on a cot and looked back at me. He coughed and sniffled and slowly rose to his feet. I wondered if he was another performing actor or a true prisoner. He wasn't much older than me and seemed physically fit. I answered my own question by peering into his mind. He definitely was for real. He did not want to be there.

"Help me. Please … help me. I'm not supposed to be here. This is all a big mistake."

His voice was scratchy and full of desperation. He looked as if he'd been working in a coal mine: Black soot covered his clothes, and his face and hands were black-streaked.

"This is Mr. Ringo," Billy said.

"As in Johnny Ringo?"

"The very same."

Even I knew of this outlaw, one of the Cochise County Cowboys in old frontier Tombstone. He was also a reputed enemy of Doc Holliday … Although history writes that Ringo, exhausted from a relentless posse chase for the maiming of Virgil Earp and killing of Morgan Earp, he had committed suicide—but many believe it was, in fact, Doc Holliday that put that final bullet into the side of the gunslinger's head.

"What's he accused of?"

"Starting a fire."

"I had my reasons!" the man behind the bars said indignantly.

Billy drew his pistol and approached the bars. "Shut the hell up or we'll forgo using the rope. It's up to you, Ringo."

The man stared back at Billy the Kid, then me, in utter astonishment. What I found interesting was that he actually had set fire to the barn in an attempt to escape a gunfight. Two horses died in the process. I had somewhat less sympathy for him. That was three dead horses just that day. *Kill each other … but leave the damn horses alone.*

Billy the Kid said, "Probably hangs tomorrow … just

waiting for the county constable to arrive."

"And who is that?"

"You may have met her. She goes by the name Calamity Jane. The two of you will determine his fate. But I warn you, going soft on horse killers won't make you popular in these parts."

I nodded and took a seat on the corner of the nearest desk. *Of course ... Calamity Jane. Could this day get any more bizarre?*

Having tapped in this morning, I had until later tonight, or the following morning, at the latest, before I'd need to tap in again. I looked around the jail, hoping to see some indication of an electrical power source connection—such as a wall outlet. No such luck. This could present a real problem for me. I thought about returning to the lodge, but that was miles back and there was the not-so-insignificant danger from patrolling, highly proficient men, armed with automatic weapons. I had no idea what I was going to do.

Chapter 28

Before leaving the jailhouse, Billy the Kid handed me several keys. The first was a large, flat-looking key with the words Tombstone Steel Works engraved on its end. "This is the skeleton key to both cells. Try not to lose it." He fished through his pockets and brought forth a smaller key, the number 27 engraved on it. "This key is for your hotel room, located above the saloon. You'll find your suitcase there—transferred over from the lodge."

Billy stepped toward the doorway, hesitated, turning back toward Johnny Ringo, and sniffed the air. "I'd say there's a full bucket that needs dumping ... there's an outhouse out back." He hesitated again. "In a perfect world, Doc, you'd be the peacekeeper around here; or, at the very least, an arbitrator for peace. But not today—now you're the champion of swift justice. This isn't Mayberry and you aren't fucking Andy Griffith. If you want to live out the week ... hell, the day, be ready to draw first and aim to kill."

I watched him leave, still seated on the corner of the desk.

"One thing he was right about," Ringo said, standing behind the cell's bars, "this bucket's heaped to the brim."

* * *

I don't know what they'd been feeding Ringo, or if he

simply had digestive problems, but the whole bucket-emptying task went far beyond anything I was prepared for. As far as I was concerned or cared, Ringo could shit on the floor from here on in. That messy ordeal was a one-time-only assist.

Returning from the outhouse, I held the bucket at arm's length. I ordered Ringo to move to the back of his cell, place his hands behind his head, his fingers intertwined—like he'd done several minutes earlier. I unlocked and swung open the heavy, iron-barred door and tossed in the bucket, then closed and relocked the door.

Ringo brought his arms down. "You know this is bullshit. It's crazy. Palmolive is crazy."

"Who are you really?" I asked. He seemed reluctant to answer, instead rubbing the stubble on his neck.

"Look, it makes no difference to me. If you don't want to tell me—"

"I'm Bobby Roper … a government lobbyist."

I continued to stare at him. I already knew about his connection to Washington, picking up on it the first time I entered his cell. He was borderline corrupt. Perhaps they all were—but in his case, it bothered him. He allowed himself to become tempted by the large sums of money at play, thus becoming a pawn of the Order and Palmolive. He'd come here wanting to move up the ladder.

"So what happened?"

He shrugged. "What he said was partially true. I did try to escape, out through the back of the barn at the OK Corral. I'd earlier told Palmolive … Billy the Kid … I no longer wanted to be part of the Order. That I'd face the music back home; even go to prison, if that's what it took. Within an hour, I was called out—told that Jude was waiting for me in the middle of the street. I'd already witnessed what that lunatic could do with his six-shooter. He must spend hours a day practicing. He's ridiculously fast and obviously enjoys killing. I don't know who they were, but he's killed several others already … out there on the street."

"How'd you end up in the barn?"

"I came out of the saloon and saw Jude. I panicked and hopped on the closest horse, then rode off in the opposite direction. But three men, holding automatic weapons, were waiting at the end of the street. I turned into the barn and … shit … I panicked. Honest, I didn't mean to kill those horses."

I continued to study him. "I can't make you any promises, I have my own problems. But if I can, I'll help get you out of here. But when the time comes, I'll expect you to have my back. Run off in the opposite direction, I'll have no problem shooting you myself."

"Fair enough."

"One more thing. This town … is there any electricity here?"

"Huh?"

"Did they run any electric power lines into this town?"

"No … it's fucking 1881 here. It's oil lamps and potbelly stoves. Just look around."

The door flew open and a woman, carrying a tray with covered platters, bustled in. "Oh … you must be the new sheriff!"

She was one of the saloon girls. Her ample breasts were on the verge of springing free of her snug-fitting bodice. Heavily made up, with rouged cheeks, ample amounts of mascara, and bright red lipstick, her face looked almost mask-like to me. I'd first thought she was wearing a wig—with piled-high, unnatural-looking red-dyed curls, but it was her own hair. Her heavy dousing of perfume immediately impacted all my senses.

"I have your lunch too." She set the tray down on the other desk and began uncovering the platters. "You can hand over the prisoner in there his meal. I don't go anywhere near the prisoners." I noticed her black net stockings were torn on one of her upper thighs. Just then, she glanced over her shoulder at me—she thought I was looking at her derriere. She smiled, still playing the part of the raunchy saloon girl, but somehow her flirtatious act didn't reach her eyes. She looked tired and … something else, too.

I let out a long breath and said, "Listen, you don't have to waste your energies on me."

Apparently, that touched a nerve. She stopped futzing with the food platters and moved in closer to me. Up close, I could almost see the real her, beneath the cosmetic mask she wore. She was actually younger than I'd first thought—maybe twenty-five. And beneath all the clown-face makeup, she was actually pretty.

She moved in, using her hips to spread my knees apart—undoubtedly, a well-practiced maneuver, done hundreds of times before. One hand moved to my upper thigh, the other brought up to stroke my face. I caught her wrist, forcing her own palm back in toward her; a simple Aikido hold that caused instant pain and allowed for me to direct her body away.

"Hey, let go … that hurts!"

Releasing her hand, she immediately swung her other hand in an attempt to slap my face. I caught that hand too, and held it firmly. I kept my voice low, but left no doubt to its sincerity. "Touch me again and I'll snap your wrist like a twig. I'm not one of your patrons, so drop the whole saloon whore act."

She pulled her arm away and I saw the pain in her eyes

that went far beyond what she'd felt in her wrist. She rubbed at it with her other hand and silently fumed—her eyes boring into me.

"Let me guess, you were sent here to deliver more than our meals."

She pursed her red lips and shook her head. "You don't know me. You don't know anything about me, so why don't you keep your big mouth shut."

But I knew her better than she thought. She was a prisoner here, just like everyone else. Her case was even worse than the black-grimed figure standing behind bars. She had a little boy and the Order threatened to hurt him—maim him. The more I probed her thoughts, the more I uncovered: Her husband's heavy gambling had gotten her embroiled in this mess. He was long dead, but she was still paying off his outstanding debt. Although she'd managed to stave-off harm to her son, she'd been forced to do things—many awful things—she'd never envisioned herself capable of. She existed in a never-ending, living, hell.

I said, "I can help you. I know what they have hanging over you." I expected relief, perhaps even gratitude. Instead, fear and tears filled her eyes. Her eyes flashed to something above me—something up and off to the right. She gently leaned forward, whispering so quietly I could barely hear her words.

"They're watching. Oh God … please don't push me away … my son."

I didn't resist as her arms came around my neck and I felt the warmth of her body, her breasts, moving against me. Her lips touched my ear. "Cameras are all over. There's one where the wall meets the ceiling, right above you."

A part of me was irritated, but another part of me wasn't surprised, even in the least. But the *smartest* part of me was thrilled. Where there were hidden cameras, there was electricity. I just had to discover where.

Both her hands rose to my face and she kissed me. Not the kiss of a saloon whore, but a kiss from a scared, desperate woman.

Chapter 29

I followed her outside where we could speak more privately. "What's your name?"

"Everyone here calls me Juniper … or June."

I knew that wasn't her real name, which was Lori. Holding on to the empty tray, she seemed hesitant to talk—somewhat embarrassed—since she no longer could hide behind her saloon-girl persona.

She looked around, squinting against the midday sun. There were faint tear tracks on her cheeks and she'd need to reapply makeup. I gave her that mental suggestion, and she immediately became more self-conscious.

"I need to go … you know … to get back there."

"Watch yourself, Lori." I spoke her real name before I could stop myself. By the startled look on her face, I knew I'd made a grave mistake.

"Who the hell are you? How do you know who …"

"I'm not your enemy here, I promise you that."

She spun on her heels and hurried off, the fragrance of her perfume lingering in her wake. As I watched her progress toward the saloon's doors, her hips began to sway more noticeably, and then, suddenly, the vulnerability I'd witnessed mere moments before was gone. She waved in the direction of an elderly man, dressed up as a dime-store cowboy, standing across the dusty street. He whistled at her and she laughed, saying something back that I couldn't quite make out.

I returned to the jail and gave Ringo his meal and ate mine, pondering what was next.

The number of lives forced under Palmolive's control was probably staggering—like Lori, Ringo, and Butch Cassidy, and the large cast of play actors trapped in this crazy, counterfeit, town. I thought of Carmen—she was probably freaking out about now, realizing I wouldn't be returning to the lodge any time soon. Would she attempt to reach me—come here on her own? Doing so could very well get her killed. And then I thought of Pippa and my heart constricted in my chest. Where was she now? Was she alive? Maybe I should go get Carmen and get the hell out of here. Then I remembered what Bridgett and Baltimore told me, about the shirt I was wearing: *"Unsnap both top collar buttons and a distress signal is immediately generated. It's your way of telling us to send in the cavalry."* Baltimore then added: *"Be damn certain you're ready to do that, because it will be the end of the mission."*

The truth was, I still didn't know near enough. I hadn't uncovered Palmolive's ultimate plan, or what the Order's future entailed. I had to remind myself he headed the Council of Five. His influence on America—the entire world, was enormous. How on earth did such a lunatic get elected to hold that high global position in the first place? I needed to move things along here … I needed to stop him.

But before anything else, I needed to find out exactly where the town's high-voltage power source was located; it was either brought in from outside town, or there was some kind of generator here. Staggering around in the middle of the night, in the throes of withdrawal, was not the time to go on a search.

I was about to turn back toward the jail when I saw a distant horse and rider. There was something familiar about him. I expected him to proceed to the saloon, but such wasn't the case. As he came closer I could see *he* was actually a *she*, wearing the same fringed-leather jacket and chaps. It was blonde-headed Calamity Jane. *Now this should be interesting.*

I took the opportunity to peruse her mind the last ten yards of her approach; and again, as she climbed down off her mount; then once again, as she tied her horse to a wooden railing.

Holy shit! I dove left, simultaneously drawing my Colt and pulling the trigger. I didn't have time to properly aim, so it was a wild shot—a Hail Mary shot. Unfortunately for me, I was a millisecond slower on the draw than she was, and I felt a stinging bite when a hot lead projectile seared the flesh on my upper back. Even in that instant, I was fairly sure it was only a flesh wound. *Christ!* She'd come here to kill me. No chit chat—no standing in the middle of the street, like respectable gunslingers did in the movies, to see who had the quicker draw. The bitch had walked right toward me and drew her gun!

I was on the ground, tasting the grit of dirt in my mouth and gasping for breath, having the wind knocked from my lungs. Even with all that, I kept the barrel of my Colt pointed in her direction. I eased my finger off the trigger. She was still on her feet but strangely bent backwards, her back lying over the hitching rail. Her arms were extended outward—almost Christ-like—her right hand forefinger still loosely on the gun's trigger.

As I struggled to my feet, others clambered from nearby doorways, and a throng of cowboys rushed out through the saloon's swinging doors. When I reached the now-obviously dead body of Calamity Jane, no less than fifteen others were standing right next to me. As if watching some kind of ridiculous ritual, one by one the men approached her, leaning over her strangely contorted form for a closer look, then stared back at me.

The bullet hole was precisely placed between her eyes, at the bridge of her nose. Her eyes were open and fixed. It was an amazing shot! I shrugged at all the open-jawed faces. "She drew down on me first." I turned to show them what I knew was a bloody mess on my upper back.

There was a commotion at the back of the crowd. "Move out of the way … let me through!"

Billy the Kid emerged jacketless, his own gun drawn. He saw me first and then Calamity Jane. It occurred to me he'd warned me—told me—that when in doubt, draw first. *Did he order her to shoot me?* How come I hadn't picked up on that earlier? Then I knew, that wasn't how the game was played here. This place was a testing ground. Only the best would survive.

Billy the Kid, following the same look-see as the others, leaned over to peer into Jane's unfocussed gaze, before turning back to study me. He smiled, then laughed out loud. Nervously, the others lightly chuckled at first, and then laughed uproariously right along with him.

Jude and Jordan approached down the raised wooden walkway. Both stopped and stared at the body for several moments, before Jude said, "You're either the luckiest son of a bitch on the planet or one hell of a gunfighter."

"Colman … you're up at bat," Jordan said, waving forward a skeletally slim man, standing off to my right. Easy guess … he was the undertaker. My guess, he was pushing seventy and, by his somewhat hunched posture, had arthritis or some other mobility-affecting ailment. Jordan and Jude eased her body from the wooden rail, each grabbing an arm. Half carrying, half dragging, they took Calamity Jane in the direction of the OK Corral where, I surmised, the undertaker's establishment was located.

"Never had the opportunity to go up against Jane. She was rumored to be the fastest draw in Tombstone but evidently, she was not." Billy the Kid holstered his gun and turned toward the others, and said, "Doc Holliday has proven himself quite proficient at aiming his pistol. I'd think twice before drawing down on him." He headed toward the saloon, then turned back to me. "Get yourself cleaned up and I'll buy you a whisky. Maybe see if you're equally proficient at twisting the tiger's tail."

What he was referring to was the ancient game of Faro. It was, by far, the most popular card game of the Wild West played in any gambling house. Although not a direct relative of poker, it was somewhat similar. I'd played it once, when I was thirteen, but for the life of me now I couldn't remember any of its rules. I nodded, and said, "I look forward to it."

As Billy the Kid walked away, the others turned and followed after him. I stayed with him, mentally watching the images in his mind flash into my own. Then I felt what he felt … felt the pang of lust and desperate longing, and I saw her face. *What the hell?* … It was Heidi Goertz.

Chapter 30

I found Room 27 at the top of the stairs in the hotel portion of the saloon. Standing next to the bed in the stillness … the stifling heat—I appraised the room, which was small and in disrepair. Faded floral wallpaper curled at seams and there were several round holes in the floorboards that looked to be about the diameter of .45 round. These authentic accommodations were a far contrast to those back at the lodge.

I gazed out the window at the street scene below. Listening, I could hear the distant, tinkling keys of the piano playing, the steady drone of boisterous, rowdy men's voices, and the occasional piping of women's laughter—sometimes screams. A large fly buzzed and skittered along the bottom of the windowpane—trapped and unaware of its inevitable fate.

A tap came at the door. In two long steps I opened it and found Lori standing there, holding a white porcelain basin half-filled with water, and a hand-towel draped over one forearm. She'd repaired her makeup and looked at me still with hesitant mistrust.

"Why don't you take a step backward?"

I did as directed and let her pass by. She moved over to a tall dresser where she set down the basin. With her back to me, she said, "Take off your shirt and I'll have a look at that wound."

"I'm sure it's nothing, I can take care of—"

Facing me now, a wet towel in her hand and brows raised, she said, "That wasn't a request … off with it."

Easing the shirt off my shoulders, I flinched, letting the cotton fabric fall on the floor. I silently took a seat on the bed and faced away from her, bristling some when I felt the moist towel gently rub at my wound.

"It's not too bad … probably could use a few stitches here and there, but you'll be fine either way," she said.

I spoke, keeping my voice a soft whisper, "Are there cameras … listening devices in here?"

She didn't answer right away. I felt her scoot closer, sitting behind me on the bed. With her lips close to my ear, she whispered, "Yes, both—be careful what you say."

I whispered back, "I'm going to get you out of this. I promise."

I felt her wet-toweled hand hesitate above the wound, then lightly pat at it, before covering it with a gauze bandage. "No one can go up against him; you'll get us both killed. Just stay out of it." She stood and went over to the dresser. "You have another shirt in there?"

I turned to see her pointing in the direction of my suitcase, sitting upright by the side of the window. "I'll put it on the bed for you. You don't want to start bleeding again."

She moved over to the suitcase, hefted it up, and placed it on the bed. I quickly moved in behind her, wrapped my arms around her waist, and pulled her close. I whispered into her ear, "I need to know where the town gets its power from … a power line … a generator … please, just tell me that much."

She giggled and spun in my arms—her face inches from my own. She kissed me gently and again I felt the warmth of her body against mine. Her nipples, through thin cloth, were erect and pressing against my chest. Her words were so faint I could barely hear them. "There's a small building across from the OK Corral. You enter it and it looks deserted." She stopped and kissed me again, this time her eyes were open and hopeful. "There's a trap door, always locked, and in-side are stairs leading below ground to a basement. That's where they watch us—there's equipment and monitors on the walls, and always a few men on duty. Palmolive spends a lot of time there late at night. I bring them their meals … and other things. Whatever they ask for." Tears welled up in her eyes and she buried her face into my shoulder. She went on, "The building next door is the undertaker's place … it's creepy. There's a door at the back, also always locked; inside is a room with, I think, electrical panels."

She composed herself and gave a light-hearted laugh. "You're a naughty boy, Doc Holliday." Then playfully, and much louder, said, "I'm going to have to watch out for you."

Lori pushed me away and made for the door. Opening it, she left without looking back.

* * *

I put my new Western-style shirt on as I stood before the mirror over the dresser. Snapping the buttons closed, for a brief moment I was startled at seeing my reflection—seeing someone else's face stare back at me. The series of microinjections I'd recently sat through at SIFTR had dramatically altered my looks. In addition to experiencing several miserable, pain-filled hours, there were other, longer-term side effects from the surgery as well. Both Carmen and Baltimore warned me, and Pippa, too, about what was coming that first time we underwent a similar procedure, months earlier, for another mission. Apparently, altering one's looks wreaks havoc on the person's total physiological state, and fucks up our sense of identity. For me, I'd made it a point to avoid looking at my own reflection; avoid touching my face. But Pippa's ordeal was even more impactful—I'd say devastating, in some respects. They altered her face, her breasts, even the contours of her body. When the mission was over, she'd lost touch with the person she really was. Part of her wanted to retain her new identity, yet the other part craved returning to her original looks and persona. Looking at myself now, the face of someone named Troy McAlister, I did what I'd found to be the most effective way of keeping my sanity: I stuck my tongue out and crossed my eyes. It's always best to keep a sense of humor.

Before leaving the room I replaced the spent round in my Colt, then took several more minutes adding bullets into the loops around my gun belt. I grabbed up my Stetson, hanging from the bedpost, and left the room.

* * *

At the bottom of the stairs, I headed directly for the bar. I was keenly aware I was being measured by those sitting at the round tables and by others, too, their elbows propped up behind them on the bar top's polished wood surface. Facing outward, toward the tables, some men were drinking whiskey from shot glasses, while others drank from large mugs filled with dark ale.

I dipped the brim of my hat in the direction of Butch Cassidy. He made room at the bar for me to join him, seeming genuinely pleased to see me. Putting a hand on my shoulder, he directed the barkeep to bring me a glass and bottle.

"Seems you're adjusting quite well to life in Tombstone,"

I said, bringing the small glass of whisky to my lips and throwing back the burning spirits.

"Hell, I'm a U.S. congressman, Mr. Holliday. A man of the people … a true people person."

"That's when you're not robbing trains and banks and such," I said, reminding him who he was supposed to be amongst the other cowboys, sitting and standing all around us.

"Of course. Speaking of which … that was quite a show you put on earlier. Had no idea you were so proficient with ancient firearms."

"Maybe it was the company … Calamity Jane. You need to bring your A game against someone like her," I said.

"From what I've heard she played for both teams—could beat most men around here in an arm-wrestle. But why she came after you like that … I don't know. Maybe she thought you were some kind of threat?"

"Nah, didn't even know her. But I imagine I'll have a scar on my back to remind me of her for a few years to come." I glanced over to Butch and saw, from his lazy-eyed, unfocused stare, that he was on his way to total inebriation. "Hey … you might want to get something to eat … take it easy on the hooch for a while."

He awkwardly lifted the bulk of his belly off the bar and turned toward me, standing up somewhat straighter: "I'm as sober as when I walked in here, my friend. A man of my girth can hold more liquor …" He stopped mid-sentence, furrowed his brow, and said, "What the fuck was I just talking about?" He lowered himself down on the bar stool and took another pull on his drink.

I laughed and signaled a man over, wearing a stained apron. "Can we get this man something to eat?"

He raised his eyes toward Butch and made an exaggerated wide-eyed expression. "I'll get him something."

I turned around and saw a white-sleeved arm give a wave in my direction. "You going to be all right here, Butch?" He turned his eyes toward me and nodded. "Fine, my good man … go have fun."

I grabbed up my glass and bottle and headed toward the table where Billy the Kid, Jude and Jordan were seated. There were five others standing, who looked to be playing. Seeing the faded-looking playing cards, I tried again to recall how to play Faro.

Chapter 31

From beneath the table, Jude kicked a chair closer to me and said: "Sit," without looking up. My eyes lingered on his scar for a moment before he glanced up at me. In his now self-conscious thoughts, I saw a rapid mental replay of how he'd gotten it—and what I saw surprised me.

I sat and watched the game of Faro unfold at a fast pace. Everything looked authentic for the game's time period with one exception: Everyone was using modern-day US $100 bills—apparently the only currency allowed here. Billy the Kid slapped a stack of bills down in front of me and said, "That was some fine shooting earlier … out on the street. Bank pays out dividends for that sort of thing here."

Almost immediately, the rules of the game started coming back to me. Faro was a fairly simple game—one played during the Civil War—also in gambling towns all around the Old West. Billy the Kid played banker, of course, and distributor of the cards, which slid out from a box or shoe—a spring-loaded contraption—that allowed only the top card to be visible, before it could be slid out onto the table. On the table were thirteen permanent face-up cards. Suits in this game were ignored. The cards' numerical value was everything—depending on where the player placed his chips—either on the cards directly, or between them, in a variety of ways. A player then places his bet. In this game you don't play against the other players, you play against the bank—the dealer: The dealer unveils the cards in sets of two—a win card and a lose card. What the banker's next card shows—whether a win card or a lose card—and where the other players placed their bet and whether the face up card they've placed their chips on is numerically high or low, will determine if they win or lose the round. The game pretty much pays out even money, with only a slight two percent edge going to the bank. What I didn't like about Faro was how little actual skill was involved to play it. It was a game of chance and the man standing next to you could win the next round just as easily as you could.

An olive-skinned man suddenly stood and left the table in an apparent huff. I shuffled my chair over to the left, taking his spot at the table. The round finished and Billy the Kid said, "Remove your bets or place new bets."

Sitting directly to Billy's left was Jordan, who wasn't actually playing but tracking each card being played with an abacus-looking device. With every exposed card released from the card shoe, he slid another little bead over. I remembered doing that when I'd played as a kid … it allowed the players, and those betting, or just standing around, to keep track of what cards were played—allowing them to better guess which cards were still inside the deck.

I handed Jordan five one hundred-dollar bills, and he gave me back an equal number of small, navy blue chips. I placed my bets around the table and put what was then called a copper, a penny, on top of several chips, to reverse certain bets.

Billy the Kid watched me with amusement. "You've played before?"

"Once … but it's coming back to me," I said.

He exposed the next win card and the men around the table either groaned or cheered, depending on how they had bet. I won and let my chips ride where they were. I noticed Billy had significantly more chips than anyone else—ten times as many. I assumed it was simply because he was the banker, but when I peered into his mind I discovered the truth, and smiled. He was cheating. The box contraption-thing was somehow rigged. It actually was a working relic from the Civil War era—and perfectly operational. He knew, through some hidden mechanical tell, what the next hidden card would be. And what he knew, I knew.

Over the next hour I amassed a sizable chunk of chips. The stacks in front of Billy the Kid were only slightly higher than my own. The crowd of onlookers around us had grown, to the point most of the other tables in the saloon were empty. Even the bar was only sparsely occupied. Side betting had increased to a point of frenzy, something Billy the Kid, Jordan, and Jude weren't pleased about.

"So … Billy," I said.

His eyes found me and then went back to tracking the progress of the game.

I continued. "There's something I've been meaning to ask you."

Billy the Kid thumbed off another card, exposing the jack beneath it. There was a mix of cheers and groans from the other players.

"I was surprised when I got the … um … invitation. You know … to come here," I said.

His response was an almost imperceptible shrug. It occurred to me that I hadn't witnessed anyone else talking business here. If Jude's glare was any indication of the inappropriateness of such chatter, I'd just made a monumental faux pas. *Screw him.* Clear in my mind was my reason for being here—I needed intel. Intel about the Order—including what was brewing with those subterranean passageways. And why the sudden activity in the buildup of military assets, of key Order personnel, such as those being vetted here, in this mock Old West era town. And where was Pippa being held and what condition was she in? The truth was, Billy the Kid didn't need to answer me directly—he just needed to think along the right lines for me to connect the dots.

"I know why I'm motivated to ... um ... have your organization support my company. But what is it about my particular business ... or me, for that matter, that is of interest to—"

The knife came so fast I didn't have time to react to it. One moment my left hand was resting casually upon the tabletop near my pile of chips—and the next, an eight-inch blade was driven down between my thumb and forefinger. The handle of the knife, black as onyx, continued to vibrate. The hush in the saloon gave way to low murmurs and then to louder, out-and-out, comments. Someone behind me laughed nervously. I dipped my hat in Jude's direction. "Looks like you dropped something, Jude. Or is this a gift for me? That's it, isn't it? This is a welcome to Tombstone gift. I don't know what to say ... but thanks, compadre."

Jude's tight smile momentarily faltered. I used my nearly impaled hand to extricate the knife from the table and examined it more closely, holding it in the fingers of both hands.

Jude held out a palm with brows raised. "Give it back ... and mind you manners on what's discussed here, Mr. Holliday. Remember the rules. That's your first and only warning."

Billy the Kid sat quietly, watching in bemused interest.

Holding the knife by the blade, I stood and made as if I were going to hand the knife back across the table to Jude. But with a rapid flick of my wrist, I sent the knife straight upward where it imbedded itself, blade first, into the ceiling directly above Jude's head. I said, "Oops ..."

"Enough! Are we playing cards here, or what?" Billy asked. "Everyone place or remove your bets." The card game continued.

All those antics weren't a total waste. Within those few seconds I mentally picked up on several visual impressions where Palmolive's plans became momentarily exposed: A nondescript brick, county municipal-type building; a huge lake ... no ... a reservoir; and a military base nestled somewhere below ground. Images that, at the very least, would be a starting point for later consideration. But as interesting as all those things were, what I most wanted to see was where Pippa had been taken—her condition. So I inserted my own image of Pippa into his mind. Nothing, but his thoughts jumped to another woman and from that point on I had trouble staying present in Billy the Kid's mind. He was way beyond fixated on Heidi Goertz. Each time I peered into his thoughts, I'd see her damn face, laughing at something he'd once said to her, or talking to or scolding someone nearby her. He watched her every movement, totally captivated by her charms. More often than not, he was recalling their most recent intimate moments; moments where they were either naked in bed, or sneaking off for an illicit encounter behind their respective spouses' backs. When his thoughts turned to their trysts, I vacated his mind as quickly as possible. Unfortunately, few of my questions were being answered, with one startling exception—something about the WZZ—Heidi and Leon Goertz's Neo-Nazi organization. Something was at play here. WZZ had grown more powerful than ever, and Heidi was becoming a real power-player now within the Order. I didn't see how both could be possible and figured I'd misconstrued the images I saw inside Billy's head. Perhaps in his mind ... his love, or lust, or both, for that horrid woman was giving her more prominence in the Order's realm than she actually held.

I'd had enough of the game and made that fact known, after winning another round, by saying, "That does it for me, gents."

I stood up, hearing the crowd groan and complain. Billy the Kid, getting more and more irritated at my winnings, unable to figure out how I'd won so often, knew that I, like him, had been cheating. In fact, I'd watched as his imagination ran wild—he considered drawing his six-shooter and shooting me in the heart—then announcing I'd been cheating and that he'd simply done everyone a favor. I almost let the game go on too long and felt lucky now to walk away still breathing.

I said, gesturing to the large stack of blue chips in front of me, "Disperse them amongst yourselves. It was never my money to play anyway." I made my way through the dispersing throng and wasn't completely surprised to find Butch Cassidy where I'd left him at the bar. Three stacked plates, shoved to the side, held a smattering of what looked liked gnawed-on barbecued ribs. I signaled the barkeep and, pointing at his plates, said, "Some of those ... and another bottle."

"You like to live dangerously, my friend."

I noticed Butch was speaking with far better annunciation than he had earlier. I wouldn't call him sober, but he was at least coherent. "Let me ask you something ... Butch."

"Shoot."

"Why are you here?" Before he could answer, I added, "I'm speaking to the congressman, now, not Butch Cassidy."

"Dangerous asking questions like that around here," he answered, reaching for a half-empty bottle of whisky. "I imagine it's for the same reason you're here, or the rest of the idiots playing cowboy in this hell hole. Power. The word's come down … things are changing. The landscape will be permanently altered, here in the great U.S. of A, as well as in the rest of the world. Either hitch yourself to the new wagon, or find yourself run over by it later."

"There ya go … rules being ignored again," I heard a familiar voice say, two paces behind me. The piano playing abruptly stopped, and the saloon quieted down to hushed murmurs. I saw their reflection in the mirror on the wall, on the other side of the bar: Behind me stood, side-by-side, Billy the Kid, Jordan and Jude. They stood with their legs apart, their hands hovering inches from the butts of their Colts. *Shit!* I glanced over to Butch and saw his typically rosy cheeks drained of color. He looked terrified. I was about to peer into their minds, hoping to find some way out of this mess, but Butch was already reaching into the air—his hands up, as he spun around. "I'm sorry, Billy … please—"

Those were the last words to escape from the congressman's lips. The threesome drew their weapons—lightning fast—and fired simultaneously. It sounded like a single gunshot. Looking over my shoulder, I saw smoke rising from three gun barrels. Butch, a trickle of blood already seeping from the corner of his open lips, had an expanding patch of scarlet on his chest where his heart was located. He toppled forward—dead before he hit the floor.

I raised my hands—my own breathing ceased—my mind a total blank.

Billy the Kid smiled: "He was warned once before. You can put your hands down, Sheriff." The three gunmen grinned. Billy was the first to holster his weapon, quickly followed by the other two. All eyes were now on me. I saw Lori in the middle of the room, sitting on a man's lap, her arms casually resting on his shoulders. Her eyes were locked on mine, showing genuine concern.

Billy gestured with his chin—at the now-familiar, skeletally thin mortician standing three feet abreast of me—at the bar. "Mr. Colman, seems you're having a fortuitous run of business today."

As Colman moved to collect Butch, I held up a palm in his direction. "No … don't touch him. I've got this."

Chapter 32

Butch, a bear of a man when alive, was now a heavy, unwieldy, corpse. Seeing me struggling to lift him, Billy the Kid smacked Jordan's upper arm. "Don't just stand there, help the sheriff."

I glared again at the approaching mortician, letting him know to keep the hell back. With Jordan now at my side, we dragged Butch's bulk toward the entrance. A glance over my shoulder confirmed that the pallid-faced mortician was indeed following, shuffling along several strides behind us—like a vulture barely biding its time. We pushed through the swinging doors and were met by a chilly, early evening breeze. I caught a final glimpse of the sun as it slid behind a colorless nearby hilltop. The street was deserted, except for a young man across the street in the process of lighting an oil lamp—one of several he'd already lit next to small storefronts along the darkening street.

Butch Cassidy's bulk was nothing compared to the weight of guilt I was feeling. For God's sake, all the poor man had done was answer the question I'd put to him.

"He wasn't long for this world, anyway, Doc," Jordan said, as though reading my mind. He sounded out of breath, struggling under the weight of supporting Butch's other thick arm. "His destiny was pretty much already set … even before he set foot in Tombstone."

"Then why even bring him here? Why not just leave him be?"

The answer came to me mentally, before he answered: Butch knew too much and he'd started to gossip about the Order organization to non-members. There was too much at stake. Big events were about to occur, in days forthcoming, and the Order couldn't jeopardize their coming to fruition by a loose-lipped congressman, causing them undue trouble. No, he'd now joined others, those similarly destined to an early, unfortunate demise—planned to occur in some kind of mass-accident soon.

"Butch just wasn't a good fit here," Jordan said, as if he'd thought better of providing me with a more in-depth explanation.

I contemplated putting an end to all this shit, calling it quits; stop the killing in this miserable place. I reached up to my open collar with my free hand and felt the two, still-clasped, snaps there. Separating the two small snaps was the only thing standing in the way of rallying the SIFTR agency's, albeit limited, forces, and closing this place down. But then what? Take Palmolive and his minions into custody? How long would SIFTR survive after that? With the CIA, FBI, Homeland Security also under the influence of the Order, it would be an inevitable bloodbath. My thoughts turned to Pippa. If she wasn't already dead, hasty actions on my part here would ultimately seal her fate as well. I wasn't ready to make that call—I'd have to play things out here to their shadowy end.

We were halfway to our destination when I felt tremors starting in my legs. I needed to tap in soon. I slowed and repositioned Butch's bulk off my injury, more onto my shoulders.

"You don't look so good, Doc."

"I'm fine ... just need to eat something, that's all." Prior, I'd grouped Jordan and Jude together as one and the same—two ruthless killers, both following the dictates of an even more ruthless, borderline psychopath-killer—Rudy Palmolive. But Jordan's mind, I was finding, wasn't nearly as bleak, or nearly as dark. Even now, as he and I dragged Butch Cassidy's body down the middle of Tombstone's Main Street, I could see Jordan had regrets. Surprised, I saw his own mental playback of the recent shooting, just as it occurred in real-time, and I realized Jordan hadn't fired toward Butch's chest, like the other two. No, in that instant, he'd chosen, instead, to put a round into the wooden floorboards, less than an inch from the back heel of the congressman's right boot. There was compassion there—or, at the very least, a sense of morality. With that insight, I wondered if Jordan could be turned.

I said, keeping my voice low, "You know, the ghoul back there ... behind us? He'll inspect the body and find only two bullet holes in Butch's chest and two exit wounds. He'll tell your boss that one of you didn't shoot poor Butch in the saloon."

Jordan's expression suddenly darkened. "You don't know what you're talking about. You should shut the fuck up before someone puts a bullet in *your* head."

But I knew Jordan's threats were only a cover for his own uneasiness at being discovered.

"Hey, I wouldn't tell him. Hell, I liked Butch. I think what you did—what you didn't do—is admirable," I said conspiratorially.

Jordan looked straight ahead as his eyes darted back and forth, like one whose mind desperately sought a way out of a tight predicament. We walked the rest of the way in silence. As we approached the front door of the undertaker's building, I noticed three coffins of varied size propped up outside the mortuary, blocking the window behind them. It occurred to me this outdoor display was more about keeping curious eyes from looking into the window, than about enticing passersby to stop and purchase a coffin.

"Colman … get the door," Jordan said.

The emaciated-looking man hurried ahead of us, pulling free a set of keys from his front trouser pocket.

The door once unlocked squeaked open on angry-sounding hinges. Colman ran forward into the murky darkness, stopping halfway into the room at what looked like a long, waist-high table. He beckoned us toward him, using outstretched arms and hand motions. I hadn't yet perused his mind—not the slightest bit interested in the inner, macabre workings of the unlikable undertaker.

"Lie him on his back," Colman said.

It took three tries before Jordan and I were able to heft Butch up onto the table. Jordan then offered me a quick nod of his head, acknowledgment of a job well done. Colman, at some point, moved away to light an oil lamp, and the room, suddenly lit, seemed even a far ghastlier place.

Billy the Kid was right—the undertaker had had a very fruitful day. The smell alone should have been my first clue that there were other dead here. Actually quite a few, I discovered, after a cursory glance around. The telltale shapes of bodies, at least six or seven, became more distinguishable in the light of the lone, flickering flame.

When my legs suddenly buckled and the room spun, I reached for the table in front of me. Jordan came around and took my arm. "Hold on there, man."

I took in a lungful of fetid air and tried to clear my head. Withdrawal symptoms were coming on strong.

"Shall I clear another table for him?" Colman asked.

Both Jordan and I answered in concert, "No!" My eyes

found two identical doors at the back of the room. One, according to Lori, would gain me access to the town's electrical panels. I wondered if it was accidental they'd been placed there, amongst these ghoulish surroundings, or an ingenious safeguard to keep curious eyes at bay. I took a last look at Butch and silently apologized to him once again.

"Come on … I'll help you back to the hotel," Jordan said.

* * *

By the time we entered the saloon I'd lost my mind-reading capabilities. I stood up tall, doing my best to hide the fact I was on the verge of collapse. The piano player was banging out a fast version of *Camptown Races*, while three brightly dressed saloon girls danced and flashed their petticoats at a rowdy, boisterous crowd. I spotted Jude and Billy the Kid at the same Faro table. Neither noticed our arrival.

"I'm heading up to my room for a while," I told Jordan, who merely shrugged and headed toward his companions. I wasted no time heading for a swinging door, which stood between the bar and the staircase. I entered the busy kitchen—the sounds of clanging pots and pans and the sputtering of flame-cooked steaks filled the air. Bright florescent lights glared down from above, my first indication there really was electrical power here. The place was packed with ten or more workers: Four men cooked at a grill, while several others prepared platefuls of food; a couple cleaned filthy dishes at an old-fashioned sink. One man looked up at me as I hurried by, his expression one of suspicion. I nodded and two finger tapped the star on my chest—an indication my presence there was for some sort of official business. I wasn't sure if he fully bought it, but he went back to scrubbing and rinsing the frying pan in front of him.

I burst through the screen door at the rear of the kitchen, staggering out into the quasi-darkness. I stopped short and leaned forward—hands on knees—and retched a series of dry heaves. Taking in several deep breaths I stepped backward to lean against the building. I needed to keep the spinning world around me at bay. Opening my eyes, I found I wasn't alone. The glow of two lit cigarettes danced ten feet away. The swath of indirect light, pouring through the screen door, highlighted two saloon girls, sitting together on an outside bench. I couldn't make out their faces, but I heard one of them say, "I've got this—go on back to work, Molly Mae."

I heard the screen door clatter shut. The other woman drew closer to me—I heard the rustling of her dress, then smelled her familiar perfume. Her voice sounded tired, just above a whisper. "What is it with you? You're like a bad penny. You keep turning up in my life."

Lori's red curls shone in the light as she stepped up to me. "Hey … you don't look so good. Why don't you go lie down or something?"

I shook my head. "I need your help. I won't make it back there on my own."

"I told you … I have a son. Helping you will get me shot. Or worse, my son will be hurt." She dropped her cigarette butt into the dirt and started for the door.

I reached out and firmly grabbed her arm. "You don't want to be a part of this—there's going to be more … a lot more."

"That's not my problem."

"I promise, I'll get you out of here. Get you back to your boy."

Lori looked up at me, searching my eyes. "What exactly do you need me to do?"

Chapter 33

Together, we headed off into the darkness, following a dirt path, paralleling Tombstone's Main Street, behind the storefronts' shabby rear entrances. Within seconds, all sounds of saloon music and frenetic, busy kitchen clanging dissipated into the night.

Lori held onto my arm, doing her utmost to keep me from toppling over. My lack of balance and worsening jitters had made it impossible to navigate the terrain without her help.

"Cut through here," I said, pulling her into a narrow alleyway between two buildings.

"I'm cold … what are we doing? This is crazy and you're going to get us both killed." Her voice was both hushed and frightened.

I slowed as we approached Main Street. Fifteen feet from the end of the alleyway, my legs wobbled, then gave out in unison, causing Lori to move in closer. She slid an arm around my waist, forced now to support even more weight, and leaned me against the building to my right.

"Just rest here for a second," she said, her face inches from mine. I felt her breath on my cheek—could smell whisky and cigarettes. Any luminescence the waxing moon above normally provided the scene was now partially obscured by the two-storied buildings. I could just barely make out her features in the darkness.

"Look and see if the street is clear," I prompted.

She stayed where she was—looking at me in the darkness for several long beats before huffing and scurrying off. I heard a loud metal clang and then, "Shit!" She'd stepped on something metallic that could be a church bell, for the ruckus it made.

When she returned she was out of breath. "It looks okay." She repositioned her arm around my waist and together we moved toward Main Street. "Watch your step here," she said, veering me around what looked like a stack of iron pipes. She halted a moment—looked both ways—then propelled us forward. "Where to now?"

I pointed off to the right. "Get us across the street."

We were now more exposed—in the moonlight's soft glow and the randomly placed oil lanterns.

"Where?" she asked, her impatience growing.

I gestured with my chin. "We're close … over there … right across from the corral."

She was holding up much of my weight and beginning to slow. "You mean the undertaker's? You're going to the fucking undertaker's?"

I nodded.

"I'm not going in there, it's stacked with bodies. No way I'm going in there!"

First one, then another gunshot loudly disrupted the evening stillness, their echoes booming down Tombstone's Main Street like a runaway train. Behind us, near the entrance to the saloon, someone hollered, "Get out here!"

Lori veered us up onto the wood-planked walkway that ran alongside the buildings' frontage. Obscured in the darkness, we paused and came to a halt. We'd been discovered.

"I'm calling you out. Come out and face me like a m … m … man, if you got any … any balls."

His slurred words trailed off, and I heard distant retching. Someone was drunker than a skunk and calling someone else out for an impromptu street gunfight.

Relieved, I said, "Keep going."

It took us another minute to reach the undertaker's. To our mutual horror, what were three empty coffins, propped up near the undertaker's front door, were now anything but empty. I didn't recognize two of the men, but the one in the middle—in the largest of the three coffins—I did. Butch Cassidy stood almost vertically upright, his eyes closed and his slack-jawed mouth agape. A handwritten sign, tied with twine, hung over his chest:

Loose Lips Sink Ships

I turned to see Lori, staring at neither the sign nor Butch, but directly at me. Her expression said it all: *What the hell have you gotten me into?*

The ruckus down the street was escalating, for which I was most grateful. Two more gunshots rang out. I tried the door—locked. With a glance back toward the saloon, I saw more men on the street, amidst loud hoots and hollering.

I drew my gun and, holding it by the barrel, used the butt to break the windowpane to the left of the door, directly behind the closest coffin. The sound of glass shattering seemed as loud to me as those booming gunshots. We stayed still and listened.

"You're not so tough. I'm going to put … put a bullet in your bl … bl … black heart … Billy the Kid."

Lori and I exchanged glances. Someone had called Billy out.

I reached an arm in and unlatched the door from the inside. I opened the door to the sound of glass shards being pushed aside.

Lori grabbed my arm. "What about me?"

"What about you?" I asked, barely staying on my feet.

"You going to leave me out here?" Her eyes flickered over to the dead man, a waxed mustache on his pallid face, less than a foot away.

"It's up to you ... I'll need ten minutes in here."

She looked as if she had eaten something foul. "What are you going to do in here?"

"I need to get close to the electrical panels."

Her features relaxed as she remembered I'd mentioned that to her before. Glancing at the dead man again, she said, "I'm coming in with you."

As if giving emphasis to her words, a single gunshot blasted out. A roar of voices cheered at what I suspected was Billy the Kid, drawing down on a drunken fool who never had a chance. Something occurred to me: They'd need the undertaker's services again tonight.

"We need to hurry," I said, stumbling into the death-scented air. "Close the door behind you."

Lori moved to my side, slid her arm around me again, pulling herself close. I suspected it wasn't entirely to help me walk. Colman had extinguished the oil lamp before leaving earlier, which made it nearly impossible to see anything in the room now. That was probably a good thing, considering Lori's state of anxiety.

"Which door?"

"Huh?"

"There are two doors at the back. Which door leads to the electrical panels?"

"I don't know ... how am I supposed to remember something like that?"

We shuffled forward—Lori kept her left arm stretched out, and me my right.

She screamed.

By the time I placed my palm over her lips, she quieted, but I kept it there just the same. Neither of us moved for thirty seconds. I whispered sternly, "What the hell's wrong with you?"

She tore my hand away. "Ugh … I touched … a face."

"Keep your hand at your side." I moved us sideways and then forward, trying to recall the room's layout, which consisted of four tables and a desk. I remembered there were bodies laid out around the room's perimeter, as well as others, propped up on stacks of old wooden soapboxes.

It took us another two minutes, in the pitch-blackness, to make it to the rear of the room. Like Lori, I'd planted my own outstretched hand onto several faces, a fact I kept to myself.

Feeling I could remain standing on my own, and knowing time was not on our side, I said, "You try the door on the left."

She let me go and I heard her step away. With my palms flat against the wall, I sidestepped to the right until my fingers brushed against a door's frame. I found the doorknob, turned it, and opened the door.

I heard a muffled scream, followed by hurried steps as Lori nearly bowled me over.

"You really need to calm down!" I grunted, between gritted teeth.

"That wasn't the electrical room. I felt—"

I cut her off, "It doesn't matter. This room is where I need to be."

"It's pitch black. How can you possibly know—"

I cut her off again: "Just stay here and don't move." I heard a desperate squeal come from the back of her throat.

"Ten minutes, then we're out of here." I pulled away from her and used my outstretched arms to navigate the room.

Like an invisible beacon, I detected high-voltages emanating off to my right. Three further steps and I felt the cold surface of a metal electrical cabinet. My hands followed its rectangular contours—first down, then beneath—where a large conduit came up through the floor. Instantly, I knew what I needed was here. I lowered to my knees and brought my head forward. In an instant, I was tapped in, and, in that same instant, knew that he, the presence, the unknown entity … was there—waiting for me.

Chapter 34

Typically, tapping in was a calming, rejuvenating experience. Sure, there were always drawbacks—drawbacks akin to those suffered by a heroin addict. While their need engendered a cost, both financial and physical, mine entailed a search, inconvenience, and what I sometimes find lurking in the dark shadows of my own mind. Whether it was a needle for the junkie, or an electrical conduit for me, if either wasn't readily accessible, then terrible and similar physical withdrawals ensued.

I no sooner entered into an altered state of consciousness than the same ominous inner presence drew near. Even as my physical form began to strengthen, like a dark cloud, unease permeated the inner recesses of my mind. Seeing the form approach, it occurred to me that I'd given it little thought while conscious. I now wondered if it was because I didn't consider it anything more than a dream figure, or if it so unnerved me, I'd relegated mere thought of it to the realm where nightmares are stored away—too awful to bring forth into the light of day.

"Stay away from me," I said.

As though there was a wall of diffused glass between us—only small areas clear enough to actually see through—the specter's out-of-focus form nevertheless appeared in repulsive clarity: greenish scales on the upper part of an arm, a lower lip fringed with wispy tuffs of hair, a small, snake-like eye.

"It is my turn."

"I don't know what that means. Stay away!"

"I can force you … make you linger here, like me, all alone and forgotten."

"Why me?"

"You know why. You pretend not to know what you know," the specter said, its words sounding wet—indicative of someone speaking through copious amounts of saliva.

I stepped back as a hazy, undefined arm above a three-fingered hand drew close, held at bay only by the nearly invisible barrier between us. The other arm came up; both hands were curled and claw-like. Then I saw it—a fracture. Like miniscule spreading branches, the hairline crack kept growing more and more visible. The ominous presence began using claw-like fingers to pry open a tiny section of the barrier.

"Where did you come from?" I asked.

"Why do you ask what you already know the answer to?"

"Tell me anyway."

"From the energy, of course. From the limitless."

"Why can't you return, go back to where you initially came from?"

A section of the barrier was spreading apart. It wouldn't be long before a hand reached through.

His answer never came.

"Doc!"

I felt her arms encircle me as she mumbled again, "Doc!"

I was consciously drawn back into the pitch black electrical room. "What … what is it?"

Lori whispered, "There's someone in the front room."

"How long have I been in here?"

"I don't know … maybe thirty minutes. Seemed to me

like forever. What have you been doing all this time?"

"Never mind that. Did you close the door to this room?"

"Of course I did."

I saw a band of soft light appear underneath the door. Colman had lit a lantern.

"What if they come in here?" she asked.

I looked around the now slightly illuminated room. Wooden buckets and a mop were in one corner, stacks of dry goods on the opposite wall, and what looked like a bundle of large black trash bags. No, not trash bags—body bags. And I saw a second door, directly across from the door we first entered. I figured it led outside to the back of the building.

I thought of the broken glass near the front door. "We need to get out of here." I took her by the hand, then hesitated. I heard their muffled, but clearly understandable voices—Billy the Kid talking to Colman. They were addressing the break in, but not coming to any definitive conclusion. Colman was on the defensive.

I turned to Lori. "Go out the back door and head for the saloon; just follow the same path back. Stay out of sight."

"What about you?"

"I'll be right behind you … go!" I whispered, putting more urgency into my voice.

Lori moved to the back door, fiddled with the lock, and quietly opened it. Moonlight filled the doorway—the voluptuous silhouette of her figure hesitated a moment before she hurriedly moved out of sight. I closed the door behind her.

I brought my attention back to Billy the Kid and the undertaker. I needed a clear sightline to read people's thoughts and I recalled the undertaker's oil lamp—the soft light it threw out. With care, I turned the doorknob, slowly easing the door into the main room open by less than an inch. Billy and Colman were standing at the same table Butch lay on earlier, talking about the next morning and something about a wagon.

"It's about twenty minutes by flatbed. Jude or Jordan will take you ... just make sure all the bodies are included in the load. None can show any indication of a bullet hole, so cut away what you need to," Billy said.

"You've already made that perfectly clear," Colman said.

"Once that's done, get them all in body bags for transporting. The smell is becoming unbearable in here."

"How many more do you anticipate—"

"Don't worry about that. Just take care of the bodies here for the time being," Billy the Kid said.

Perhaps due to the extended amount of time I was able to tap in, I peered into Billy's mind with surprising clarity. His thoughts were preoccupied by a hand-delivered message he'd received from HQ in Denver. The new co-leader, his elected counterpart, would be arriving in the morning. Billy the Kid—*Palmolive*—stood trancelike in the semi-darkness, watching the undertaker assemble the tools of his trade on top of the drunken, dead, gunslinger's chest—a rusty handsaw; a long, thin-bladed knife; and some kind of pliers or forceps.

Billy the Kid leaned back against an adjacent table. As he chewed on a stubborn hangnail, his eyes watched the undertaker's bony thin fingers pluck the sharp knife up in one hand and the forceps in the other, though his thoughts were somewhere else. The news he'd received was bringing out a small measure of forbearance, but something else, too ... yes, both a longing and a lust. Again, I saw the naked image of Heidi Goertz. Then I saw her dressed the way Palmolive had last seen her, wearing a smart-looking, dark gray uniform. A band on her upper left arm held a black swastika on a field of red. She'd promised him that the Neo-Nazi bullshit would be left behind, agreeing that the WZZ, and its fanatical Adolf Hitler-reborn prejudices, had no place in today's modern realm. But she had lied. She never really intended to let go of her precious WZZ's true directives. He cursed his own weakness. *How had she so captivated him?* The Order—the shadow-government—secretly influencing geopolitical circumstances for nearly a century, was an organization disliked but readily accepted by corporate moguls and world leaders alike. Considered a necessity of modern times—the underlying glue—that bound and kept geopolitical, and all unstable powers from going too far astray in any one direction. The Order was very possibly being derailed, now that there was a new co-leader—Heidi Goertz.

I watched as Palmolive mentally conjured up long-past images of World War II: Hitler in his motorcade—arm defiantly outstretched toward a frenetic cheering crowd; the death camps, where thousands of emaciated, half-naked Jews were herded into large, windowless, brick buildings. Palmolive pondered on a new-world-order-to-be under the influence of the WZZ. Even now, the subterranean thoroughfares beneath the United States and Europe buzzed with activity. Armies, not huge, but highly trained, were being positioned to seize control of major municipal electric and water works across both massive geographic areas. Those actions alone would bring the United States to her knees, Palmolive had little doubt about that. The world was heading into a very dark and menacing era. Was his obsession with Heidi that powerful, he asked himself? Yes, the answer was yes. He would do anything to keep her. It was far too late now, anyway. The WZZ had managed to slither its way into the most powerful organization in the world. He and Heidi would rule the world together.

I found it difficult to extricate myself from Palmolive's

crazy mental ranting. At least I had the intel I'd come here for. Now I could get out of here and, at the very least, warn Baltimore.

I touched the snaps at my collar. *Time to bring in the cavalry?* No—not yet. Tomorrow Palmolive and Heidi Goertz, together, would be dealt with. Both needed to die … then I'd contact SIFTR.

Chapter 35

Rudy Palmolive, aka Billy the Kid, left the gore and stench of the undertaker's storeroom convinced that together, the saloon girl and Doc Holliday were responsible for the break in there. They were spotted together behind the saloon earlier and neither had been seen since. Why? He didn't know, but all too soon he would. The woman, the vulgar whore with the big tits, would easily be dispensed with. Hell, she was here on a one-way ticket, anyway. But Doc, or Troy McAlister, was far more important—a crucial addition into the ranks of the Order.

Billy the Kid crossed the street and heard a loud metallic sound, akin to the gong of a church bell. He drew his Colt and slowed his pace. The street was clear—no one else around at this ungodly hour. He moved with caution, slowing as he approached the nearest alleyway. He raised the barrel and eased back the hammer until it clicked into place. At the building's corner he peered into the blackness of the alley beyond. It was faint, but he was hearing something … breathing? In a quick, well-practiced movement he stepped out into the open, his weapon raised.

"Whoever you are, come out with your hands up. Do it now. I'm a very good shot … you don't want to test me."

There was movement, fifteen feet back in the alleyway. Billy adjusted his aim—tracking the sound with the barrel of his gun. The culprit emerged, looking guilty—ears down and tail between his legs.

Billy continued to hold the animal in his sights. Ol' Yeller approached and after taking two steps forward, sat down. As he looked up, he tilted his head first to one side, then the other.

"Fucking mutt … I should …" his words trailed off. He released the hammer and re-holstered his gun as he turned away. Then, taking two steps, he suddenly drew his Colt, whirled back around, and pulled the trigger in one fluid motion.

* * *

Billy the Kid entered the saloon and caught the eye of Jude, back at the Faro table. Interestingly, Doc Holliday was there too. By the size of the stack of chips in front of him, he was winning—again. That, by itself, since the game was rigged, was a mystery. Added to the fact he'd been snooping around didn't bode well for the man's longevity. More and more, the man was becoming a real concern … least of which was his obvious familiarity with firearms and edged weaponry.

Billy headed for the bar, arriving at the same time a shot of whisky was placed down on the polished mahogany bartop. Downing the whisky without acknowledging the bartender, he turned and watched the large crowd huddled around the Faro table. Holliday seemed to be popular with the other men. He raised his glass toward the bartender—signaling for another. He found it strange: McAlister, thoroughly vetted, was simply a nerdy tech genius; he'd capitalized on several inventions, making millions in the process. Repeatedly, he had showed interest in the Order, being introduced to it by another longstanding member. Arriving here, facial recognition software confirmed his identity. Billy the Kid's eyes narrowed as he took in the room, before focusing on McAlister again. *So what the hell game are you playing?*

Jordan entered through the swinging door. Spotting Billy the Kid, he joined him at the bar.

"Check the monitors like I asked?" Billy questioned.

Jordan nodded. "McAlister's been nosy. He and the whore were inside the undertaker's place. It was too dark to see what they were doing."

Billy made a face as if he'd smelled something foul. "You say they were there together?"

Jordan nodded.

Billy the Kid let out a breath with a perplexed expression.

"Dolan says the whore's been in her room ever since." Jordan added, "She told one of the others, going on shift, that she's not feeling well."

Billy the Kid considered the news. Dolan, who monitored the security feeds all around town, though mostly in the saloon, was known to nod off. The saloon ladies were housed in the building next door, unless entertaining guests in the rooms upstairs. Everything was recorded, but the whole point of having a manned security station was to catch issues when they first arose.

"What is she doing … specifically?"

"I checked her room feed and rewound the tape. She was lying down for a while then turned off the light. It's not one of the rooms with a night vision camera. So we have to assume she's still in there. Do you want me to go and check on her?" Jordan asked.

Billy considered it a moment before saying, "Yeah, go check on her, then put a bullet in her head while you're at it."

Jordan held up mid-step, checking to see if his boss was dead serious. Billy the Kid, from his grim expression, made sure Jordan understood he was. "Clean up any mess you make," he added. "Then tell Colman to collect the body."

* * *

Lori was well aware of the ill-disguised camera in her room. From being in the security room with all its monitors, when bringing that fat fuck Dolan his food, or having to service him in any number of humiliating ways, she knew that all cameras in the dorms were totally blind once the lights were turned off. Doc had told her to run—that he'd run himself if he were in her shoes. He couldn't guarantee her safety any longer. From what he'd mentioned, there were armed security teams always on patrol on the outskirts of town, so she'd need to be extra careful—stay out of sight and keep quiet. He told her once back again at the lodge to find someone named Carmen there, who would know what to do to get her to safety. Doc also mentioned, if all else failed, to head into the town of Guffy and find the sheriff there, someone named Corki.

Lori left as soon as she'd turned off the bedside lamp in her room. There wasn't time to change or pack a duffle bag; the only saving grace—exchanging high heels for flats. Taking advantage of the time she'd spent in the security room, she moved between the buildings in obscurity. She knew where to go to avoid the night-vision cameras. Hearing approaching footfalls, she held up in an alcove and watched as the mortician hurried down the middle of Main Street toward the saloon.

Her heart pounded in her chest—it was now do or die

time. She could make it back to her room unnoticed, if she went back now. She looked back the way she'd come and bit her lower lip. *God! How did I get myself into this mess?* Who was she kidding … she knew exactly how. Desperate, a single mother of a ten-year-old boy, in debt up to her eyeballs because of her ex-husband's gambling losses, now hers, she wasn't making it on her measly, corporate administrative assistant's salary. So she borrowed money from the petty-cash bin; then did it again, and then again. When caught red-handed, her boss was more than willing to work out some kind of *arrangement*. Lori was well aware of the effect she had on men—the good ol' boy nudges between the gawking assholes in the break room. Going to jail wasn't ever an option. Thus, an arrangement with her boss was made that seemed to be never-ending, until an opportunity arose that would wipe her slate clean—one last, final, humiliating deed. He promised her.

She heard the saloon's doors swing open and closed—Colman was back inside. She darted across the street and disappeared into the dark space between the Guns and Ammo shop and the building next door. She slowed, coming to the end of the alleyway. Beyond was an open field that stretched toward distant foothills. She thought back to the bank of monitors and couldn't recall ever seeing that particular vista in any of them. Was it the right direction to the lodge? Yes, she was fairly certain it was. She thought briefly of the man called Doc Holliday and wondered if she'd ever see him again. Then, she thought of Ben, her boy, and ran for the hills.

Chapter 36

I wasn't just conflicted, I was furious with myself. Had I actually done that, told that poor woman with the alabaster skin and fiery-auburn hair to head out on her own, in the dead of night, and try to escape this treacherous town? What chance could she have against highly trained, roving, special ops teams? I flashed back mentally to the sounds of gunfire, and Butch Cassidy's bulk hitting the hard saloon floor. Another misjudgment, on my part. And now Lori's body, I feared, would soon be added to the stacks of other dead bodies at the undertaker's. Christ! I made a move to stand and go after her, then saw Billy the Kid entering the saloon, heading toward the bar. Out of the corner of my eye I watched him and entered into his mind.

Billy had suspicions about me, but for now, at least, that was as far as they went. He wanted what Troy McAlister—I—could bring to the Order. Jordan entered the bar and joined Billy the Kid's side. I mentally listened in on their conversation—heard Billy the Kid tell Jordan to go to her room and shoot her in the head. Suddenly, I was very glad I'd told her to run. *Run Lori … run like hell!*

I brought my attention back to the Faro table and the men around me. Apparently, I'd missed the last round and let everything ride. I lost and, subsequently, so did all the others—the players sitting around the table, and the ones standing around us and making side bets.

"Nobody wins every hand, that's why it's called gambling," I said, offering up a shrug and a crooked smile.

The game resumed and Jude, playing banker, said, "Place or remove your bets."

His palm, hidden beneath the table, rested on his gun. Apparently, I'd been winning to the point he was ready to call me out. I wondered how Billy the Kid would react to one of his potential indoctrinates being gunned down by one of his subordinates. Jude glanced at me, then toward his boss, still standing at the bar. It was time for me to cash in my chips.

I stood, and like before, gestured toward the small mountain of chips in front of me. "That's it for me, all you swindlers and shysters. You can have my chips. Play nice now, boys." I rose, hearing more than a few groans and grunts spewed, some insults about my manhood, then something about a goat that I didn't quite catch. I headed for the exit; I needed to check in at the jail.

* * *

"Where the fuck have you been?" Johnny Ringo blared, his white-knuckled fists wrapped tightly around the bars of his cell.

I crinkled my nose—the smell in here was even worse than before. "What, nobody's come in here … since—"

I cut myself short, seeing his crazed expression. "What? What is it?"

"You mean besides the fact that the shit bucket needs emptying and I haven't eaten since morning? Oh, and how about the fact they're going to fucking string me up first thing tomorrow?"

I shook my head: "No, Calamity Jane's no longer—"

Ringo, on the verge of hysterics, spat, "I know, you shot her between the eyes. Old news and that makes … no … fucking … difference!"

"What do you mean?"

"Jude or Jordan … I don't know who the hell is which, was in here less than an hour ago. As soon as they get back tomorrow from the silver mine, I'm to be taken to the top of the saloon. Then it's all over for me!" He made a hanging gesture—one hand clutching an invisible rope above his head, letting his tongue extend outside his mouth.

I shook my head. "You think they're going to hang you? Without a trial?" Then I remembered Billy's recent words to Jordan: *Shoot her in the head.* No, he was right. Any thought of a trial actually taking place here was quite ludicrous.

Ringo's anger quickly dissipated and he just looked beaten. "Come on, man," he said. "This isn't a real town … this isn't Tombstone, and I doubt I was ever supposed to leave this hellhole alive."

What he was saying was probably true. "Tell me, who are you, really? And how did you get involved with Palmolive?"

Ringo looked at me as if considering how much to share. "Guess it doesn't matter at this point. I'm Bobby Roper, a Washington lobbyist."

"For whom, what industry?"

"The gun lobby … NRA."

"How did you help Palmolive—the Order?"

He shook his head. "Palmolive wasn't sitting at the table then. All correspondence went through a woman, a Mrs. Gulliver. I never met her in person."

"What did you do for her?"

Again, Ringo hesitated: "I greased the wheels. I influenced, as much as any lobbyist could, that certain bills were fast-tracked—those dealing with legal procurement, and the use, if necessary, of automatic weapons for private security firms, other than the U.S.'s military personnel."

"You mean firms such as the Order? Shit, you helped arm the same organization that is now poised to overthrow the U.S. government."

"I didn't know the scope of things then. Hey, there was a lot of positive buzz behind the scenes about the Order. It was the answer to government gridlock … the huge U.S. debt, and America quickly becoming China's bitch amongst the world powers."

"So what happened? Why are you here?"

"Look, I may look like a dirty guttersnipe now, standing next to a bucket of shit, but I'm Harvard educated, pulled down a solid two mil a year, and lived in a three-story D.C. brownstone. I got greedy—crossed the line. I started to realize what the Order was really about. I complained to too many people—the wrong people. When I got the invitation to bring the family here, I thought it was their way to make amends, maybe hash out my concerns."

"Tell me about this trip to a silver mine. What's that all about?" I asked.

"It's like … um … a field trip. Everyone's been talking about it ever since yesterday. Rumor has it Billy the Kid is going to assemble the lot of us inside the mine to announce key new positions within the Order. It's what everyone is fucking here for. It's the big reveal."

More like a one-way ticket to an early grave, I thought. But, there again, not everyone here was to be killed—so something didn't add up. I said, "You sure everyone's to be included in the mine trip?"

"Yeah. Well, it's supposedly a small space. There'll be two groups, one before the other."

"Let me guess, your invitation was for the first group."

Ringo nodded, as realization reached his face. "Yeah … until I was arrested and thrown in here. You're thinking the early group will be killed in an accident or something … maybe a cave-in?"

I nodded. That was exactly what I was thinking.

"Then why hang me? Why not simply include me in the first group to the mine? Be done with me right there."

"My guess, provide an example to those left alive—the ones chosen to be indoctrinated into the Order. Another opportunity for Palmolive to show what disloyalty looks like."

"So I'm fucked either way?"

I didn't answer him, instead musing that I hadn't received an invitation to the mine for either time. I reached into my pocket and came out with the master key to both jail cells. Ringo instinctively took a step back while I unlocked the door, swinging its metal bars open. Ringo's eyes flashed toward the jailhouse door behind me.

"You don't have to make a run for it, at least not from me. I'm letting you go, but with one condition."

"What? Anything! Just ask. I'll be in your debt—"

I cut him off, "Shut up and listen to me. Lori, the one bringing you your food—"

"You mean June?"

"Just listen to me. June, as you call her, is on the run. They were going to kill her. She's heading for the lodge, then to the sheriff in Guffy."

"There are patrols. Palmolive's armed security is out there."

"That's right. She chose to take a chance, make a run for it rather than sit around and wait for Jordan or Jude to shoot her here. I'm giving you the same opportunity. But I want your word you'll help the girl if you see her. Help her get back to her son." I weighed Ringo's thoughts carefully. Even the slightest indication of deceit and I was prepared to shoot him where he stood.

"I promise. She seemed okay. And, by the way, I'd have helped her without your fucking ultimatum," he said angrily.

He was telling the truth. "I believe you. If you find her, you'll both need to stay out of sight … long term. The Order isn't going to forgive and forget."

"I've got some relatives in Denver …"

I stepped outside the entrance into the street and looked in both directions. "It's clear. Best you head on out. Stay in the shadows, close to the buildings."

Without another word, Ringo sped away from the jail.

Chapter 37

Out of breath and scared, Lori ran to the tree line and entered a forest of dense, tall evergreens. For the tenth time she chided herself for her hasty decision not to change out of her dress. *Damn! How much time could it take to slip on a pair of jeans and grab a sweatshirt? A couple of minutes?* Now, even with her arms wrapped tightly around her, her shivering became uncontrollable. She knew that maintaining a quick pace would keep her from freezing her ass off. She cupped her fingers to her mouth and breathed hard to warm them. As her steamy breath quickly dissipated in the chill, her fingers still felt as if they were going numb.

Thirty minutes earlier, she'd made it safely across the open grassy expanse, between the rear of town and the lower foothills. She'd always been a fast runner—in high school she'd preferred sports, such as track and field, to other activities like cheerleading. Not that she'd been pretty enough for that then, anyway. She thought back to those times, when life was so much simpler. Boys hadn't known what to make of her then—with freckles and flaming red hair and rather shapeless—a thin, boyish body better suited for unisex gym shorts than short cheerleading outfits. That was until things started to change her mid-senior year. Her flaming red hair mellowed to a more attractive auburn, and her boyish body gave way to more feminine curves. She well fit the epitome of the term *late bloomer*. From then on, like now, men pursued her in one way or another.

Lori stumbled over a low tree stump, stifled a scream, and caught herself just in time from falling to the ground. Before becoming engulfed in the forest's thick growth, she was able to keep her bearings by sighting on Pikes Peak, off in the far distance. She knew it was the highest summit of the Colorado Mountains around her and roughly in the direction of the lodge. But the further into the trees she went, the taller and denser the trees became. She was afraid she'd come so far off course that she'd bypassed the lodge entirely. Her heart pounded in her chest and her lungs burned to the extent she feared she'd keel over from a heart attack. *I'm not remotely in shape for this kind of workout.* Then, thinking of her son and determined to see him again, hold him in her arms, she persevered on.

Seeing a small clearing up ahead, Lori allowed herself to slow down to a fast walk. From there, she hoped to reestablish her sightline. She stepped into the open glen and found herself standing in a bright swath of silver moonlight. Looking toward the horizon, she glimpsed Pikes Peak, off in the distance, left of where she'd thought. She realized she needed to substantially veer left to get back on course. *Shit, getting lost in this wilderness is not an option.* She picked up her pace, hoping and praying the tree growth would become less dense, helping her to not lose sight of the ridgeline completely.

Startled, she heard a noise ahead that sounded like the distant snapping of a tree branch. She brought her steady jog down to a slow, cautious walk. The ground was covered in a cushion of pine needles, thankfully masking her footfalls. Her dress, though, with its stiff petticoat under layers of material, made a pronounced rustling sound that was anything but stealthy. Again, she cursed herself for not changing. Coming to a full stop, she waited and listened. Immediately, the chilly air enveloped her—the chattering of her teeth was joined in cadence with her body's acute shivering.

Movement! Something dark was moving directly in front of her. Lori's muscles tensed—ready to run for her life—her eyes widening when she realized what she was seeing: A patrol of five … no six armed men, dressed in black. They were moving quietly, perpendicular to the direction she was heading. She heard the soft murmurs of voices—then someone chuckled. They were no more than twenty paces ahead of her. *That's right … just keep going, assholes.* Relief washed over her as the team of armed killers slowly proceeded onward. She stood perfectly still, knowing all it would take was one man to turn his head and catch a glimpse of her bright scarlet dress—so completely out of place in the middle of nowhere.

Lori took one tentative step forward and then another, then stopped. The rustling of her skirt seemed as loud to her as a jet engine compared to the cold night stillness. She opted to give it a few more minutes, letting more distance expand between her and the patrol.

Oh God no—she heard scuffling and fast footsteps. Then, running feet and elevated, excited, voices. *They must be coming back for me!* Lori squinted into the darkness, trying to get some indication the direction they would be coming.

Multiple gunshots cracked and echoed into the night around her. Lori spun, paralyzed by fear—wanting to run, but not certain which direction would lead to safety. She heard someone excitedly call out *Ringo!* Or, *it's Ringo*. The only Ringo she knew of was Johnny Ringo, sitting in a jail cell several miles back. Had he escaped? She hoped he had and that he'd keep them occupied all night long.

Gunshots continued to ring out but seemed farther

away now. Lori listened and determined the security team was definitely heading away from her. She let out a long breath, spotted Pikes Peak right where it should be, and ran toward it.

* * *

Johnny Ringo ran flat out for fifteen minutes straight—running like he'd never run in his life. As far as he knew, his wife and little girl were back at the lodge, still waiting for him. Tomorrow, Mandy would receive the devastating news that her husband of eight years was killed in a freak accident; some kind of silver mine cave-in. Nope, that was not going to happen.

After what he estimated to be about two miles—crossing the field into the foothills, then climbing higher into the mountains and tree line—he saw no sign of the armed patrols. He wondered if they called it quits after a certain point at night? Maybe start up again at first light. With luck now, it would be clear sailing all the way to the lodge.

Ringo thought of the pretty girl, June, whose real name was Lori. She'd been good to him. He could see she didn't want to be here, either—was just as much a prisoner as himself. He kept an eye out for her and had every intention of keeping his promise to help her, if he spotted her. But he wasn't going out of his way to do that; wasn't about to get caught in the process.

Ringo, feeling encouraged, jumped over a toppled tree trunk with renewed enthusiasm. Unfortunately, he didn't quite clear it with his right boot and landed awkwardly on his left foot. There was the unmistakable crack of his tibia fracturing. He'd heard that same cracking sound twenty years earlier, after jumping off old man Cowley's tin-roofed chicken shed. Same bone … different leg. The sound preceded a searing, agonizing burst of pain. Johnny Ringo let loose a combination of howls and cries that carried for several miles. Lying on the ground holding his damaged leg in both hands, and doing his best not to move an inch, or chance bringing on additional, racking, pain, Ringo could do little as the approaching team of men descended upon him.

A substantial section of a nearby tree trunk exploded into dust, along with the simultaneous sounds of automatic weapon fire. Ringo felt the first three rounds enter his body. The fourth one killed him.

Chapter 38

In the early dawn hours I awoke to some kind of commotion below on Main Street. It took me a moment to realize where I was. I recognized the faded, yellowed wallpaper covering the wall on the far side of the bed. I was in my room above the saloon, still wearing yesterday's increasingly ripe, smelly clothes. Listening, I heard the sounds of horses and squeaky rigging, probably an old wagon, and the raised voices of more than a few rowdy men.

My thoughts first flashed to Lori, then over to Ringo, with dread. Did they make it safely out of town or had Palmolive's security team gunned them down like stray dogs? My hatred for Billy the Kid—*Palmolive*—was elevating to new heights. I mentally vowed to put an end to that lunatic soon. I sat up, suddenly remembering what was to happen this morning—Billy the Kid's scheduled field trip out to the silver mine. I wasn't officially invited, still I needed to get up there. Then I noticed something beneath the door. *A piece of paper?* I scrambled out of bed and snatched-up the envelope. It was addressed from Billy the Kid. I tore it open and smiled ... *better late than never.* It was a last-minute invitation, probably delivered earlier this morning. It looked like I'd be going to the Silver Mine after all.

I needed coffee to get my brain working. Short term, I

needed to figure out how to throw a wrench in Billy's plans to thin out the herd of potential candidates into the Order. Beyond that, stopping what was appearing more and more like a nationwide cataclysmic attack on the rise was paramount. In any event, I'd come to the conclusion that no matter what happened, I was calling it quits on the mission. Whether that meant simply riding out of town to join Carmen back at the lodge, or going so far as to unsnap my collar snaps, thereby bringing in the cavalry, was still up in the air.

* * *

Ten minutes later, spruced up and wearing a clean shirt, the pinned-on sheriff's star on my chest, my black Stetson on my head, and my holstered Colt worn low on my right hip, I descended the stairs to an empty saloon. Tempted to follow the smell of hot coffee into the kitchen, I reluctantly veered right toward the saloon entrance and stepped through its swinging doors to a flurry of activity outside. There were almost a hundred men preparing for the big hayride out to the mine.

"Morning, Doc," one of the ever-present Faro gamblers said, atop his horse.

"Hey Doc!" the barkeep said, a broad smile on his face as he loaded the back of a flatbed wagon with supplies.

"Get enough beauty sleep in there, Doc?" another cowboy joked, whose face I didn't recognize.

I tipped my hat to each and saw Jude on horseback, riding down the street from the corral, with two saddled horses tethered behind him; one was the gray, Gunner, I'd ridden into town on.

"Go ahead and grab your horse, Sheriff," Jude said, maneuvering Gunner closer to me.

I took the reins and walked the horse away from the other one I recognized as the chestnut, Ticker. To my surprise, Billy the Kid appeared next to me and grabbed the reins of his horse too.

"Morning," I said.

"Good morning, Sheriff," he answered, with a pinched expression that only emphasized his bird-like demeanor. In the early morning sunlight, even more noticeable now, were the scores of tiny black moles distributed spottily over his face and down his neck. At first glance, they appeared to me like immobile black gnats.

Billy's horse, Ticker, began acting up, resisting the direction Billy the Kid wanted to lead him. He yanked hard on the horse's reins, violently jerking Ticker's head sideways. Instinctively, my hand moved to the grip of my six-shooter. I tried to think of a reason not to put a bullet in the back of the sadistic fucker's head right then. Leaving Heidi and Leon Goertz solely in charge of the Order—not to forget Pippa's still unknown predicament—was reason enough to hold off, as tempting as the desire was.

"You may want to find Butch's horse. That pinto, Potts, is a good horse … easier to manage," I said, adding, "Butch certainly won't be needing him."

Billy the Kid glared at me. "No. This is my horse and it'll stay that way until I decide otherwise."

The chestnut whinnied, both nostrils flaring, as he began walking backwards, tugging against the reins tightly held in Billy's outstretched hands. I stayed present in Billy the Kid's mind, ready to intervene. I wasn't going to stand by while another horse was mercilessly euthanized.

The surrounding crowd suddenly quieted, watching with fascination as the situation quickly spiraled out of control.

Digging in with his heels, Jude spurred his own horse forward, getting in between Billy and his now completely riled-up chestnut. "I got this, sir," he said, grabbing the tautly-held reins away from his boss, and bringing the horse back under control.

Looking into his mind, I saw that Billy the Kid was furious and contemplated shooting both the horse and Jude for humiliating him in front of everyone.

The abrupt sound of an approaching helicopter, bizarre and out of place in this 1880s-era environment, pulled Billy the Kid's attention away from the tussle with his horse. Again, I saw Heidi Goertz's face spring into Billy the Kid's mind. *Shit.* I now knew what Billy knew: The leader of the WZZ—the newly appointed co-leader of the Order—was inbound on that very helicopter. Both horse and Jude now forgotten, Billy couldn't be more excited. *Shit.*

The little man looked up, and spotting the helicopter coming in fast over the horizon, spun toward Jude.

"Just hold the fucking horse still while I mount up. Can you at least do that much?" Billy the Kid climbed up onto the saddle and wrenched the reins away from Jude. "Get that pinto … Potts … saddled up for Ms. Goertz. Have her join us up at the mine when she's ready."

* * *

Our excursion, close to one hundred of us, I figured, to the silver mine took nearly two hours. Mounted on Gunner, I was three horses back from Billy the Kid, riding on Ticker, who was leading the long procession. He periodically turned in his saddle, sometimes standing upright in the stirrups, to check on the progress of the caravan following behind him.

Jude brought up the rear, behind the two supply wagons, bumping unevenly along on what was more of a wide trail than a road. Earlier, I'd witnessed the bartender load food supplies onto one of the wagons; the other wagon had a canvas sheet strapped over its contents. I first wondered if it carried the remains of Butch Cassidy, Calamity Jane, and six or seven others, kept stored at the undertaker's. But no, they must have carted those remains up the mountain earlier—well out of view of curious onlookers.

"So what's your story, Doc?"

I turned to see a man about my age coax his horse up next to mine. He touched the brim of his hat. "I'm Clancy ..." He stopped, then began again, "I'm Sundance. We haven't officially met yet."

I'd seen him numerous times since I'd arrived, typically within earshot of Billy the Kid. I figured he was either an employee, or a confidant of some sort—maybe even a bodyguard. With a peek into his thoughts, I saw that he was all the above. He looked nothing like the sandy-haired actor Robert Redford, who played the folklore Sundance character in the movie. This Sundance had dark eyes, short black hair and a stocky build. Not only was he one of the few knowing what today was really about, he'd spent much of the previous afternoon and evening preparing this site.

I've peered into the minds of thousands of people since I'd acquired this ability. Each mind unique—not only the way in which information is processed, but also the way the information is stored. Emotions play a large part in what the mind's imagery draws on. Strong emotions, positive or negative, sometimes produce too intense a scene to look at for more than a moment or two, such as deadly car wrecks or the violent vestiges of a recent battlefield. You want to look but you need to turn away from them just as quickly. There is never an imagery shortage with emotional people.

I don't read minds, per se, in the same manner most people would assume. It's not like scanning a computer's hard drive and picking and choosing information. It doesn't work that way. No … I interpret imagery clips: Most are like three- or four-second video loops, where things, people, or events currently of importance to the person are replayed over and over. It can be disconcerting to view—especially when it obviously is a self-destructive, sometimes manic preoccupation I'm scanning. I spend as little time as possible in such minds. It is all too easy to get sucked into the drama—making his or her issues my own.

Sundance was a very emotional person, although looking at him, you'd think the opposite. His mind was a kaleidoscope of vivid images and color and conflicting thoughts. This tough guy, whose background was similar to my own—armed forces, then special ops, that eventually led to a career in one of the world's clandestine organizations. For me, it was SIFTR; for him, I guessed, CIA.

Sundance and I talked about the game of Faro, the lack of showers at the hotel, and the saloon girls. But he was only half-invested in the conversation. He had several repetitive mental loops reeling on constant replay. First, was an emotional goodbye—of him standing on the threshold of his Maryland suburban home; his two small tearful boys—their arms tightly wrapped around his legs—not wanting him to leave on another extended mission. Another loop, more recent, involved the firing of his six-shooter, nearby in the Colorado Mountains. It was a woman—a saloon girl. I recognized her—she'd taken a long drag on a cigarette and in its soft glow her attractive face was illuminated. Last night, she'd sat next to Lori in the near dark, outside the saloon's kitchen. Sundance had a relationship with her—was apparently in love with her. Sorting through the imagery was difficult, but from what I could piece together, Billy the Kid, informed by Jude of Sundance's relationship, ordered Sundance to kill her. She was a loose end and would not be allowed to leave Tombstone, in any case. So he'd put a bullet in her head late last night. Suffering, sleep deprived, and on the verge of unraveling, he was talking now about inconsequential things. Of even more importance, the man despised Billy the Kid as much as I did.

Chapter 39

The silver mine was pretty much what I'd expected it to be: A leveled-out stretch of property, just before the rise of a near-vertical scraggly hillside, with a dark, gaping mine opening that was supported by thick, re-purposed railroad ties. A set of train tracks led into the orifice, soon swallowed up in the darkness further on. Three wooden structures, all in splintered shambles, stood nearby. One, the furthest away, looked to be some kind of barrack—housing for the miners. The other two, closer in to the tracks, looked to be more crucial in the process of extracting silver ore.

While the mine's backdrop was mildly interesting, the abundance of pre-party setup decorations took center stage. Countless large and colorful helium balloons, all tugging at their strings to escape into the blue sky above, and scores of red, white, and blue triangular flags, fluttering on long guide wires, crisscrossed ten feet above our heads. Multiple picnic tables were oriented in a semicircle, close to the mine opening. One held tall brown liquor bottles, all lined up like erect soldiers, standing at attention. Another table provided plates and cups and eating utensils, and another held the still smoldering carcass of a wild boar. A chef of sorts, in a white apron, was cutting generous slices and placing the meat onto a platter. The other tables were dedicated to offering up cobs of corn, watermelon slices, platters of burgers and hotdogs, and heavy metal serving vats—their lids still secured. Off to the side, away from the festivities, stood five, empty, flatbed wagons. *Seems this is the feast before the reckoning to come …*

We were directed toward a makeshift corral, where we promptly dismounted and handed our reins over to the equivalent of an 1880s parking attendant. I watched as Gunner trotted off, not a care in the world. Sundance and I headed toward the picnic area where I immediately inhaled the aroma of fresh-brewed coffee. One table supported several industrial-sized coffee urns. Sundance apparently had the same idea, and together we made a beeline toward the stack of ready mugs. It was a help-yourself setup. After Sundance filled his mug to the brim, I did the same.

"Gather around, gentlemen." Billy the Kid, standing on an overturned wooden box, waved his hands over his head in a come-toward-me motion—only adding to his bird-like characteristics. "Before you run off to fill your bellies, I want to take a few moments of your time." Billy waited for a few men to leave the corral and join the assemblage. He looked down from his platform and scanned the crowd of close to one hundred men. The silence became a bit uncomfortable. In the pause both Sundance and I exchanged a quick glance. Billy finally continued on in a louder voice, "Well … you've made it!" He smiled and held out his hands, palms up, in much the same way countless church statues of the Messiah were presented—both fatherly and accepting.

"Let's dispense with all the pretense. I can now say it outright … welcome to the Order!"

The crowd cheered in unison—fists punched into the air while others high-fived the man next to him. Smiling, I watched as Billy the Kid again made exaggerated eye contact with every man there. What the men here did not know, but I did know, was that Billy was making a mental checklist who would, and who would not, survive through the afternoon. He knew each man's real name, along with his assigned Tombstone moniker. He knew each man's profession and what he meant to the advancement, if any, of the Order. I watched, through Billy's eyes, as the progression of two words flashed before his eyes when he glanced at each man: Live ... Die ... Live ... Live ... Die ... Die ... Die ... continuing on and on, till eventually his eyes reached mine. His eyes fell on me, wavered, then passed on, mentally condemning the man in front of me to die. By the time he finished, I was the only one he'd passed over. *A deliberate slight?* Yes ... I was certain it was. Perhaps he hadn't made up his mind yet, or was conflicted in some way I wasn't able to determine. What I was certain of was almost half the men here had been condemned to die.

I turned and found Sundance, standing off behind me, three men to my left. I zeroed in on his thoughts and looked for specifics on how the imminent cave-in would take place. Here, my ability to make mental suggestions became vital. Typically, I gently and unobtrusively guide another's thoughts in a certain direction, imparting my own influence—something visual—that will conjure up in them their own relative image loops that I'll then be able to decipher. In most instances, simply offering up certain visual words is all that's needed to start the progression of images forming within. I used the words *Explosives*, *C4*, and *Detonator*, and watched for Sundance's response. His mind quickly returned to the previous night spent here at the mine. The image loops I was observing were dark: Within the confined tunnels of the mine, multiple flashlight beams, like miniature spotlights, shone down on a singular small box, filled with wires, a circuit board, and a pasty chunk of c4 explosive. Interpreting what I was viewing, along with the steady progression of other images, it seemed that Sundance, along with three accomplices, had placed a total of six charges within the mine's interior—hidden close to crucial support structures. The charges, connected wirelessly, were set to explode simultaneously. *Huh … wirelessly? Through solid rock, plus all the twists and turns inside the mountain?* That, I knew from my own experience in the military, would take government-grade equipment. With a little more probing, I discovered the Order was using the latest high-tech mining system—one involving magnetic radio waves, whereby a signal is generated through a loop that's wrapped around a pillar placed deep within the mine. When the signal is sent through a loop of wires it creates a momentary magnetic field. That magnetic field, essentially, creates a bubble of magnetic energy, which rises to the surface. Somewhere here, external to the mine—perhaps higher up on the mountain—was another antenna, an inductor. The way I saw it, I had two options: either find the wireless detonator switch, or find and destroy that second antenna. I scanned the mountain along the ridgeline, far above the opening of the mine. All I could see were tall evergreen trees. Hell, it could be anywhere. The crowd began to dissipate around me, everyone moving off toward the food tables. Glancing back, I noticed Sundance lurking behind, unmoving, watching me as I scanned the ridgeline. *Shit!*

I nodded toward him. "Ready to grab some grub?"

"Nah … go ahead, Doc. Enjoy yourself." He took a steely glance in Billy's direction before heading off alone toward the corral. It was clear to me that the guy was quickly losing it. And why shouldn't he be? Only last night, he'd set up charges within the mine in order to commit mass murder. Finished with that chore, he met up with his girlfriend and promptly fired a bullet into her head. He'd never slept—everything done in the pursuit of loyalty to Palmolive and the

Order. But his conflicting emotions were exacting a toll, plus a heavy dose of self-loathing. What I was witnessing in Sundance's mind was akin to a volcano's eventual eruption. When that happened, I wondered if I'd be able to use the fallout to my advantage.

Using one of the empty flatbed wagons as a stage, two young cowboys—one with a banjo, the other a guitar—started playing a familiar folk song. I headed in the direction of the mine, where Billy the Kid and Jude were speaking together in hushed voices. I figured it wouldn't be long now before the men would be ushered into the mine, under some pre-planned pretense. I needed to find the detonator switch before it was too late. They both glanced up as I approached, neither looking particularly pleased to see me.

"What do you want? Grub's that way," Jude said, gesturing toward the picnic tables.

"Thought you might want to know … I let Johnny Ringo go last night."

They silently looked at me for a moment and I knew from their similar expressions that this wasn't news to them. They already knew full well what I'd done; had probably watched the whole thing on security video.

Billy looked in my direction. "What you did is not news to me, but *why* is another matter."

I didn't answer him right away, as if contemplating the question. Instead, I mentally inserted my own question—*where did I leave that wireless detonator*—into Billy's consciousness. Immediately, looking nervous, he patted his front vest pocket. Okay, there was one of them. I mentally inserted the same question into Jude's mind—*where did I leave that wireless detonator?* Jude didn't reach for a pocket, like Billy. Instead, he looked toward Billy the Kid's vest. That was promising. There seemed to be only one detonator switch and Billy was pocketing it.

"Look, you appointed me sheriff, Billy. With Calamity Jane out of the picture I went ahead and made a management decision. Added to that, I had enough of emptying his shit bucket. Tell me … how is it possible for any one person to shit that much?"

Billy the Kid continued to stare at me for several long beats before abruptly laughing out loud. He slapped me on the back and shook his small, bird-like, head. "Doc … I don't know if I should be impressed by your initiative, or if I should shoot you for flagrant disobedience." He continued to laugh, then, looking over to Jude with raised eyebrows, asked, "What do you think, Jude? What should I do with this guy?"

Jude hesitantly smiled, which was, of course, only for his boss's sake. In a blur, he drew his Colt .45. I had a feeling he was well practiced using a six-shooter, but this guy was fast—very, very fast. With a steady hand, he kept the gun pointed at my chest. "My vote would be to shoot the S-O-B dead … right here … right now."

Billy the Kid looked at Jude and then at me. "Put the gun away, Jude … this is a celebration. We'll deal with all this unpleasantness later." He looked out at the festivities, noticing that most of the men were finished eating. He then studied the trail we'd arrived up on, anxiously looking for Heidi and Jordan to arrive. "A few more minutes … then I think it's time we move on to the main event."

Chapter 40

Before actually seeing them, I heard their approach, coming up the mountainside—first, the distant whinny of a horse, followed by the barely audible sound of a woman's voice. Billy, consumed by the prospect of seeing Heidi Goertz again, brushed past me and ran to meet them—needing to ensure he'd be the first there, the one standing in front, once they turned that final bend.

Whereas Palmolive was on the verge of pissing his pants with anticipation, I was anything but looking forward to her presence here; to being anywhere near her. The Neo-Nazi leader was responsible for untold thousands of deaths. She'd recently watched with amusement as Pippa was nearly beheaded. Now, evidently, she was the catalyst taking the Order in a far more ominous direction than its former, behind-the-scenes, mode of operation. She was true evil incarnate. The mere thought of her presence made me feel sick.

Jude, pointing his Colt at me, wasn't the slightest bit distracted, like his boss, Palmolive.

He holstered his gun and said, "Later … you're all mine." He too brushed past me and headed for the group of three mounted riders, just coming around the bend.

Billy the Kid stood, his arms apart, a welcoming gesture that Heidi mirrored with her own arms, also held wide open, while siting atop her horse.

"Polly, my love!" she said affectionately.

Obviously, that was her pet name for him. *How cute.* Jordan held the reins of her horse as she slid down from her saddle. She wore tan, skintight riding pants that emphasized the curve of her small, well toned behind, and a snap-down, pink-plaid shirt that was open enough at the top to expose her ample cleavage. Her long hair was probably tucked into her bright-blue cowboy hat. She looked tan, fit, and beautiful—ready for a photo-shoot. Even more than killing Palmolive, I wanted to kill the woman, and I wouldn't think twice about doing so. The thought of looking into that wretched mind of hers revolted me. There'd be plenty of time for that later.

The musical duo was now playing and singing, *The Yellow Rose of Texas.* I watched as Heidi ran into Palmolive's arms, kissing him passionately on the lips. I was struck by the seeming inappropriateness of it all: Not just the prolonged kiss—well, that too, but they were such a mismatched couple. He—small, twitchy, and bird-like, and she—strikingly beautiful and, simply put, way out of his league. Yes, he was wealthy, but so was Heidi. But what he possessed was raw power. Perhaps more power than any one person on Earth. Power she'd manipulated her way into and was now part of.

The onlookers applauded her, with several hoots and hollers, and more than a few whistles. Jordan held onto the reins of the other man's horse—the third rider. I recognized him immediately as the man who placed a garrote to Pippa's neck.

I moved quickly, weaving in-between the numerous cowboys. My hand hovered an inch above my six-shooter—my eyes locked on the large, pretty-faced man.

"Hey ... watch it!" someone said, as I nearly toppled him over.

He must have seen movement in the crowd—me, heading right for him. We locked eyes. A bemused smile crossed his lips before he went stone-faced serious. Heidi, several paces in front of him, saw my approach, her eyes suddenly going wide. I ignored her … I had someone else in my sights.

An outstretched arm brought me to an abrupt standstill. Then, that same arm pinned my drawing arm to my side.

Sundance held fast—his face inches from my own. When he spoke, his voice was just above a whisper, "Not … now!" His eyes conveyed his seriousness. "Your gripe with the guy will only get you killed. Suggest you bide your time."

Heidi said something then spun around, giving everyone another good look at her outfit. She laughed as more catcalls came from the crowd. Unknowingly, she'd also kept their attention off me—a welcome coincidence.

I said nothing, but continued to stare at the man who'd arrived with Heidi. Just as I was about to enter his mind, Billy turned and addressed everyone.

"Now that Ms. Goertz has arrived we can proceed—can formalize your membership into the greatest organization this world has ever known. You will vow allegiance, and utter the sacred pledge. Those not ready, or not inclined to do so, should leave now. Jordan will accompany you back down the mountain. No hard feelings; I wish you well."

Billy the Kid surveyed the crowd—looking for anyone not willing to officially join the ranks of the Order. There were no takers. Billy smiled broadly, reached a hand out to Heidi, and raised their clasped hands high into the air. "Together, we will anoint you all into the fold … into our family." With that, Billy the Kid and Heidi Goertz headed toward the mine's opening. We all watched them until they disappeared into the darkness.

"We'll do this in two separate groups!" Jude bellowed, now standing on the flatbed wagon where he'd displaced the singing duo. "Space is cramped in the mine." Holding a sheet of paper in his hand, he looked at it as he spoke: "When I call out your name I want you to assemble near the opening of the mine. Those names not called will be in the second group … so be patient."

Sundance, at some point, had released his hold on my arm. He was still close and I gave him a slight nod.

Jude began to call out the men's real names; apparently, there was no longer a need to use our gunfighter aliases.

"Thomas Wright … Terrance Crow … Larry Sanders …"

One by one the men, jubilant at being chosen to enter in first, hurried over to the mine. I contemplated shouting something, telling them they were all going to be killed—that they were not the chosen ones. But nothing I'd say would be believed, and I'd only get myself shot by Jordan, holding a Winchester rifle, and moving about the ranks of excited men.

Unceremoniously, I reached a hand up to unsnap my two collar snaps. It was time. Sure, I'd still have to overtake Palmolive—snatch the wireless detonator off him—within the next few minutes. But the time had come to bring in SIFTR … bring in the cavalry.

Startled, I saw movement off to my left. In a blur, I saw Jordan, who, two handed, rammed the stock of his rifle into my face. Everything went black.

* * *

Pippa walked alongside Palmolive, her hand still grasped tightly in his. She caught him for the umpteenth time staring at her; felt his grip tighten on hers—an unspoken gesture of his love for her. So far, she'd carried it off. Palmolive was none the wiser that she was an imposter. Walking between the rails, they moved deeper into the dimly lit mine.

Why did Rob look at me that way? Didn't he look into my mind … hear my repeated message, explaining that it was me in Heidi's disguise? She knew that look—he'd wanted to kill her, was prepared to do so right then. She couldn't think about that right now. Baltimore's words were playing over and over in her head: *You need to think and act exactly like Heidi … take control of every situation … every conversation … just like she would.*

"Tell me about your preparations here. I don't like being left in the dark," she said.

"Everything's exactly as we discussed. We will welcome them into the fold … have them all take a knee position and close their eyes. As they repeat the sacred vows, we will move toward the exit."

"And the cave-in?" she asked, slowing her pace and looking down at him. She wasn't one hundred percent sure a cave-in was planned, but it seemed logical.

"Again, just as we discussed. Everything's handled, so why concern yourself with—"

Pippa angrily turned to face him: "Who do you think you're talking to? When have I ever left the details to someone else?"

Palmolive stared back at her. Like a wounded child, his eyes searched hers for forgiveness. "I only wanted to convey to you that everything is going as planned." Without moving his eyes from hers, he reached into a pocket on his vest and held up a small device, similar to a remote garage-door opener. He then placed it back in his vest pocket and, patting it twice, said, "All is well, my love."

She softened her features, letting the smile return to her face. She reached up and took the man's mole-infested face in both hands. "You are so amazing, my little Polly." Tenderly, she kissed him on the lips while fighting back a gag.

Chapter 41

Together, they entered an expanded, quasi-circular juncture, sited within the roughly cut walls of the mine, approximately thirty yards in diameter. Looking up, the cavern ceiling was so high it was lost in the blackness above. Three tunnels, slightly smaller than the main artery they entered in from, branched off in different directions. Pippa's mouth fell open and then, just as quickly, she composed herself.

Palmolive was watching her every expression. "I thought you would be pleased. Is it not exactly what you requested?"

What she was seeing would have warmed Heidi's heart. The cavern had been transformed: Special lighting—high-mounted spotlights—along with four blood red banners hanging down from high above. Each banner, at least forty feet long, prominently displayed the Nazi emblem. Actually, not the old, familiar, Nazi emblem for that one had been modified. Here hung the twenty-first century version of the nefarious swastika—overlaid now with an added pyramid symbol, and an all-seeing eye above it—as depicted on the back of the U.S. one-dollar bill.

Pippa moved to a waist-high lectern, made of white marble, and ran an open palm along its cool flat surface. Looking up at the banners, she realized she didn't have the complete picture. Why had they gone to so much trouble for a group of men they were going to exterminate in the end, anyway? Then she remembered there were two groups—all this would be for the second group. "Walk me through what comes next, Polly."

Palmolive looked momentarily flustered by her question. "We've spoken about this … numerous times." Seeing her impatient expression, he continued, "The first group will be brought in here, where they will assemble together, and you, standing there at the lectern, will administer the oath … the oath into the WZZ."

Pippa's eyes flashed over to Palmolive and she hoped he hadn't noticed her alarm. She never anticipated that the Order would be folded into the WZZ—she'd just assumed it would be the other way around.

"Once the men in group one give their oath," he went on, "each will shake my hand, then yours."

As Palmolive spoke, Pippa spotted several small, disgusting spit-bridges in his mouth—little bands of saliva, spanning his upper molars to his lower molars.

"One by one they will be instructed to proceed into that center tunnel, where they will walk in silence one full mile, entering deeper and deeper into the mine. There, in another chamber, not so very different from this one, they will complete the second part of their indoctrination. At least, that is what they will be told."

As he spoke, Pippa noticed the large metal hanging door. Four six-inch rollers, evenly placed along the top edge of the massive door, hung from a ten-foot-long rail. Using both hands, Palmolive pulled the door along the rail until it closed—separating the cavern from the tunnel. He walked back to Pippa, moved in behind her, and slid an arm around her waist. He pulled himself close to her, bringing a hand up to cup her left breast. He fumbled with her shirt and bra and found her nipple and squeezed it tight between thumb and forefinger. He said in a low tone, "I know you like that … I know exactly what you like."

The cosmetic procedure Pippa had recently undergone, for the second time in her life, was extremely painful. To match Heidi's anatomy, her face and all key areas of her body were modified—careful scrutiny given to every detail—along with too many injections to count. Her breasts were now firm and far larger than her normally small, albeit perky, ones. They were still extremely sore and ultra sensitive to touch—even the fabric of her bra was hurtful. The ride up the mountain on horseback had been miserable. Now, with tears filling her eyes, as his boney fingers pinched … pinched … pinched … it was all she could do to hold back a scream.

She felt his erect hardness, slowly, rhythmically, thrusting up against her. He buried his face in her neck, kissing her there. She pushed herself into him, turned her face to let him kiss her mouth, then asked in a low, husky voice, "So … what then? Tell me the rest."

His breaths were coming faster and deeper now. He was moving to unbuckle his belt but she shook her head and pulled her face away from his, letting him know there would be no more fondling until he spoke.

Frustrated, he looked over to the main tunnel: "Well … at that point, the second group will be ushered in here by Jude. They will be told that the first group has moved deeper into the mountain to complete their processing. We will then administer the same oath to group two—to the men actually being accepted into the WZZ."

Palmolive pulled the small remote switch from his pocket. "Inside the mine, it takes approximately twenty minutes for a person to walk a mile. So we'll give them … the first group … thirty minutes, to ensure they are deep within the mountain." Smiling, Palmolive mimed pushing the remote's button: "Click," he said.

Pippa smiled—emulating what she guessed would be Heidi's sick glee at the prospect of fifty men being escorted to their death.

Palmolive said, "There are enough explosives planted over there that the whole damn mountain will shake. Dust will fill the air and we'll quickly usher this second group of scared men from the tunnel, back out the same way they entered. A horrible accident … a horrible cave in." Palmolive made a mock sad face, then said, "Having a mountain literally cave-in on top of them will make any extraction of bodies impossible."

"What about us … will we—"

He raised a reassuring palm. "We'll be perfectly safe here … far too removed from the actual explosions." He propelled the hanging door back along the rail to open it.

"And notifying the proper authorities, the next of kin?" Pippa asked, extricating herself from his grasp when he returned, and moving toward the open cavern.

"We'll give it a couple of days. We'll be far away from here by then. Let Jude and Jordan deal with the fallout. They're being well paid for that sort of thing." Palmolive pulled a pocket watch from his pocket and stared at it momentarily. "It's time. Time to bring in the first group."

Pippa bit the inside of her lip. She had to get that remote switch away from Palmolive before things progressed further. "I'll be the one to trigger the cave-in. Give me the remote," she demanded, holding out a palm, eyebrows arched.

Palmolive stared at her, and said, "That's not what we discussed. I think that it's best if—"

"You think?" Pippa mimicked, all playfulness absent from her face. "Do you really want to make me angry at this stage of things? I thought we were partners, partners for life. Wasn't that how you phrased it? This is just another indication of your lack of trust in me."

Palmolive continued to stare at her, nervous and looking hurt. He tentatively fished out the remote, looked at it, then back at Pippa. "What other indications?"

Pippa pursed her lips and tilted her head. She'd seen Heidi make the same petulant gesture and she did her best now to mimic it.

"Seriously … what other indications?"

Her heart rate leapt. She almost had him—was on the verge of getting the information she came here for. Pippa looked down, making a little-girl-pouty-face—another manipulative Heidi Goertz antic. "I've risked everything by joining with you again. My organization … my very life. All for you!"

"What … what do you want?"

"I need to know what's going to happen. I mean exactly. What targets are going to be hit, the timetable. What if I don't agree with your decisions?"

Palmolive looked confused, then spoke slowly: "We've already agreed to this. You had no problem with me handling this aspect—"

Pippa flared at him, "Well, I do now! There are too many secrets. Far too many. Are we leaders together, in every aspect, or not?"

He looked to be contemplating the question when Jude hurried in from the main tunnel. "Natives are getting restless. Ready for group one?"

Pippa answered before Palmolive could say anything, "I don't know … perhaps it's best if we forestall the whole thing …"

"No! Bring them in." Palmolive, still holding the wireless

remote, held the device out to Pippa, making another mock sad face. "Our first fight … here, take this. I want you to be the one to initiate World War III in … a war that will be won without a single bullet fired."

Chapter 42

Waiting silently, Pippa positioned herself behind the lectern, her eyes fixed on one of the long, gently swaying, red banners. She was, for the moment, alone in the cavern. Her heart pounded in her chest as she considered all the negative repercussions if she didn't properly handle things right. Her thoughts turned to Rob. Why hadn't he made contact with her? She recalled the way he'd looked at her—no—the way he'd looked at *Heidi.* She was fairly certain he hadn't peered into her mind yet. There'd been murder in his eyes, and knowing Rob, knowing what he was capable of, it occurred to her in that very moment that her life was in just as much danger from him as his was from Palmolive. Could his hatred of Heidi be so fervent it actually kept him from looking into her mind? She closed her eyes and shook her head.

"Are you still upset with me?"

She opened her eyes to see Palmolive standing there.

"No. I'm fine," she replied, smiling back at him.

The first group of men were already filing in. Heads first turned right and left, until their eyes caught sight of the hanging red banners, and the modified Nazi swastikas. She put herself in their shoes, seeing the despicable symbol. Personally, she'd have spun on her heels already and made for the exit. But these men, with the exception of a few sideways glances at each other, held fast. Whatever their individual reasons for being there, being accepted into the Order or the WZZ trumped everything else.

While waiting for the last man to enter, she counted them off. So far, there were a total of forty-eight men, all wearing several days' stubble on their faces. Dressed as cowboys, some were young, some in their late sixties. What seemed a cavernous space to her just moments earlier now seemed near-claustrophobic—hot and sour-smelling, from co-mingling body odors. The men looked at her with anticipation. She wondered what they were told about her—about Heidi Goertz. There was no sure way of knowing—but if their rapt faces were any indication, their expectations were high.

Palmolive looked at her and nodded. If there was some kind of special oath she was supposed to deliver, she had no idea what it was. She hadn't thought of acquiring that bit of information from Heidi. *Crap!* Times like this, she really wished she had Rob's mind-reading capabilities. She looked over to Palmolive, as an uncomfortable stillness fell over the space.

Another man entered the cavern, approached the lectern, and stood beside her. Mr. Taffy nodded to Pippa, to Palmolive, and then gazed out at the group of men.

"We will now commence the oath taking," Taffy said. "Ich schwöre bei Gott diesen heiligen Eid, dass ich die Führer der Zehnte Reiches und Volkes, Heidi Geortz und Rudy Palmilive, der Oberbefehlshaber der Streitkräfte unbedingten Gehorsam und als tapferer Soldat will jederzeit bereit zu geben, um mein Leben für diesen Ich schwöre bei Gott diesen heiligen Eid, dass ich die Führer der Zehnte Reiches und Volkes, Heidi Geortz und Rudy Palmilive, der Oberbefehlshaber der Streitkräfte unbedingten Gehorsam und als tapferer Soldat will jederzeit bereit zu geben, um mein Leben für diesen einzusetzen."

Pippa, although somewhat rusty, was fluent in German. Taffy, with his numerous syntax and pronunciation mistakes, obviously was not. Not that any of the men there noticed the difference. But there again … this was not Mr. Taffy … it was Curt Baltimore, who had undergone his own last minute set of facial injections. The real Mr. Taffy was German—a discrepancy Palmolive had not seemed to notice. Pippa chastised Baltimore with a glare. His shrug was subtle enough to go undetected by everyone else. What Baltimore spewed forth was an oath to God—swearing unconditional obedience to Heidi and Palmolive—the joint Fuhrers of the Tenth Reich.

Now, having a better idea what words needed to be expressed, Heidi said, "Please repeat this oath after me: I swear to God, my unconditional obedience to Heidi Goertz and Rudy Palmolive, supreme commanders of the armed forces of the WZZ, and that I shall, at all times, be prepared—as a brave soldier, to give up my life to protect this oath."

The men swore their obedience, line by line, repeating the oath aloud. Now, looking somewhat bewildered, they silently waited for what more was to come.

Palmolive said, "Now you will be led into another tunnel, where you will hike a mile further into the mountain, to a cavern similar to this one. There, you will wait for the arrival of the second group, who will join you within the hour. At that time, each of you will be provided with your individual leadership position within the organization."

The excitement in the room was palpable and there was a low murmur of voices as the men congratulated each other. Palmolive and Heidi moved out from behind the lectern to shake each man's hand. Jude slowly slid open the hanging metal door and ushered the men forward. "Keep going along this tunnel, all the way to the end," he said, repeating over the same words several times as the first group of men filed past. He waited a full minute before re-sliding the door closed, and latching it securely with a locking mechanism.

Palmolive, looking exhilarated, caught Jude's eye. "Go ahead and fetch the rest of them."

Pippa interjected, "But wait five minutes before you bring them in."

Jude looked back to Palmolive, who gave him a nod: "You heard her … go!"

Palmolive noticed Taffy, standing off to the side of the lectern. "You too—out with you. Give us some damn privacy."

Palmolive waited for Mr. Taffy—*Baltimore*—to leave before turning back to Pippa. "What is it? I would have thought you'd be ecstatic by now."

"I told you, I need to know all the specifics before this goes any further."

"Right now? It's a lot of information … subterranean deployment of combat teams and military assets throughout the country. I assure you, everything is just as we discussed. All that awaits is for me to give the final order to deploy."

"Well, I need to know everything—"

Palmolive cut her short by drawing his Colt and pointing it at her. "Let's dispense with the charade, shall we, Ms. Rosette?"

Pippa looked at him blank-faced. "What … what are you doing …"

"Come on, now. I knew you weren't Heidi Goertz the second I laid eyes on you. I admit the resemblance is remarkable. But there were subtle giveaways, the least of them being your height. I'm guessing you're at least two inches taller than Heidi. And your voice … close, but not the same." Palmolive eyed her up and down. "I'll enjoy determining other subtle differences between the two of you in private."

Pippa didn't respond.

"The truth is, I was forewarned about your presence here. Especially, since your partner's true identity was confirmed earlier today—Rob Chandler. After witnessing, first-hand, capabilities not found in your usual entrepreneurial nerd, I had his prints lifted from a whisky glass. Surprise surprise, his prints didn't match the real Troy McAlister's. Perhaps even more telling was that our imposter's prints didn't show up in any database. As you and I know, clandestine operatives' fingerprints, as well as other personal details, are often redacted. I had to go so far as to use one of my own high-level NSA contacts to come up with a match. Once we nailed down who Rob was—a decorated war vet, then a CIA agent of almost infamous acclaim—stemming first from suspicion he was a Russian double agent, from which he was later exonerated, then his subsequent induction into SIFTR. The one notable person tied to Chandler throughout his career, as well as in his personal life, was one Pippa Rosette … also a SIFTR agent."

For a moment Pippa continued to glare like she didn't know what he was talking about, but they both knew she'd been made. She shrugged.

"So I have one question for you: What have you done with Heidi Goertz?"

Pippa shrugged, "I'm sorry to inform you she's dead. I actually shot her myself … in the head … between those conniving, bitchy eyes of hers." She smiled, seeing the alarm on Palmolive's face.

After composing himself, his smile returned. "You know, I don't think she is dead, and let's be frank—when one has the kind of influence I have over virtually every clandestine organization on Earth, finding that out will not be difficult."

"I wouldn't be so certain of that," Pippa replied with confidence.

"In any event, I have you ... remember? I can be very convincing. Sure, you may hold out for a time, but rest assured, everyone has a breaking point. I'll personally enjoy exploring just where your breaking point resides."

Pippa's last hope of turning things around evaporated, upon seeing Baltimore being manhandled into the cavern by Jude. Clearly, they knew he too was not who he'd represented himself to be. With a monumental shove from behind, Curt Baltimore was sent sprawling to the ground with a grunt.

Palmolive cocked his head sideways at the disguised Curt Baltimore and said, "Three little piggies captured with ease, and now one of them must pay the price."

With surprising speed, his arms outstretched, Baltimore sprang toward Palmolive. In a blur, the bird-like man drew his weapon and fired once. The sudden impact from the round catapulted Baltimore backwards, head over heels, where he dropped, dead, near Pippa's feet. A circular blotch of dark red blood had replaced his left eye socket. Palmolive holstered his pistol and raised his eyes to Pippa.

Pippa didn't even try to hold back tears as she stared down at the body of her friend and colleague, Curt Baltimore. When she glanced up, she saw both Jude and Palmolive looking pleased with themselves. Jude approached her, found the wireless remote in her pocket, and handed it over to Palmolive.

"Please don't ... there's no need to kill anyone else," she pleaded. "I'll help you. Do whatever you ask ... just don't—"

But his hand was already moving—Palmolive depressed the button: "Click."

Pippa didn't hear an explosion—didn't feel the ground shake beneath her feet. Perhaps the device hadn't worked? Maybe something malfunctioned?

With an index finger pointing into the air, Jude said, "Wait for it … wait for it … wait for it …" and then it came: The sound of a distant explosion, quickly followed by flickering lights, billows of dust, and what seemed like an 8.0 earthquake. Pippa lost her balance, falling atop Baltimore's lifeless body, and thought about the forty-eight men who'd just lost their lives.

Chapter 43

. . . And here I am—back where this story began—precariously perched outside on the Tombstone saloon's top floor balcony. The noosed rope around my neck is still affixed somewhere above me, and I'm still awkwardly canted forward, waiting for my feet to slip out from under me. Of course, the rain has started coming down in buckets and I've come to the conclusion I'm pretty much fucked.

Jordan's two-handed blow to my head with the butt of his rifle at the silver mine knocked me out cold for what I'm guessing was several hours. Then came the dream: Actually, calling it what it really was—a nightmare—would be more accurate. It was the first time the entity infiltrated into my everyday life. What once was relegated only to my tapping in states had, somehow, crossed over, and it was more than a little disconcerting. The theme of the dream was similar to those before, but the scene was playing out in a different location, right here in the high mountains of Colorado. I was lying face down on a flatbed wagon. There was a repetitive chirping sound, coming from one or more wagon wheels in need of grease. My body bounced as we hit a large pothole on what I guessed was a downward sloping trail. Not more than a foot from my nose was Taffy. I knew instinctively he was dead—his eyes glazed and fixed as he started to speak. I needed to wake up. *Why can't I wake up?* My heart raced and I tried to move away from him.

I watched Taffy's lips move to speak, but instead heard the voice of that awful inner presence.

"It's my turn, Rob. It is time."

"No. That will never happen. You need to find someone else to help you."

"I saved you. Plucked your essence back from the wrangling grip of death herself. I pulled you into the vastness and there I nurtured you for a lifetime. You were mine. I should never have put you back … back into that dying body."

"You saved me? The car wreck?"

"Yes … and now I share your life. I see what you see, feel what you feel. It is my turn!" Taffy reached out a limp hand toward my face—cold fingertips brushed my cheek. I tried to pull away. The wagon hit another pothole and I awoke. The presence was gone, and my heartrate settled down.

The body of Taffy still lay there—obviously dead. Around me, I heard the sounds of multiple horses trotting and the rustling of tree branches, somewhere high above. I inhaled deeply, then let out my breath. I wondered why Heidi Goertz's bodyguard, or whatever the hell he was to her, would be lying dead next to me?

I tried to sit up and immediately discovered my skull was in no shape for any kind of movement at all. Also, my hands were bound behind my back. Using my similarly bound feet for leverage, I scooted my body around in such a way that I could see out the back of the wagon, and witnessed a second startlingly strange sight in as many minutes.

Rudy Palmolive was sitting atop his chestnut, Ticker, who was periodically doing his best to nip at the man's legs. Riding next to Palmolive, on my horse, Gunner, was Heidi Goertz. Her button-down shirt was partially ripped to the waist, leaving her ample breast semi-exposed, and, like me, her hands were bound behind her back.

Whoooa … almost lost it there. My left boot slipped from the railing and I watched several large, splintered-off pieces of railing free-fall toward the muddy street below. Feeling nauseated, I retched again and felt hot bile at the back of my throat. Just one of a thousand dry heaves I've been experiencing over the last three or four hours, while stranded helplessly up here on my narrow perch. I *really* need to tap in.

Back to Palmolive and Heidi and me, lying in the back of the flatbed wagon. In addition to the nipping chestnut mount, Heidi's semi-exposed boobs, her bound wrists—there was something else that was odd. While Palmolive was preoccupied with Ticker, yanking the reins this way and that, Heidi tilted her head to one side and made an exaggerated, wide-eyed, expression in my direction. Finally, I looked into her mind.

I AM PIPPA, DAMN IT! Are you getting this? I'm cosmetically altered to look like Heidi.

Her thoughts, directed at me, were received loud and clear and I was dumbfounded. I stared at the woman, who looked so much like Heidi Goertz. And then, I could see the real Pippa Rosette behind the series of what must have been extremely painful, face and body altering, injections.

Reassessing her torn shirt and partially exposed breasts, I inwardly prayed she hadn't been violated. I inserted that mental picture into her mind.

Did he …?

She shook her head. *No—not yet anyway.*

I gave her a nod and hoped my expression conveyed my regrets at how things had turned out. I looked again at the dead man lying next to me, Taffy. Suddenly, adrenalin began coursing through my veins. A part of me knew this was not Taffy. I looked back toward Pippa and peered again into her mind.

I'm so sorry. Palmolive killed Curt Baltimore.

My eyes locked on the man sitting next to Pippa. He was looking back at me, a bemused smile on his face. Only a few other times in my life had I wanted to destroy someone as much as I wanted to kill this pompous little fuck. His smile broadened as he saw the hatred on my face. The world around me was spinning and I felt on the verge of losing consciousness. I needed to tap in; my mind-reading capabilities were failing fast. But I did have sufficient time to insert one more, subliminal, suggestion into Palmolive's mind before blacking out: *Doc Holliday will kill Billy the Kid.*

* * *

I'd awoken as they dragged me into the saloon and up the stairs. Now, perched on the slick railing, the hangman's noose ever-tightening around my neck, I felt more raindrops splatter against my face. I retched again from worsening withdrawals. The homely saloon girl behind me had come and gone. Below, on the muddying street, the wind was blowing a Stetson end-over-end in the direction of the corral. The sound of distant low rumbling transitioned into an ear-shattering thunder clap that seemed right on top of me: CRACK! … CRACK! … CRACK! The sound was deafening as bright lightning illuminated the staged town of Tombstone below, seeming like a series of magnificent, bright-white flashbulbs going off, one after another. I felt the coarse rope around my neck, and again used the minimal tension it provided me to help keep my balance. The railing below my boots was slick with rainwater, giving me the precarious sensation of standing on skates.

Below me, through sleeting rain and an ever-darkening sky, I caught the faint outline of someone standing in an alcove, directly across the street. He suddenly moved and I saw the tall skeletal figure come into view—Colman—the undertaker.

I yelled into the wind, "You'll just have to wait … asshole!" I doubted he heard me, but it felt good shouting out just the same.

I thought of Johnny Ringo and the vulnerable saloon girl, Lori. Had she made it out? I then thought of Baltimore who, over the past year, had become one of my few close friends. Now he was gone and his murder unavenged. I next thought of Pippa, who'd endured a painful series of facial, and body-altering, injections, in order to save me. What Baltimore and Calloway—hell, SIFTR—hadn't known, was that the physiological impact on her the first time she'd undergone physical alterations to change her persona almost drove her to suicide. These latest surgical changes could easily put her over the edge. But, like me, she probably didn't have all that long to live now, anyway.

There was more movement on the street below and Palmolive's helicopter, barely discernible in the misty rain, was on the ground at the far end of town, its large rotor blade spinning. They'd be leaving soon—he'd accomplished what he'd come here for. Fifty men—high government officials, business moguls, millionaires and billionaires had conveniently been slain—weeded out of the Order … or was it the WZZ?

The wind was strongly buffeting my pants now and, with both arms tied behind my back, I was increasingly losing my balance. More thunder, like immense bass drums, resounded all around me. With one final, uncontrolled wobble, I slipped from the railing.

It took less than a second for me to fall the sufficient distance for the noose around my neck to go taut and for the wet hangman's knot to squeeze tight about my neck. The sudden jerk, as my downward momentum came to a dead stop, should have broken my neck right then and there. Apparently, though, that doesn't happen in every hanging—especially those that are non-professionally rigged, like mine was. The gagging—struggle for air—came first; tunnel vision, resulting from restricted carotid arteries no longer able to feed the brain necessary blood flow, came second. I was only slightly aware that the pole I was suspended from had partially given way—undue stress from my sudden added weight upon it—and dropped my body down another three or four feet. That sudden drop almost succeeded in breaking my neck for the second time. What came next could not have come at a more fortuitous moment.

It was only a matter of time before the wet, metal flagpole I was suspended from attracted one of the hundreds ... thousands ... of lighting bolts going on in the air around me. The wet pole and the equally wet rope acted as perfect conductors—the hot bolt of electricity entered my body through the neck, ran through my body, and exited through my wet, soggy, boots. From there, as physics surely attests, the lighting arc continued downward in its direct pursuit of ground, in order to complete its singular, instantaneous, sole mission in life.

As my body went rigid I felt the agonizing effects of electrocution. Even as the horrific electrification came to an end, I was still faced with the ongoing, although quickly coming to an end, peril of hanging. Even then, through my quickly fading consciousness, I could smell the tinge of burnt flesh invade my nostrils. *Flesh and ... hemp.*

The rope partially separated, then quickly unraveled somewhere above my head. Once again, my now-dancing, convulsing body was lowered another ten feet. When the scorched rope broke completely apart, I was a mere eight feet above the ground.

* * *

I awoke thrashing—gasping desperately to draw in a deep, burning, lungful of air. I felt hands working the noose away from around my neck then up over my head. My hands were freed from behind me. My head lay upon my savior's lap. I opened my eyes to see Colman, concern on his face, staring down at me. He brought a flask up to my lips. I greedily gulped at the burning liquid—only to cough most of it back out again.

"Sorry … it's all I have. Small sips … that's it … just a little, now."

I tried to speak, but the words caught in my ravaged throat. He brought his face lower to mine and turned an ear to my lips.

I croaked out one word, "Why?"

Confused at first, he then smiled. "Rudy Palmolive is truly a monster. You're the only one he's tortured here. It's gone too far … there's no one else …you need to stop him!"

My words came out somewhat better this time, but still a whisper: "I'll need a gun."

"Can you stand?" he asked.

"Yeah … I think so." I let him help me to my feet. When he let go, he still kept his hand poised to catch me. Standing upright, I realized the world around me was no longer spinning. The nausea, too—all gone! Of course—I'd just survived the ultimate tap-in fix. I quickly tested my mind-reading capabilities and saw real concern within the undertaker's mind. Not wanting to hang around there too long, I gave him a reassuring nod. "Thank you. You saved my life."

Colman drew the six-shooter from his holster and briefly pointed it at me. Then, flipping it around and turning its handle toward me, said, "Take mine … it's loaded."

I took the Army Colt .45 and slid it into my empty holster. "Where's Pippa … the woman Palmolive took prisoner?"

"The corral. He's got her tied up there. He's got his boys with him—Jude and Jordan and several others. I overheard him talking on a radio … to his security forces; they'll be returning from the outlying areas. Most everyone has been sent back to the lodge. Palmolive and his men want to head out within the hour."

I let that sink in.

"There's something else. This town … it's rigged to blow."

"What do you mean?"

"Explosives. He doesn't want any trace of Tombstone to be left behind."

"Do you know when?"

Colman nodded. "I heard him say 6:00. It's about 5:00 now."

"I can't do this alone. Will you back me up?"

"No … don't ask me to do that. I'm a coward. It took all my fortitude just to help you this much. I'm sorry."

I heard someone approaching from the corral, at the opposite end of town. The near-vertical barrage of falling sleet made it impossible at first to make out his identity. Nearing us, with a steady gait, he wore a black Stetson pulled low over his eyes. Armed with two holstered Colts that hung low on his hips.

"Best you step away from me, Colman …"

Chapter 44

I anticipated the man approaching us to come to a stop—let the gunfight play to its inevitable, deathly, outcome. To my surprise and relief, considering my condition after being both hung and electrocuted, as he drew nearer he raised his chin up and, for the first time, I could see his face beneath the Stetson's brim: It was Sundance.

"You can stand down. I'm not going to draw down on you," he said.

I already knew that for I was in his head. Just like before, conflicting emotions were running rampant within him. He said, "I don't know who you are. What I do know is you're here to stop Palmolive."

I didn't say anything for several beats. "Look … I don't trust you. I know what you did. Killing the saloon girl and the wiring of the mine."

His brow creased, suspicion crossing his face. "How could you know that?"

"Let's just say a little birdie told me."

"The girl?" he scoffed. "Did you also know she pulled a gun on me? A small derringer pistol was strapped to her thigh. She'd been play-acting, following orders to manipulate me. When she threatened my kids, I took the gun away from her and killed her."

I hadn't delved into his mind far enough earlier to see all that—only viewing those last few seconds before he'd shot her, which endlessly looped now through his thoughts. A memory eating him up.

"And the silver mine—the fifty men you helped bury beneath a mountain?" I asked with contempt.

"It's true, I did rig the explosives. And yes, Palmolive blew up not one, but two tunnels. They just happened to be two other tunnels those fifty or so men were not anywhere near. They'll still need to dig themselves out, but I suspect it won't take them more than a day or two, at the most."

I verified his words as he spoke, and he was telling me the truth. "And the reason you're here in the first place?"

"That part of it I'm not proud of. It was greed—pure and simple. I'm a single parent, in debt up to my eyeballs, and CIA operatives don't make that much money. Someone told me about the Order and got me an interview. But it's obvious I'm not cut out to be a criminal, so I'll stand with you. You do have a plan, I'm assuming?"

"What is your real name?" I asked.

"Matthew Carver … Matt."

"Okay, Matt, I'll take you at your word, for now, not that I have much choice. I've signaled my people, but I can't guarantee they'll make it here in time. According to Colman here …" I turned to the undertaker, who'd stood behind me only a moment before, and found him gone. "Well … so much for him. Anyway, Palmolive is readying to leave anytime now. And the whole town is rigged to blow within the hour."

"So we'll need to make a move on them right now," Carver said.

Out of the corner of my eye I saw something move and promptly drew my gun, then eased my finger off the trigger. Limping, his tail wagging, and wearing what looked like a little dog smile, Ol' Yeller hurried over to me. On his left rear flank was a bloody, six-inch-long gash. The dog wiggled in close, flipped on his back, and barked. I scratched his tummy.

Are you okay, little guy?

I like my belly scratched.

I took a closer look at his injury. Undoubtedly, it must hurt like hell, but the gash wasn't life threatening. Someone had attempted to kill the dog.

Who did this to you?

Bugs on face.

It took me a moment to understand. Palmolive—his face covered in small, gnat-like, moles. *Will you do something for me?* I asked.

No. Scratch my belly.

I'll scratch your belly all you want if you help me.

Ol' Yeller flipped back onto his feet and looked up at me.

Sneak into the barn and see what's happening in there. I need to know where the woman is so I can help her.

Ol' Yeller ran off—his limp somewhat less pronounced.

"I'm afraid to ask what the hell that was all about," Carver said.

"Let's go," I responded.

We hurried over to the right side of the street, staying close to the buildings. Visibility in the pouring rain was nearly zero, but my guess was Palmolive had one or more lookouts strategically placed close to the barn. Some fifty-foot distance away from the wide-open barn doors, a series of gunshots rang out.

Carver and I instinctively crouched down, holding up where we were. A second later, Ol' Yeller came running out of the barn, heading down the middle of the street toward where we'd stood moments earlier. I whistled once and the little dog, spotting us, changed direction. He no sooner reached us than he rolled onto his back and began to squirm. I scratched his belly and told him: *Good job … what did you see in there?*

Female sitting on hay bale ... hands and feet tied.

Where is she?

All the way in the back. Man with gun near her. Scratch more now.

I gave the dog several more good scratches and stood back up. "Pippa's held in the rear of the barn, her hands and feet tied."

Carver looked at me as if I were crazy. "Okay ... this is getting really weird."

"You have no idea," I said, gesturing for us to continue moving.

"I don't suppose you were told how many—"

I stopped and looked at him. "Dogs ... animals, in general, are not great at counting."

"Oh—okay, but carrying on silent conversations with humans is fine," he answered sarcastically.

"I got the feeling there were more than five guards, but less than ten," I said.

Slowly, we continued toward the barn. I mentally told the dog to keep well behind us, but then had an idea.

"Carver, do you have a knife?"

"Just a pocket knife."

"Give it to me," I said.

He pulled a small black knife from his front pocket and handed it over. "I'll want that back."

I crouched down to the dog. It took me several minutes to convey the message, implanting the appropriate mental images to him, but eventually Ol' Yeller took the knife in his teeth and scurried back toward the barn. A pang of guilt fell over me. They'd already taken potshots at the little guy, I only hoped his luck continued to hold.

I stood and held up a hand, remembering something: "Wait up—what do you know about Palmolive's plan? Some kind of military operation or deployment by the Order?"

"Only what you just said. Nobody knows the specifics, other than selected municipal water works are being targeted. You know about the underground highways and hydro-passages?"

"Somewhat," I said. "We need to keep Palmolive alive—he seems to be the only one with critical deployment information."

"We're about to walk into a firefight. If he shoots at me … I'm firing back. Just saying."

I couldn't argue with that. I opened my weapon's cylinder to verify it was loaded. "You ready?"

Carver nodded and drew both guns. "Ready as I'll ever be."

We walked only three steps before passing an open alleyway. I spotted the glow of a cigarette first. As the cowboy's hand touched his side, I pointed my Colt and pulled the trigger. The gunshot was loud, and echoed into the storm.

"Fuck!" Carver said, startled. "I didn't even see him hiding in there."

I hurried toward his slumped over body and checked his pulse. He was dead—a bullet hole in his left temple. I pried the six-shooter from his still-clenched fingers and holstered the gun. Spotting a second gun on his other hip I took that one, as well.

"So much for a sneak attack," I said.

* * *

Pippa used the tip of her tongue to explore the crack in her lower lip, the result of a recent backhand from Palmolive. She saw her guard eyeing her.

"I need to go to the bathroom."

"You went an hour ago. You can hold it," he said, with a glance in her direction.

"Well I need to go again," she said, holding up her bound wrists, "so how am I going to escape … there's nine of you here and I'm tied up."

"Fine. You know where the bucket is. But hurry it up." He gestured toward the stall, adjacent to where she was seated on a hay bale. She stood and, with her ankles also bound, shuffled over to the empty stall. Two men, standing beside Palmolive, looked over at her, then back to their boss, who was angrily barking orders into what looked to be a satellite phone. She disappeared behind the wall, leaned her back against it, and lowered herself down to the hay-strewn ground. Tears filled her eyes as she recounted what had transpired hours earlier. She was forced to watch, from the street in front of the saloon, as Rob, hands bound behind his back, was manhandled up onto a second-story railing. A hangman's noose was placed over his head, then secured around his neck. She could tell he was barely hanging on, suffering from the effects of the blow to his head, as well as undergoing withdrawal symptoms. How he was able to keep his balance for the few minutes she'd watched him was a miracle. Palmolive had assembled those left—the second group of men who'd safely exited the silver mine after the blast—as well as his own men.

"Take a good look, my friends," Palmolive said. "This is what disloyalty looks like. I had such high hopes for Doc, hanging up there. Actually, he's Rob Chandler, an agent of sorts, from an insignificant little agency that will soon cease to exist. Let this be a reminder to you how any deception, among those within the Order, is dealt with."

As if accentuating his words, thunder cracked above, and it began to rain. They dragged her away, as Rob teetered on the railing high above them. Their eyes briefly met before she lost sight of him in the storm's pending gloom.

There was no way he could survive this long. Right now, his dead body was surely hanging limp from that pole. She brought her arms up and hid her face in her tied together hands. Between gaps in her fingers she saw the small dog, staring up at her. They'd shot at him, laughing as the poor animal ran one way and then another—terrified. She was surprised to see him still alive.

In a hushed voice she said, "Stupid dog, why'd you come back here?"

The dog tilted his head, wagged his tail, then dropped something by her feet. Pippa studied the small object, lying before her, not sure what it was. She picked it up and turned it over in her fingers. As the beginning of a smile reached her lips, she heard a distant gunshot.

Chapter 45

Gunshots erupted and Carver took a hit to his upper arm. I grabbed on to his shirt and together we dove and landed behind a wooden water trough. I didn't expect to see men also positioned on a rooftop across the street from the barn, especially in this storm. Bullet rounds continued to pummel the ground all around us, and into the quickly emptying-out trough, now riddled with holes.

"They both have rifles," I said.

"And they know how to use them," Carver replied back, grimacing.

"How bad?" I asked, returning pistol fire in their general direction.

"Grazed … hurts like the devil, though," Carver said.

"We need to get out of here … we're sitting ducks." I peeked my head around the side. Two more rounds impacted the muddy street, mere inches from my face.

"I'm open to ideas."

I scanned the street and the next building, standing between us and the barn—where a large, overhead mounted sign read, O.K. Corral. I looked more closely at the barn. It was dark, nearly black in color, and made from distressed wood; its high-pitched roof topped a second story. Surely, that meant a loft was up there. A smaller access door was positioned four feet above the barn's main entry door.

I looked over to Carver. He must have been following my sightline, because he said, "I think I can make it up there from the alleyway."

"You?"

"Arm's hurt but it's working just fine. I was a gymnast in my youth. Wait for me to get into position … and give me some cover. I'll enter from the roof. You find a way in from down here." With that, Carver was gone, sprinting back toward the alleyway where the dead cowboy still lay slumped over.

I fired several more shots across the street, in the direction of the two gunmen. To my surprise, I next saw Carver precariously standing on a propped-up wagon wheel, as he pulled himself up to the lowest section of roofline. He hung there for a moment, before swinging his legs up and over sideways.

The gunfire increased, not just from across the street. At least two, maybe three, men were firing from the open barn door. As all traces of residue water drained from the trough, several rounds exploded right through to my side of the wood planking—one struck, lodging in my gun belt.

The rain was easing up now, the visibility better—enough that I could clearly make out one man, shooting from the barn. I had one predominant hope—that he was an idiot. My whole mind-control talent was limited to simple things—like suggesting someone scratch his nose, or inserting certain mental images to help in two-way communications. I discovered over the last year that the less intelligence a person had, the more easily they could be influenced to do things by merely inserting mental suggestions. Pippa, highly intelligent, was not suggestible in the least; neither was Baltimore.

A subsonic round flew past my right ear, leaving a *pssst-* sound in its wake. I zeroed in on the gunman, standing furthest to the left in the open barn door, and concentrated:

Run … run to the middle of the street … you'll have a better vantage point … hurry … go now!

Apparently, he wasn't very smart. In what seemed an impromptu show of bravery, the man darted from his position of relative safety, firing off three shots in my direction.

I fired once and watched him tumble over dead into the street. I turned back just in time to catch Carver crawling into the loft's access opening.

Two men were firing toward me from the barn's entryway, and another two from the roofline across the street. The emptied water trough was quickly turning into woody Swiss cheese. Using my toes, I eased up just enough to see around the trough, and got a good look at one of the gunmen on the roof. He, like me, was lying on his stomach, taking aim with his Winchester. I entered into his mind and saw what he saw—me—hiding behind the trough. Then, through his eyes when he glanced sideways, I could also see the others, positioned at the barn doors. As though his rifle was held in my own hands, I quickly readjusted his aim an inch to the left and pulled the trigger. I'd never made that kind of a mental suggestion before and allowed myself a quick smile. One of the men, standing in the barn doorway, staggered forward and grabbed his throat. I cringed: *a nasty way to go.*

Another gunman took his place and began firing—alternating between my position, and the rooftop's second gunman. I tried several times to repeat my successful, remote-shooting technique, but apparently it was a one-time-only phenomenon.

Two more rounds erupted through the disintegrating wood planks and I decided I needed to make my move. I rushed back to the open alleyway, where I momentarily held up behind the dead cowboy. Almost immediately, his slumped body was riddled with a handful of bullets. I sprinted down the long alleyway, waiting for the next round to get me in the back. It never came and I didn't stop running until I turned the corner. My intent was to move toward the backside of the barn, then enter through the fenced horse corral on the barn's other side. There, hopefully, I could get a better angle at the enemy's positioning at the barn doors.

Halfway around the back of the barn I held up to reload my three pistols with the spare bullets on my belt. With that accomplished, I moved off, but then quickly held up. There was a blackened section of siding and I could smell the acrid tinge of charcoal in the nearby air. I flashed back to what Johnny Ringo'd related of his foiled escape attempt from the barn. Apparently, he'd nearly succeeded.

Knowing seasoned gunmen could come running around the corner at any second, I used the barrel of my Colt to poke at the blackened wood siding. With almost no resistance, it passed right through. I continued scrutinizing the little hole. It all came down to this moment—I would either survive or not, but I had to try. I needed to crash through the siding, guns blazing, and hope I didn't kill Pippa, or Carver … or the dog, in the process.

Chapter 46

All gunfire outside the barn suddenly ceased and Pippa could hear Palmolive's high-pitched voice reprimanding someone on the other end of the line: "Get your fucking men back here … No! … No! … let me put it to you this way, you have ten minutes; after that, you're dead … you're all dead."

She guessed he was talking to his outlying security team—calling them back in to help fend off whoever was out there shooting at them. Several of Palmolive's men had just been killed and he was quickly becoming unhinged.

Pacing back and forth and grumbling, every so often Palmolive strode past the opening of the stall she was sitting in. Pippa waited for him to pass by her again, then awkwardly flipped the small knife over between her fingers and began moving its blade up and down—slicing through the leather binding on her wrists. Stopping, just before cutting all the way through it, she inspected her handiwork. A good tug would tear the leather apart. She duplicated the same maneuver on the strap binding her ankles together. Frowning at her dirty bare feet, she realized that somewhere along the way she'd stepped in horse shit.

Startled, she heard a board creak directly over her head—someone was moving around up there. She might have missed it, but she couldn't recall any of Palmolive's men going up there. She tried to keep her hopes in check—that the delivery of the knife was … well … just a fluke. Maybe the dog was showing off a trick he'd learned or … no, that was no accident. Could she dare hope Rob was still alive? Was he one of the gunmen shooting outside? *But how?*

"Hey! What's taking you so long?"

Pippa nearly jumped out of her skin. Standing at the stall's opening was her guard. She looked down at her hands and the knife was clearly visible. Then, most fortuitously, she realized the guard's face was actually turned away—apparently, giving her privacy to pee.

Pocketing the knife, she stood. "I'm all done."

The guard turned toward her and, gesturing with the long muzzle of his rifle, silently told her to return back to the same hay bale.

"Leave us," came another voice.

At first obstructed by the bigger man's form, Pippa now saw Palmolive—he was off the phone and standing by impatiently. He repeated the command again, "I said, leave us!"

The guard hurried away.

Palmolive's face was flushed with anger, and he stared at her with murder in his eyes. "Who's out there? Who's shooting? Tell me now!"

"You're asking me?" Pippa said with contempt, then laughed.

Catching her by surprise, he punched her in the face. The blow landed squarely on her left cheekbone—knocking her backward into the stall and up against the wall. With his fists up, like a boxer, he punched out again—this time hitting her in the mouth. She tasted blood and tried to raise her hands to defend herself. But the violent blows were coming faster and faster now. She was only slightly aware that she was losing consciousness.

She snapped awake, feeling as though her scalp was being ripped from her head. Palmolive was dragging her by her hair. Desperate, Pippa kicked and screamed and reached out to grab ahold of his tightly clenched fingers, then felt the leather strap on her wrists pull apart. He'd no sooner dragged her into the center of the barn than all hell broke loose.

Like an inward explosion … something … no … someone crashed through the back of the barn. In a blur, the man—a six-shooter in each hand—began firing.

Suddenly, she felt the grip on her hair release as Palmolive ducked away to take cover. She covered her head, curling into a ball, as the mayhem around her continued. More gunfire erupted from above in the loft. The man with the two six-shooters ducked behind a six-foot-tall stack of hay. Did Palmolive recognize him? … Oh my God!

* * *

Bursting into the back of the barn, I immediately assessed the situation. First, I caught sight of Palmolive, five paces ahead of me, dragging something behind him. There was a scream. Jude and Jordan were standing to my left, at a makeshift table of wooden planks supported by two sawhorses. Two of Palmolive's armed cowboys stood by the barn doors; three others, all armed with rifles, were arbitrarily positioned around the large barn.

Palmolive ducked and scurried away as I shot the closest rifleman to my right in the chest. Gunfire came down from above—that would be Carver, joining in the fight. I scrambled behind a stack of hay bales to my left, as more gunfire, aimed in my general direction, erupted all around me.

Thump … thump … thump—fired rounds buried deep into the wall of hay I hid behind. I stole a quick glance and froze: Heidi Goertz—no, Pippa—was curled up in a ball on the ground. I could see enough of her face to see blood. My heart nearly seized in my chest—did he shoot her in the face? She moved and we made brief eye contact.

I glimpsed movement of something red—Jordan's red shirt. He was coming around the left side of the barn in an attempt to flank me on that side. I shot at him and missed, as he ducked behind a stack of cut timber.

There was enough of a gap between my barriers of hay to glimpse Carver had taken out both men in the barn's doorway. Looking up, I saw him change his position in the overhead loft. With another glimpse to the right, I noticed Pippa was gone—then saw her slide in the dirt right by my feet. I pulled her back behind the haystacks, and she rose to her feet.

"Give me a damn gun!"

I pulled the spare third Colt from my holster and she snatched it from me. Crouching low, she fired three successive shots and I heard a man groan. We exchanged a quick glance.

"God, that felt good," she said, already back to shooting.

I concentrated my aim on Jordan, who'd moved in several feet closer from behind the stack of wood. I felt fingers prying bullets from my belt—Pippa's gun was out of ammunition and she was quickly reloading. I checked both my guns—only five rounds left between the two.

It was a little while since I'd heard gunfire shoot down from above. I shouted, "Carver, you okay?"

His reply didn't come from above. A shot rang out, followed by another groan. I looked over, seeing Carver standing near the table, his Colt pointed toward the stack of wood off to my left.

Carver said, "That's all of them … the ones who haven't escaped."

I moved out from the stacks of hay and saw Jordan's staring eyes, fixed; a bullet hole in his cheek. Pippa joined my side. “I count seven dead in here.”

Bodies were strewn about and I hurried over to each one, confirming he was indeed dead. “Damn!” I said. “Palmolive’s not here.”

“I saw both Jude and Palmolive hightail it out through the barn doors. I think I winged Palmolive, though,” Carver said.

“Look at this,” Pippa said, standing at the makeshift table. She’d wiped most of the blood from her face, but the swelling on her cheeks and lips was significant. She was holding an iPad-type tablet in her hands, with a satellite interface affixed to it.

Carver and I joined her side. “That blood … is that yours?” I asked, noting a large red smear on the screen.

“Nope,” she replied, wiping at the screen.

“It’s Palmolive’s,” Carver said. “He was grabbing for the tablet when I shot him. He dropped it and, with Jude’s help, ran for it.”

Pippa looked up at me and smiled. “He must have been in the process of deploying—this is how he keeps in communication with the individual assault cells.”

“Did he …”

Pippa shook her head. “No, I don’t think so. There’s still a flurry of incoming messages, coming in from different locations. They’re asking for orders to commence their attacks.”

I looked at the screen as two new messages popped up. “Answer them … answer them all. Tell them to stand down.”

Pippa nodded and began tapping on the screen. An *Enter Passcode* prompt popped up. “It’s security protected. I can’t do anything with this thing.”

I turned to the table. There were hand-scribbled notes all over the margins on various blue-line diagrams. “What the hell is this?”

Carver said, "It's the U.S." He pointed to the obvious contours of the Eastern Seaboard. "What we're looking at is a nationwide operational schematic."

He was right. I counted no less than thirty different operations going on across the nation. The thickness varied on some of the dotted lines that traversed across the country. My guess, these were subterranean passageways, connecting to major city sub-stations.

Pippa pointed to the New York area on the plans and leaned in closer for a better look. "It says Croton, Catskill, and Delaware?" She looked up with a questioning expression.

"Those are reservoir systems … the primary reservoirs that supply New York City and much of the rest of the state." I'd spotted a satchel lying half open on the ground near my feet. I snatched it up and started to rummage through its contents.

"Well, if I'm reading this right," Carver said, looking at the opposite end of the table, "Palmolive's got military assets positioned at key locations … the primary water supplies, all over the country." He stood up. "This is …"

"Bad," I interjected. "This plan shows a clear-cut methodology to control the masses. Within a week every man woman and child will be at the mercy of the ones who control the water flowing to their faucets."

"The good news is, it doesn't appear from the flurry of incoming messages that the 'Go' command has been issued yet," Pippa added.

I gestured toward the tablet. "I'm sure Palmolive will get his hands on another device … it's only a matter of time." Still rummaging in the bag, the only thing I found worthwhile was Palmolive's sat-phone. I placed it back inside, grabbed the tablet from Pippa, and shoved that too into the satchel—which I handed back to Pippa. "Hold on to this."

I heard the sound of an engine springing to life. "Pippa, keep looking for a passcode in the margins … maybe someone jotted it down. You never know." I headed for the barn doors with Carver close behind. We came to an abrupt stop at the front of the barn and stared.

A helicopter, a Sikorsky S-76D, was situated at the end of the street—about seventy-five yards away. The rotor blade was quickly picking up speed. Its rear door was wide open and I could just make out the pilot, seated at the controls. Standing on the ground was a small tactical team of five men—each outfitted with an automatic weapon. Wind from the spinning rotor was now kicking up thick brown dust. In the middle of the pack of five men stood Palmolive, his shirt-sleeve bloodied, and Jude standing next to him. Palmolive was yelling over the noise, then pointed in our direction. His Stetson flew off his head and disappeared into the dust as his tactical team dispersed. *Shit!* They were coming for us.

"We're not going to last long, not armed with pistols." Carver shook his head at me.

I said, "I have an idea. Back inside now, let's close and latch the doors."

With that done, I moved over to the closest of Palmolive's dead cowboys. "Let's re-arm ourselves." I retrieved the dead man's shotgun, then, rifling through his pockets, I came away with ten shells. I also took his holstered Colt. Pippa and Carver grabbed up shotguns and shells from the other dead men.

"Out the back … hurry!" First Pippa, then Carver, ran out through the same splintered opening I'd smashed through earlier. I followed close behind them. I figured Palmolive's men should be reaching the front of the barn by now, and that they'd split up—at least one man moving around to cover the back.

As quietly as possible, we moved to the corner of the barn closest to the corral. I peeked around the corner and saw the helicopter in the distance and one of the black-clad men stealthily moving closer to us from inside the corral. Several horses nervously skittered away. One whinnied and reared up on his hind legs.

Out front, multiple hard-soled boots were kicking at the barn doors and making a racket. I let the man in the corral get closer, concentrating my focused attention on his head. At three paces away, staying low and moving far slower now, he saw me. I was in his mind then: *Hey, someone's coming up right behind you!*

It's an instinctual thing. You can't be instructed that there's someone sneaking up behind you without you turning around to protect your six—I've seen it time and time again. It's nearly impossible to ignore the impulse. The soldier's head and upper torso spun around, spotting nothing amiss. Then, while he was turning back, I drove the stock of my shotgun into the bridge of his nose. He dropped like a sack of bricks.

Moving fast, I relieved him of his M16 and passed it back to Carver. Below the unconscious man's armored vest was his battle belt, with pouches filled with a combination of M84 flashbang grenades and M67 explosive fragmentation grenades. I unclipped the belt and swung it over my shoulder.

"You best get some distance away from the barn. I'll be right back," I told Carver as I retraced my steps to the barn. Coming to a stop at the door opening, I peered inside and saw four men methodically clearing the space.

I figured three would more than do the trick. I withdrew the fragmentation grenades from their pockets and pulled the pin on the first one and immediately threw it all the way to the front of the barn. I did this two more times—throwing one to the mid-left side and one to the right. To give Carver and Pippa warning of what was imminent, I yelled, "Fire in the hole!" The combatant nearest to me spotted me—raised his weapon and fired. Mere inches above my head, a round tore through the back of the barn leaving a hole the size of a man's fist. I spun and ran while mentally counting down the seconds. I dove just as the first of the grenades blew—quickly followed by two more. The blasts propelled me five more feet and I fell hard in a heap with my ears ringing. My M16 and battle belt were gone—out of reach. Smoldering embers rained down from above. I saw much of the barn was on fire and a large section of the roof had fallen in on itself.

"Doc!"

I spun left to see Jude had come round the other side of the barn. He was standing no more than twenty feet away, and he was poised to draw his Colt.

Chapter 47

I glanced around me—spotting the M16 lying on the ground—too far to reach. Gunfire erupted in the distance. I figured Pippa and Carver were going up against Palmolive. I remembered there had been at least one ... maybe two additional men positioned up on the rooftops.

"Think it's a good idea leaving your boss unprotected like this, Jude?"

He smiled and shook his head. "Nah ... another team's inbound. Your friends are pinned down. It's just a matter of time."

"And what's this? You missed me? Wanted to say goodbye?" I asked, keeping a close eye on his right hand, now hovering an inch above his pistol.

"Something like that. This won't take long—been waiting to put you down since you got here. You know ... you're a cocky fuck."

Slowly, I got to my feet, not taking my eyes off Jude. The distant gunfire had stopped. Only the sound of burning timber was left.

"You're not the first person to bring that to my attention."

"Shut up and ..."

I didn't let him finish his sentence. Reading his thoughts, I knew he was planning on drawing any second. He was fast—normally, a bit faster than me. But I had the advantage of drawing my gun a fraction of a second before him. Both guns fired simultaneously—both of us took a bullet: Me in the shoulder, and he—like Calamity Jane—right between the eyes.

I watched as Jude crumpled to the ground, his gun still clenched in his hand.

I heard someone clapping. Behind me was Palmolive. Behind him were Pippa and Carver, held at gunpoint by two of Palmolive's remaining security team. Pippa's expression said how sorry she was they'd gotten themselves taken.

"Jude was fast … very fast. I commend you, Mr. Chandler. Makes me wonder if I could take you myself."

"There's an easy way to find out," I said.

Palmolive offered up a courtesy chuckle and became serious. "This is the end for you. You do know that."

I shrugged. "So what, you're just going to execute us?"

"That's exactly what I'm going to do." Palmolive gestured toward Pippa. "Do her first. I want him to watch."

His security man shoved Pippa hard, nearly sending her sprawling. Her eyes were on me. I saw a tear roll down her cheek.

"Wait. Let me do it."

Palmolive raised his brow. "Come again?"

"We're all toast. She's toast. Let me be the one to do it … you can drop me right afterwards. I guarantee you, she'd rather it came from me than from this asshole."

Palmolive continued to look at me blank faced. I saw Carver, two paces behind, make a pained, *this is fucking sick*, expression.

"Fine … this is something I'd like to see. Try something and you'll only quicken the inevitable."

The Colt was still in my hand. A fact I was reminded of, seeing Pippa's steady gaze upon it. The two security guys raised their weapons—one toward Carver—the other me.

Slowly I lifted my arm and pointed the muzzle of the .45 at Pippa's head. I read her thoughts. *You better not be actually doing this … so help me …*

I pulled the trigger.

The gun clicked but didn't fire. Everyone took in a breath at the same time.

Palmolive laughed out loud. "Holy mother of God! That was fucking mind blowing. You've got some real stones, man … I have to give you that much."

"I guess I'm out … Jude took my last round." I held up one palm. "Wait … just hold on …" My shoulder throbbed where I'd been shot and I was losing blood. Slowly, I opened the cylinder and let the spent casings fall free. I reached into my forward left pocket and pulled out another .45 bullet—all without losing eye contact with Palmolive. I snapped the cylinder closed with a quick twist of my wrist and nodded. "Let's try this again."

"You're really going ahead with this?" Palmolive asked. His own pistol was pointed at my head as he moved around, positioning himself away from the gun's fire behind me.

"It's best this way," I said. I looked at Pippa … "I'm so so sorry." I raised the gun again, and pointed it at Pippa's head. I pulled back on the hammer and let it click solidly into place. Feeling the smooth curve of the trigger on my finger, I inserted a new image into Pippa's mind and, with her head no more than three inches away, I squeezed the trigger.

In that split second, as a small flame burst forth from the gun's muzzle, I heard a near-ear-shattering report echo off into the distance. Pippa tumbled to the ground.

I stood with my arm held straight out, my Colt pointing to a spot Pippa's head no longer occupied.

"He did it … he fucking did it," I heard Palmolive say. I

looked back at him and smiled. "Got some stones, huh?"

He huffed and shook his head. With a sardonic smile he peered down at Pippa's still form. He tilted his head, suddenly becoming alarmed.

Pippa was already moving—the M16 coming up in both hands.

Tat Tat Tat.

Somewhere along the way, in the span of two, maybe three, seconds, Pippa managed to snatch up the weapon, switch it to full-auto mode, rise up and pull the trigger. Three taps went into Palmolive's torso. She then rolled to her right and shot the other two men before they could react.

Carver and I stood mesmerized as Pippa got to her feet. She took three steps toward me and delivered a perfect roundhouse punch to my jaw.

I staggered backwards.

"I thought I was dead! I felt the burn of the round. You're an ass hole … by the way … you know that?" She glared at me.

I nodded. "Sorry."

Carver was still standing in the same spot. "How … I don't understand?"

Before I could reply, two Sikorsky helicopters suddenly descended downward from the skies above. Apparently, the racket I'd created, from blowing up the barn, and the subsequent gunfire, affected my hearing.

Although unmarked, I recognized the old SIFTR aircraft. It no sooner touched down than the rear door slid open and an assault team hurried out. The team fanned out all around us. I wasn't surprised to see Calloway, dressed in a smart, navy pinstriped suit—not a gray hair out of place—following close behind.

The second helicopter, a bigger and later model, landed moments later. Here, too, another armed team deployed with well-practiced efficiency. Then a middle-aged woman, dressed in a gray business suit, jumped down from the craft and made her way toward us.

She met Calloway and they shook hands. Together, they both hurried toward us. The woman signaled two of her own men to attend to Palmolive. Surprising to me, he was still alive. Pippa had fired a round into his left shoulder, his right thigh, and clipped his right ear, which was no longer there. Unfortunately, he'd live. Lifted up by his arms, he was half carried, half dragged, away. He and I made eye contact. I smiled and flipped him the bird.

"Who are you?" I asked the woman in the gray suit, now standing before me.

Calloway said, "This is Ms.—"

She scolded Calloway with a stern glare and said, "My name is Mrs. Gulliver, Mr. Chandler. This is quite a mess you've made here." She looked over to the barn, now fully engulfed in flames, stoked by not one, but two, still-spinning rotor blades. Her eyes roved-over to Palmolive's two dead men, eventually coming to rest on fallen henchman Jude—emptily staring into the sky above.

"Perhaps it's time you came to work for me."

I looked over to Calloway, who shot back, "That's not going to happen. Remember our agreement, Anne?"

Pippa unslung the satchel from one shoulder and handed it to Calloway. She said, "Palmolive was coordinating the attack from a tablet in here. It's passcode—"

Interrupting, Mrs. Gulliver said, "I'll take that," as she grabbed it away out of Pippa's hands before Calloway could reach for it. "Rest assured, my people are already closing down the operation."

Calloway, about to protest, was interrupted by me teetering. He reached an arm out to steady me.

Pippa moved in close to help keep me upright. "He was shot by Jude … already lost a lot of blood." She looked over to Calloway, who signaled to two of his men, who rushed in to assist me. Then I remembered something and held up a palm … "We need to get out of here."

"Why?" Ms. Gulliver asked, obviously not accustomed to taking orders.

"Palmolive … rigged everything to blow. The whole damn town."

* * *

When I awoke next I was on a stretcher and we were lifting off. Ol' Yeller, whom I'd completely forgotten about, was on my stomach and licking my face. I pushed him off and saw Pippa smiling down at me. She had a bandage on her scalp and seemed to have forgiven me.

Suddenly, everyone looked out the window. With some effort, I pulled myself up to see out, too. The first explosion started at the far end of Main Street, where I'd first ridden into town with Palmolive and Butch Cassidy. The next explosions below us were coming rapidly now, one right after another. I watched as the saloon exploded in a fireball—I lay back, feeling dizzy, and said, "Good riddance."

Epilogue

I've been stuck in some dingy hospital room, in the hee-haw town of Canon City, for the past two days. The shoulder wound bullet had driven through and through—not bad enough to warrant surgery—but with so much blood loss, the doctors decided to keep me under observation, just the same.

Apparently, my shirt unsnapping-signaling thing did work and had called in the cavalry. I definitely needed to thank Bridgett Bigalow the next time I saw her.

Carmen, who'd waited back at the lodge, felt she was going berserk after not hearing from me for several days. Since phone service was not available at the lodge, she eventually headed out to get help from the local Guffy authorities.

Around that same time, a woman, wearing a soiled and torn saloon dress, and nearly frozen to death, staggered into town. Sheriff Corki wasn't inclined to buy her bizarre, crazy, accounting of events happening in a Western town called Tombstone, of men running around shooting each other. A town he was not completely convinced even existed. Only when Carmen arrived was he set straight. He finally agreed to contact the Canon City PD, but warned they were four hours away and typically didn't respond all that quickly. Corki did allow Carmen to use his telephone, and she contacted SIFTR, who'd already dispatched a helicopter to the ranch site.

From my hospital bed, I heard voices in the corridor and

a moment later Pippa, followed by Calloway, entered my room. She still looked like Heidi Goertz and like she'd gone five rounds with Evander Holyfield. She moved to the right side of my bed, nearest to the window overlooking Pikes Peak in the distance, was about to take my hand, but seemed to change her mind. Calloway, looking dapper in a pristine navy blue suit and pewter-colored necktie, moved to the other side.

I looked at him quizzically. "Well? Disaster averted?"

He and Pippa exchanged a quick look. Pippa said, "Yes and no."

"Yes … the Order's attempt to take control of key municipal water supplies has been thwarted. That feat alone made your mission a significant success," Calloway said, giving my leg a couple of pats.

"And?" I probed.

"We now have significant intelligence about the inner workings of the Order. More than a few of the men we extricated from the silver mine are speaking freely about the organization. After nearly being buried alive, any loyalties they once held are no longer a factor. Other than that, not much else has changed."

"What are you talking about? That's certainly enough to bring down the Order. Plus, we have proof of their plans; hell, we have Heidi Goertz—"

Calloway didn't respond back for several moments. "No … what we have is the WZZ and another foiled attempt at domestic terrorism. Everything's blamed on the WZZ—all of it. There's no official admittance that the entity called the Order ever existed. What little intel we've pieced together tells us the Order, that elusive organization, has retreated for the time being behind the scenes back under the leadership of Mrs. Gulliver—who was next in line to sit at the head of the table. She has distanced herself from anything to do with the Goertzes' and Palmolive's radical intentions to invade key U.S. municipalities."

"What about the underground thoroughfares … the hydro-passages?"

Calloway shrugged. "I'm sure they are still there. Look, the influence of the Order into international mega-corporations, and virtually into every aspect of the U.S., and other world governmental agencies, is staggering. That's not going to change as a result of what happened up in Guffy. That's a fight for another day. With luck, we'll get some help."

"Is SIFTR still operational … away from the Order's influence?" I asked.

"As long as I'm heading things up, the Order will stay out of our business. Time will tell how long that remains so."

"What is it you said to Mrs. Gulliver … you have something on her, don't you?"

"Never mind that," he said, his expression relaying to me the subject was closed.

"And what about Rudy Palmolive?" I asked.

Again, a furtive glance was exchanged between Pippa and Calloway. This time she answered: "Palmolive, according to our sources, has been ousted from the Order. His prospects for survival are not good. Mrs. Gulliver has taken over his seat at the head of the table. Leave it to say, there is some major house-cleaning going on now within the Order. There's one other thing …"

"What's that?" I asked, without enthusiasm, feeling we'd taken two steps backward for only one step forward.

"Both Heidi Goertz and Taffy escaped from our safe house in upstate New York."

I shook my head in disbelief. "I thought SIFTR was out of reach—"

"No … safe houses are shared government resources. It was actually an FBI breach. The Order had a mole in place and well before Palmolive was taken into custody, he had their escape plan in the works. But I should have known better. A mistake I won't make again," Calloway said, reprimanding himself.

"They won't get far, not with the resources the Order has," Calloway said. "I need to leave now. Curt Baltimore left behind a family and they've not been notified yet. I want to handle that task in person. He had an ex-wife and two teenage kids," Calloway said.

He stood for a moment in the room's silence, then said, "But first I need to know something. I've now heard the same story from multiple points of view—but not yours." Calloway looked at Pippa, then back to me. "How'd you do it?"

"Do what?"

"Shoot her in the head … and not kill the poor woman in the process?"

"Oh … that," I said, as if it were no big thing. "When I first arrived in Tombstone, I was encouraged to replace my blanks with live rounds. While standing in the Guns and Ammo Shop, and for no particular reason, I decided to hold on to the blanks. Shoved them into my pocket and forgot about them. That is, until Palmolive and his men had us dead to rights at the back of the barn. With a little sleight of hand, keeping a red-colored blank from view, I was able to reload and … with the necessary dramatics … shoot Pippa in the head."

Pippa reached for the bandage on the side of her head and scowled down at me.

"Apparently, it convinced Palmolive, and everyone else, that I'd shot a real live round."

Calloway shook his head and smiled. Saying his goodbyes again, and that he expected me back in service within two weeks, he left.

I looked up at Pippa. I wondered how she was dealing with the physiological aspects of her Heidi Goertz-like appearance. This had to be incredibly difficult for her. I had to force myself to stay out of her head. "You doing … okay?"

She looked down at me, the smile gone from her face. "What do you think?"

I shrugged, but before I could say anything, she continued:

"I know how you feel about Heidi. You hate her; detest her. Probably more than any other person alive."

I nodded, not knowing what to add to that.

"You're going to look at me … and hate me! At least until these fucking injections dissipate. I should just disappear for a while. We were already having problems, Rob … this just makes things impossible for us." Pippa looked toward the door and pursed her swollen lips—I could tell she was thinking about leaving.

I shook my head. "Hey … don't shut me out! I love you." The words just came out … three words I'd never said to her before.

Then I noticed she was back to wearing her hair in her former style and right then I realized I was already looking past the Heidi Goertz physical alterations. Heidi exuded ego and nastiness, while Pippa was not only beautiful on the outside, but inside, too.

Before I could say anything, which I was certain would come across as condescending, she said, "Well, then I've decided to make the best of it." She pointed to her own face and shrugged. "Maybe even have fun with it … I don't know. Hell, I lived through this once before … right? I'll survive this time too." She touched my face with the back of her hand … "Calloway said we have two weeks off. How about taking us back to that mansion-in-the-rocks of yours and we—"

At the risk of pulling out my stitches, I pulled her into the bed with me. She laughingly screamed once, then kissed me.

The End.

Thank you for reading Deadly Powers, Tapped In, Book 2!

If you enjoyed Deadly Powers, *please leave a review on Amazon.com—it really, really helps!*

To be notified of the third book in the Tapped In *series, as well as other new releases—such as the next installment in the* Star Watch *series, please join my mailing list. I hate spam and will never, ever, share your information. Jump to this link to join:*

http://eepurl.com/bs7M9r

Thank you, again, for coming along with me on these Sci-Fi and Thriller romps.

Other Books by MWM

Scrapyard Ship
(Scrapyard Ship series, Book 1)

HAB 12
(Scrapyard Ship series, Book 2)

Space Vengeance
(Scrapyard Ship series, Book 3)

Realms of Time
(Scrapyard Ship series, Book 4)

Craing Dominion
(Scrapyard Ship series, Book 5)

The Great Space
(Scrapyard Ship series, Book 6)

Call To Battle
(Scrapyard Ship series, Book 7)

Mad Powers
(Tapped In series, Book 1)

Lone Star Renegades
(Lone Star Renegades series, Book 1)

Star Watch
(Star Watch series, Book 1)

Find Ricket
(Star Watch series, Book 2)

Deadly Powers
(Tapped In series, Book 2)

Acknowledgments

I am grateful for the ongoing fan support I receive for all of my books. This book—my twelfth, Deadly Powers—came about through the combined contributions of numerous others. First, I'd like to thank my wife, Kim, for her never-ending love and support. She helps make this journey rich and so very worthwhile. I'd like to thank my mother, Lura Genz, for her tireless work as my first-phase creative editor and a staunch cheerleader of my writing. I'd like to thank Mia Manns for her phenomenal line and developmental editing ... she is an incredible resource and friend. A special thanks goes out to L.J. Ganser, who produces the audiobook versions of my books. Anyone looking for a truly immersive, not to mention 'fun' reading experience—with all his wonderful character voices ... you have to try the audiobook version. I'd also like to thank those in my writers MeetUp groups, who have brought fresh ideas and perspectives to my creativity, and elevating my writing as a whole. Others who provided fantastic support include Lura and James Fischer, Sue Parr, Stuart Church, and Chris Derrick.

www.ingramcontent.com/pod-product-compliance
Lightning Source LLC
Chambersburg PA
CBHW071300170626
46809CB00001B/301